A Celtic warrior's wo

MW00914062

Gryphon wondered why the Sorceress' latest summons contained the unusual words, '*Come without delay...no time for explanation.*' Her instructions usually gave him dates, times and places for his next assignment, but she had never used language indicating such urgency. Every instinct told him he should have probably left already, but the Sorceress could damned well wait. Any mission she had in mind required preparing his body and spirit and that preparation could only be accomplished by cleansing at leisure in an enchanted pool. Besides, what was she going to do if he didn't jump at her command as he'd always done? Turn him into a creature everyone in the Order feared? Well, it was too bloody late for that.

To my husband, Lee Sams, who has always stood beside me. To my Mom, Winifred Thompson, who taught me to never give up. For my two brothers, Lester Bashaw and Jim Thompson, who helped me learn a sense of humor and have kept fun in their hearts our whole lives. For their families, Carol, Joni, Kelly, Angela, and my friends, including Mika Boblitz, and Chris Roberts. Without them, this book would have been impossible. Finally, for anyone who ever wanted to believe in something when common sense told you not to...magic, myth, legends, and heroes...I dedicate this book.

Reach for the Moon. If you fall, you may land on a Star!

Learn more about The Order in
upcoming books from Candace Sams

The Gazing Globe
Coming in August 2002

Stone Heart
Coming in 2003

Goblin Moon
Coming in 2003

Gryphon's Quest

***

Candace Sams

GRYPHON'S QUEST
Published by ImaJinn Books, a division of ImaJinn

ISBN: 1-893896-72-2

10 9 8 7 6 5 4 3 2 1

PUBLISHER'S NOTE:
This book is a work of fiction. Names, characters, places and incidents are products of the author's imagination or are used fictitiously. Any resemblance to actual events or locales or persons, living or dead, is entirely coincidental.

Books are available at quantity discounts when used to promote products or services. For information please write to: Marketing Division, ImaJinn Books, P.O. Box 162, Hickory Corners, MI 49060-0162, or call toll free 1-877-625-3592.

Cover design by Patricia Lazarus

ImaJinn Books, a division of ImaJinn
P.O. Box 162, Hickory Corners, MI 49060-0162
Toll Free: 1-877-625-3592
http://www.imajinnbooks.com

One

Gryphon O'Connor watched the Nymphs stroll by and enter the woods. They were the only ones daring enough to get so close, but if their sexual appetites weren't recently satisfied, even he'd seem approachable. He continued his ritual bathing and knew they watched. He could hear their incessant giggling from the shrubs. What difference did it make if they chose to ogle him? They were almost as nude as he. Their race loved nothing more than to expose themselves to anyone in the Order. Many a man whose eyes wandered in their direction had to answer to a jealous mate when he arrived home. But Gryph would never have that particular problem to worry about. There would never be a mate waiting for him. Even the damned Ogres had mates, and they were as lacking in looks as they were brains. Being one of a kind might not have been so bad except he'd had no say in the matter at all. He shook his head and continued to wash. There was no point rehashing that particular subject. His parents' mistake couldn't be undone.

He glanced toward his black cape and the message secreted within its folds. It had only arrived at his home in the abbey ruins an hour ago. He wondered why the Sorceress' latest summons contained the unusual words, '*Come without delay...no time for explanation.*' Her instructions usually gave him dates, times and places for his next assignment, but she had never used language indicating such urgency. Every instinct told him he should have probably left already, but the Sorceress could damned well wait. Any mission she had in mind required preparing his body and spirit and that preparation could only be accomplished by cleansing at leisure in an enchanted pool. Besides, what was she going to do if he didn't jump at her command as he'd always done? Turn him into a creature everyone in the Order feared? Well, it was too bloody late for that. The way he saw it, anything she could do to him would only bring a release from thirty-three years of being a freak. Even in a world where outsiders would deem all inhabitants of the Order as unbearable monsters, he would be labeled the most monstrous of all.

He swam to the opposite side of the pool, reached for his leather crane bag and began to search within its recesses. A large measure of whiskey usually took the edge off his depressive feelings. Let the old woman wait. He'd done everything she'd ever asked of him, and she still couldn't manage with all her persuasive powers to have him accepted as an equal. He was tired of helping her settle problems within the Order, only to be shunned for having done so. If no one else gave a bloody rat's ass, why should he? After taking a long drink from the bottle, he reached back into the bag for some food. His hand glanced against a heavy object, and he drew it forward.

Gryphon closed his hand tightly around the quartz crystal and felt its cold edges bite into his palm. Lore had given it to him for luck. He suddenly felt a small measure of shame at having forgotten his friend. Even as a child, the Fairy had sided with him and attempted to befriend Gryphon as best he could. No sooner would the two of them begin to play than Lore's parents would quickly call their son away and chide him for getting too close to *The O'Connor*. It was on one rare occasion when Lore's parents weren't present that Lore had given him the crystal. Since then, Gryph kept the stone close and carried it with him almost everywhere. It was a constant reminder that one person in the entire Order wasn't afraid of him. Now, these many years later, Lore was leader of his people. Gryph's responsibilities kept him from seeing the man as much as he'd like, but the Fairy Leader had done more to try to gain his childhood friend's acceptance than the Sorceress ever had. Still, most of the Fairies had minds of their own. The most Lore had been able to achieve was the lessening of tensions when Gryph approached their territory. For that he was grateful, and his feelings of gratitude intensified his guilt. The protection he provided the Order helped Lore and the other Fairies every bit as much as it did the Druids, Elves and the others who disliked him. He just wished they could get over his ability to shapeshift into something unusual and let him be.

"I didn't ask for this," he mumbled.

More giggling from the trees and bushes alerted Gryph to the fact that the Nymphs were nearby and still watching him.

"What didn't you ask for, creature?" one voice asked.

"I was speaking to myself, Nymph. Go away!" Gryphon took another long drink of whiskey, angry he'd spoken his thoughs aloud. Angrier still that he was, to them, a creature. Not just another member of the Order.

"Do you want some company?" the disembodied voice questioned.

"Go away," Gryph repeated, emphasizing the words so she'd understand he didn't want them near.

Gryphon watched as one black-haired Nymph crawled toward him from her hiding space. Her full breasts swung from beneath a thin white veil of fabric. This, in turn, was twisted about her slim, blue body as if she'd been writhing in the nearby ferns. Even from several feet away, he could tell he wasn't the only one in the sacred woods to have been drinking. Maybe that was the reason the little chit had the nerve to come near him. The smell of alcohol clung to her like gum to the bottom of a shoe. It wasn't a very flattering come-on when a damned woman had to drink herself into a near stupor just to approach him.

"What part of *go away* did you not understand?" Gryphon snapped at the approaching figure.

"Don't be so abrupt with me, O'Connor. I'm only offering a little...companionship."

"You're drunk."

She laughed and fell forward. Her outstretched hands reached for him. "I know. I have this wager with my sisters."

"Wager?" Gryph snorted.

"They want to know if you're as well endowed as the other Druids we've known. I'm betting you are. I mean...a creature like you must be well-favored, so to speak. Everyone says you're huge when you shift. We can see you when you fly, but can never get close enough to really get a good look at your bottom half. We're just waiting for you to leave the pool so we can see."

Angrier than he could remember being in a long time, Gryphon pulled the woman forward and into the water with him. Her shrieks of laughter did little to calm his rage. "Go back to where you came from and tell your little bitch sisters to leave me alone. I don't have to take this from you. ANY OF YOU!"

He pushed her away and reached for his clothing. The woman's laughter and that of the others rang in his ears. Gryphon grabbed his belongings as he hefted his weight from the water. This was the last, the final outrage he was going to put up with. He should have just taken the girl right then and there, but something in him couldn't sink so low as to have sex with a woman who didn't know what she was doing.

"I win. He's marvelous," one of the Nymphs observed as she caught site of Gryphon's exposed body. Her sisters joined her in a round of bawdy whoops and whistles.

"Bloody damned Nymphs," he muttered as he stumbled away while pulling his clothing on.

To cool his anger, Gryph took the longest route through the ancient forest, or *Shire*, as it was known to the Order. Doing so cost him more time, but he found himself wanting to see the Goblin Meadow. It was here that his heart always found a little peace. Glancing up at the sky, he knew it was about time for the children to be allowed out to play, and he dearly wanted to watch. His warrior's soul found a calming influence in their innocent antics.

He waited by a nearby tree until their laughter reached him. In spite of his anger with the Nymphs, a smile drifted across his face. Tiny forms approached as they danced and cavorted with Pixies. Some of the Fairy children had their wings out and they glittered like jeweled gauze. In the deepest part of him, Gryph desperately wanted a child of his own. But he'd long since resigned himself to the fact that what he wanted just didn't matter. So, he assuaged his longings by watching the children of others.

A little girl ran straight toward the tree where he waited. She had a tiny fistful of flowers and laughed as if there were no problems on Earth too terrible or demanding. Her life was one beautiful adventure. Gryph's tough heart reached out to her, wishing he could have been that carefree in his youth.

Sensing the presence of another, the girl stopped and looked into the edge of the woods. She walked straight toward Gryphon and stopped when her eyes made out his form.

"Hello," she smiled up at him.

There seemed to be no fear in her at all.

"Hello, little one." He stooped down so he could speak to her on an even level.

"I got some pretty flowers. Want some?" She handed part of the bouquet of wild trillium to him.

Gryph laughed and brought his hand forward to take the small offering. He abruptly stood when a loud voice rang out.

"Lily, get over here this instant!" A tall woman ran forward and pulled the little girl to her. She glared at him and walked away with the child, scolding her for getting too close to the *'gryphon.'*

He stepped back as though he'd been slapped. There was no way, in this life or any other, he'd harm a child. That the toddlers were being taught to stay away from him hurt far worse than anything the Nymphs could have possibly said or done. It wasn't as though he was a stranger to these people. He swiftly turned so that those adults who were entering the meadow couldn't see the tears in his eyes. In that instant, he hated them all.

Gryphon strode away without acknowledging a soul. Had he looked back, he would have seen Lily waving at him and ignoring the condemning remarks made by her mother. After all, *The O'Connor* had been there before and hadn't ever hurt anyone. And Lore, the Fairy Leader, had said the big man was nice. That he was safe. Though Gryphon didn't see her, Lily just kept waving and vowed to pick some flowers for him on some other night. He didn't look like someone who would ever hurt her. And if Lore said the gryphon was okay, then he was okay.

***

"You know I wouldn't completely ignore a summons from the Sorceress." But the thought had occurred to him. Gryphon shook his long hair back over his shoulder as he spoke.

"I know, Gryph." Gwyneth O'Connor sighed. "But you're late, and there's a dangerous situation evolving. She'll be terribly angry with you."

"So...she'll be miffed. She'll get over it. It's my job to be here. I'm here."

From the backseat of the large luxury car, Gryphon O'Connor watched the guilt-ridden glances exchanged between his two parents. Thirty-three years before, James and Gwyneth O'Connor had meddled with powers that should have been left alone. Gryph's *condition*, as he referred to his shapeshifting ability, was the result of that meddling.

"Don't worry about me. I'll be all right. Shayla will give me the information, I'll handle the problem and be back before you know it." Gryph quickly changed the subject to spare his parents' feelings. "The flight from the English countryside was long. I'd have gone the entire distance, but there was no sense taking the risk of being seen during the daylight hours. And besides, I wanted to see my two favorite people before meeting with Shayla tonight. How have things been these past weeks?"

"Well enough, Son," James said over his shoulder, keeping his eyes on the winding and narrow Irish road. "Your mother and I have had a wonderful time in France. There are many of our kind still practicing there, you know."

Gryph smiled patiently at the two people he loved more than anything in the world. He stretched his six-foot-four inch frame as far as the backseat area would allow and listened to his parents' latest travel exploits. The flight from England to Ireland had been more tiring than he wanted his parents to know. He had to practice great care when he traveled, avoiding overly populated areas and the eyes of those who constantly looked toward the heavens. As a result, covering distances sometimes took longer than expected and could be strenuous.

He'd had to avoid several British army helicopters on routine maneuvers the night before, and keeping his distance had added miles to his trip. The human world wasn't ready for him and his highly unusual alter ego. He knew his presence, should it ever be detected, wouldn't be explainable or tolerated.

He listened to his parents converse. That they loved him had never been questioned. It was the extent of that love which had brought him to his current, painful circumstance. Blaming them was unthinkable. They had no knowledge of the responsibilities the Sorceress heaped upon him. He rarely shared the nature of his dealings with anyone and went out of his way to keep Gwyneth and James O'Connor from knowing. He let them think he simply helped out when called upon. They needn't know any more. It would crush them to learn Shayla Gallagher had him doing every dirty little deed she didn't feel like handling. He tried hard while in his parents' presence not to make much of the Sorceress' assignments or his part in enforcing rules within the Order. For their part, he felt sure they tried to pretend he wasn't such an outcast. It was a game they all played. He pretended not to be hurt by what others in the Order said. His parents pretended the situation wasn't all that serious. That their son was just like any other Druid. For them, Gryph's latest residence, a dilapidated English abbey, was just a retreat their son had chosen as a resting place. For Gryphon, it was one of the only places left where he didn't feel like such an outcast. Like someone who was so different. There, he had been left alone to read and decipher ancient tomes in an effort to learn more about his own history. No one had asked many questions of him. There were outsiders who lived nearby, but they rarely ventured into that part of the forest.

"Son, are you listening?" James looked through the rearview mirror at Gryph, repeating himself to be heard.

"Sorry, Father. I was woolgathering. A bad habit of mine, I'm afraid." Gryph smiled at his father.

"I was asking if you thought the full moon tonight might make whatever Shayla has in mind more conspicuous?" James spoke, enunciating each word to make sure Gryph was paying attention.

"I doubt it. Shayla hasn't practiced in anonymity all these years without learning how to be crafty," Gryph responded as he watched the passing scenery. He tried to keep the sarcasm out of his voice and hoped he succeeded.

"But we'll be meeting with her at the ancient stone circle on the hill." Gwyneth turned in the front seat to see Gryph better. "Anyone will be able to see what we're doing under the light of the full moon."

"I promise you, Mother, Shayla knows what she's doing." *The old crone always has,* he thought to himself.

***

Gryph stood in pretended reverent silence as Shayla Gallagher, Sorceress of the Ancients, spoke the words which preceded the meeting. His parents wore the long white robes of their Druid ancestors while he was dressed in a similar robe of brown. Shayla lifted a crystal to the night sky with one hand and threw herbs into a small fire at her feet with the other. The evening breeze lifted the older woman's long, silver hair from her shoulders. While still beautiful, she looked every bit the wizened, prophetic conjuror she wanted others to revere. But Gryph was past the point of respecting her. Her wiles had worked on him as a boy, and the small tasks she'd given him seemed important yet simple. The tasks and their importance had grown, however. And he wasn't a boy to be tricked any longer. He knew the older woman for what she was S a user.

Gryph pulled his hood up as his long dark hair began to drift about his own shoulders. In customary fashion, he had braided long strands of it next to his face. Celtic symbols were painted on his forehead and cheekbones in a shade of garish, blue woad as ceremony demanded. They matched the Celtic knots which had been tattooed at childhood on his biceps and inner thighs, marks of his position as a warrior.

Finally, Shayla turned to Gryph with a smile on her face. He walked forward and, more for the benefit of his parents, kissed her outstretched hands. She gave him a disparaging look, and he knew she wasn't fooled.

"Gryphon, I was told you received my message two days

ago. I trust you have a plausible excuse for your delay?"

"There's no excuse except I simply couldn't get here any faster." He just wanted her to get on with it.

"I couldn't have made myself more clear. Circumstances here are very serious," she replied with condemnation.

"Sorry, Shayla. I wasn't able to file a flight plan with the local authorities. I got here as soon as I safely could."

"That had better not be sarcasm, young man. I don't tolerate it well," she warned.

Gwyneth placed a hand on Gryph's arm. "Please, Gryphon, don't make her angrier. This isn't the time."

Gryph heaved a sigh, glanced at his father's reproachful countenance and decided his exhibition of disrespect could wait until another time. A time when he and Shayla were alone, and he didn't have to guard his words for his parents' sake. "Just tell me what you want me to do, Sorceress."

She raised her eyebrows imperiously and shot Gryphon a look that would have sent less bold men into hiding. For now, their personal battle could wait. She took a deep breath to quell her anger, then proceeded.

"Several weeks ago, friends from the North sent word that an ancient burial mound had been desecrated."

"You want me to find out who did it?" Gryph asked.

"We know who it was. What we didn't know, until quite recently, is what was taken." She walked toward the largest of the stones in the circle. "Along with ancient jewelry and weapons, three stones were taken. While it was criminal enough that the personal items were stolen, the stones are the most serious of the missing objects."

Gryph's eyes narrowed. "Why? What's their meaning?"

"The stones are old. They are so ancient, at one time these stones were referred to as having Ogham markings. They date to the time before the Romans came. They were buried with the remains of an ancient Celtic family who were sworn to protect them at all costs. Their power is unspeakable. Should they fall into the wrong hands and their original use be discovered, horrors will walk the Earth." She paced back and forth in front of the fire. "Unless we undo what's been done, the entire Order is in danger."

Gryph felt his skin grow cold. For the first time in his life, he saw Shayla show signs of fear. He'd never seen her in a state of agitation. She never paced, never clutched at the crystal she used to call forth her spirit guides, and he'd never *ever* heard her voice shake as it was now. This wasn't the normal assignment. Now he had second thoughts about delaying his response to the Sorceress' summons. Behind him, he heard his parents' gasps.

"Shayla, what were these stones?" James asked as he walked forward and stood beside Gryph.

"Marks of the oldest of our Druid kind were chiseled into them," Shayla answered. "These were the marks of making, of shape shifting."

"*By all that's sacred. No*!" James whispered. "The Rune Stones of the Tuatha De! Danann."

Gwyneth grasped her husband's hand in fear, the blood pumping through her veins visible in her flushed features.

Seeing his parents' response, Gryph looked at Shayla. "Explain," he demanded. "I know of the old ways and have studied ritual objects, but I've never heard of these stones."

"That isn't surprising, as they were kept very secret. The name your father has given them is what they are now called. Their magic may have been derived from wisdom within ancient Ogham writings. The Tuatha used these writings to embed powers into the rune stones. Anyone who deciphers the stones for honest intent will be able to move about in a form reflecting their true soul. However, those seeking to use the stones for evil intent will take on the form of something monstrous," Shayla told him. "Your job, Gryphon, is to retrieve the stones before that can happen. Only you, with your special power, can bring back the stones. They must be hidden away, once and for all, where no human can find them. No single being was meant to have that kind of power."

And yet, that burden has been inflicted upon me, Gryph thought, feeling old bitterness in his heart. His powers were something that, given the choice, he'd never have accepted.

As if she knew his thoughts, Shayla looked him straight in

the eyes. "Your soul, however embittered it may be, is clean and unfettered, Gryphon O'Connor. Your ability to shape shift came from the mistake your parents made with a minor enchantment. Can you imagine that power being magnified one-hundred fold and being used by someone whose nature is corrupt?"

"The stones are really that powerful?" Gryph asked, turning to look into the distance, his eyes attempting to pierce the darkness.

"Yes, and they must be returned here as soon as possible," Shayla warned.

"You said you knew who took them?"

"Yes, Gryphon, and I know where you should begin looking. But be warned. It won't be easy to retrieve them. You may have to break the outsider's law in order to do so. Even so, since this task is more than I've ever asked of you, I'll make sure the reward for recovering the objects is great."

"I want no reward. Just a promise, Shayla. Since I'm fairly sure you know what I want, and since I feel reasonably sure you'll grant it, I'll find the stones and bring them back." In return, he wanted no more asked of him. That was the only request he'd make. "Where do I have to go?"

Gwyneth ran forward. "He's my only son, Shayla. The power he might face is too great to confront alone. This must be the most dangerous thing you've ever asked of him."

"Then you and James may follow him. While you're Druids and not warrior class, he'll need some sort of backup. If he should fail, then the task will become yours to complete."

"*Absolutely not*!" Gryphon swiped his hand in immediate dismissal of this new turn of events. "I refuse to have them responsible for an assignment meant for me. You said it yourself, they're not warriors, I *am*."

"Then I suggest you start acting like one," Shayla proclaimed in a loud voice.

"If this is so critical, what will you be doing?" Gryphon placed his hands on his hips and looked down at the older woman. "Shouldn't the person with the most power be present to help bring back the stones?"

"*Gryphon*! I didn't raise my son to be so disrespectful to the Sorceress of the Ancients." James placed a hand on his son's forearm and forced him to turn and look at him.

"It's all right, James," the Sorceress placated. "Your son should know that if his and your attempts to bring back the stones are unsuccessful, I'll be doing what I can here to save the rest of the Order."

Gryph turned away from his father to look at her. The woman wasn't exaggerating. There was a solemnity in her voice, a look of urgency on her face. "I'll bring the bloody things back."

"You'd better, or the rest of the world will learn of us. And while you take exception to me and my methods, Gryphon, surely the others shouldn't be endangered because of our differences. Surely you don't blame everyone for the way some treat you?"

Gryphon glanced at his parents, unwilling to have the Sorceress continue the conversation while they were within earshot. He didn't want his parents to feel guilty over the way others behaved toward him. What the O'Connors had done couldn't be altered. He lowered his voice. "I've promised to do as you've asked. We'll talk about our differences, and the way anyone else behaves, later."

Undaunted, the Sorceress continued, "Surely the children aren't to blame for how you and the others feel toward one another? You don't want harm coming to them, do you?"

"Of course not," Gryphon snapped back. The woman knew his weakest point and wasn't above exploiting it. "I've told you I'll go. What else do you want?"

"Damn you, Gryphon. I want your heart in the task. It could mean the difference between success and failure." She looked at Gryphon, then James and Gwyneth. "You all play this silly little charade where Gryphon pretends no one cares what he is. I can't make people like or accept you, Gryphon. Only you can do that. And I can't keep your parents from feeling guilt. Only they can deal with those feelings. What I can do is protect the Order. And this I'll do at all costs. Our children have the right to grow up in safety. To that end I've given you a task to perform. It'll take everything you have to pull this off. Without your full cooperation and willingness...well, there's nothing left to do but see to the safety of the others. But *try* to think of the them, Gryph. While some have shunned you, others have tried to help. You won't see it because you're so wrapped up in self pity. I could almost hate you except I haven't time for the distraction. Alternate plans need to be made in case you fail. In your current state, I can easily see that happening."

Gryphon watched her stalk off. Anger not withstanding, the Sorceress had never spoken to him so bluntly. Part of him wanted to run after her as he had when he was a boy and she'd been displeased with some small thing he'd neglected. He wanted her to care about him. Not just what he could do for her. He felt empty, then shame crept in. He had to lay his personal problems aside and do his best. While he wasn't exactly as popular as he might have liked, he had no business endangering anyone because of his attitude. Especially since the Sorceress seemed so certain only he could carry out this assignment.

He sighed and turned to his parents. Gwyneth's eyes shimmered with tears. James' head was bowed as if he were deep in thought.

"I have to gather some things for the trip. Ask the Sorceress if she'll meet me back here in one hour." His head went up. "I won't let anyone down. But I'll need to know everything. Where to go, what she wants done. Tell her...just tell her I'll do it only for the children. She owes me nothing." He walked away and hoped the message would be taken as an apology for his behavior. If he couldn't come out and say it, he'd let his actions speak for him.

***

Two hours later, Shayla, James and Gwyneth looked into the night sky. They saw the clear, menacing outline of an ancient being against the pale reflection of the moon. They heard the unearthly cry of a beast of legend. He was the only one of his kind. Gwyneth turned to her husband and buried her head into his chest. James held her as she cried. Because of their foolishness, their only son would be forever alone.

TWO

"*Jeez*, Heather, you work far too hard." Niall Alexander complained to the young woman walking slowly beside him. "We're hardly ever alone anymore."

Heather sighed in frustration. His attention was beginning to interfere with her work. "I know, Niall. But if I'm ever going to be allowed to do my own research, the way you and Professor McPherson are, then I have to prove I'm worth the grant money." She brushed a falling leaf from her hair. "Besides, I love what I do."

"That's your father's influence. There wasn't a better archeologist in the field of Celtic studies than he was. Still, I want more time with you," he remarked, his posture slumping as it often did when she denied him something. Her gracefully slim, five-foot-six inch frame made other men stare when she walked by and her clear, silver-blue gaze even had the old security guard straightening his tie. Niall made it known she was having a relationship with him, and that it was strictly hands off where she was concerned.

Heather turned to look up into Niall's green eyes. "If you're so worried about having more time together, why don't you give up some of your research?"

When Niall ran a slender hand through his blond hair and looked at her like she was crazy, Heather knew that, like always, she would be doing most of the giving in their relationship. Niall wasn't at all receptive to giving up any part of his career in acquisitions to have more time with her. No. The guy definitely wasn't the knight-in-shining-armor type she'd always wanted to find. No hero material there. But maybe she was judging him too hard. Nobody could ever come up to the image of the hero her imagination conjured.

"What about this weekend? There's a big party at the Professor's house for some of the more prestigious donors. I just received my invitation in the mail. You will be coming with me, won't you?" he pleaded.

"I don't know, Niall. I want to get a look at those new artifacts sent in from Ireland and Scotland. I'm lucky Dr. McPherson is letting me have the first shot at deciphering some of the find."

Niall wrapped his arms around her waist, keeping her from walking across the parking lot to her car. "You're much too beautiful to have your head buried in ancient history all weekend. Come on, babe, go to the party with me."

"We'll see," Heather sighed with resignation. Niall would never take her love for her work seriously. It was that way with most of the men who worked with her. Not many of them looked beyond what they saw on the outside. She suspected that had she been born plain none of them would even notice her at all. Niall was right about one thing. Her love for the antiquities she studied was deeply instilled by her father's work. She'd grown up around Celtic objects. Not the least important of which was her Irish mother. She smiled to herself as fond memories invaded her thoughts. The stories the woman told her gave her a deep sense of belonging when she handled particular artifacts. It was like stepping into another world of magic, myth and mystery. Something she deeply wanted others to feel.

"That's my girl. I'll call later about when I'll pick you up." Niall kissed her soundly then turned and walked away.

Heather mentally shook herself back into the present. She hadn't been listening to a word Niall had said. Sometimes she really just wished he would shut-up all together. He was a brilliant technician where artifacts were concerned, but her thrill at having a man with his academic reputation pay her attention was wearing thin. Occasionally, however, he'd turn on his brain, act like a regular co-worker and allow her some leeway in dealing with the categorizing of the Professor's finds. Niall could be exasperating and remarkably astute all within the space of a few minutes. So...he wasn't Mr. Perfect. Was there any man who was? At least he loved the artifacts as much as she.

From her mother's stories, she'd conjured an image of a hero like Cu!chulainn, The Hound of Culann, warrior of Ulster. She'd dreamed, in her romantic school-girl days, of meeting a man with that kind of magnetism. That kind of machismo. She laughed to herself. Being a little older and wiser had definitely dulled that particular image. There were no heroes. Just regular men with regular needs and flaws. Even some of her beloved artifacts sometimes had chips. That didn't make them less valued. Just more realistic.

"Hi, Ned." She waved when she saw the museum's night-time security guard approach. The older man shuffled slowly down the steps toward her. His balding head was covered with a baseball cap and had the word *Security* inscribed on it in gold letters. His body was stooped, and the hand he offered to her was wrinkled and gnarled with age.

"Evening, Miss Green. Was that your young man?" Ned squinted his eyes when he got near the lights from the parking lot.

"That was Niall," Heather responded, reluctant to have him or anyone else refer to Niall as her "young man."

"Well, if you don't mind my saying so, I'm kind of glad he's gone."

"Why is that?" she asked in surprise.

"Well, it isn't often an old coot like me gets to walk a pretty girl to her car. I'd hate to think that young buck took my place. This is my favorite part of the job."

Heather laughed. "No one could take your place, Ned." She looped her arm through his. "And how many years have we known each other that you still call me Miss Green?"

"Well, we can't have rumors starting, can we? You know what a gossip den this place is. I wouldn't want anyone knowing we've been meeting like this." He winked. "We have our reputations to think of. No, I'll just settle for the formality of Miss Green. That's about all my old heart can handle."

Heather smiled brightly at his humor and pulled her jacket more tightly around her to shut out the night chill. Ned Williamson had been her close friend since the day they had first met over five years before. Most people didn't pay any attention to the old security guard, but that was their loss as far as she was concerned. He was a dear, gentle soul. "Well, we'll have to be careful about these clandestine meetings," she joked. "As you say, someone might start an ugly rumor."

"Anybody ever says anything bad about you, and they'll answer straight to me." Ned patted her arm in a fatherly fashion.

"Thanks, Ned. It's nice to know I have such a loyal friend."

"Well, I'll see you in the morning." He stopped as she reached into her jacket for her car keys.

"Good. I'll be in early. I'm anxious to get into those crates Professor McPherson had sent from overseas."

"You work too hard. You should be out more enjoying life. Believe me, you're only young once."

"Well, what can I do? I can't stay away from you, Ned. Seeing you every night and then again in the mornings makes my day."

Ned laughed, then turned more serious as he opened her car door for her. "You know, Miss Green, not many people here would give me the time of day. We joke and all that, but I think you're one of the nicest people who's ever come to work here. If that young man doesn't know what he's got, he's a fool."

Heather felt tears sting her eyes. "Thank you. That means a lot to me. Not many people have a good friend like you." She gave him a friendly hug. "Good night and stay warm."

"Good night, Heather," he said, finally dropping the formality. "Drive safely."

Ned stood and watched her drive away. He was turning to continue on his rounds outside the museum when a strange sound from the upper floors caught his attention. He walked inside the main exhibit room, up two flights of stairs, and into the hallway leading to the shipping and receiving room. Crates of all kinds of new artifacts had been placed in the musty, cavernous room according to their country of origin. Ned stopped, but didn't hear anything. The room was dark toward the far end. He walked to the circuit box to turn on the ceiling lights for that area. Suddenly, he was blinded by a bright green light. He covered his face with his hands until his eyes could adjust. When he was finally able to focus, he stared in horror.

"My God...what in the name of...*Oh sweet Jesus! No...No...don't...Nooooo*!

***

Heather got up early the next morning. She wanted to beat Niall at having a look at the newest artifacts from Professor McPherson's latest trip. Of all the things she unpacked first, those from Ireland and Scotland always took precedence. She was like a kid in the candy store when it came to any Celtic objects. Getting her hands on them before some of the other technicians arrived was her priority. Turning into the parking lot, she was shocked to find police cars parked everywhere. People were standing about on the museum lawn, pointing toward the main building. She quickly exited her car and walked toward the nearest police officer.

"Excuse me," she spoke above the din of radio transmissions, "can you tell me what's happened?"

A young officer turned to her. "Do you have some business inside, Miss?"

"Yes, I work in the research and acquisitions department. What's happened?"

"I'm sorry, Miss, but we're not letting anyone inside just yet. We're investigating a homicide."

"*A what*!" she gasped.

"Heather," Niall called.

She turned to see Niall and Angus McPherson walking toward her.

"Niall, Dr. McPherson, what's happened?" She watched as the Professor bent his greying head and his usually tall shoulders drooped. Niall stood tall and faced her. His boyishly attractive face was uncharacteristically serious.

Niall spoke softly. "There's no easy way to say this except to just spit it out. Ned Williamson was murdered."

Heather stared at both of them. McPherson's gaze never left the ground. "But I just saw him last night. He walked me to my car like he always does. He was fine when I left. Why would anyone...I mean, he wouldn't have harmed a living soul. Why would someone want to hurt him? That doesn't make any sense. *Why?*" Heather's voice broke, and she began to cry.

Niall pulled her into his embrace while Professor McPherson stared into the distance in disbelief.

A stocky, brown-haired man in a dark business suit approached them. "Excuse me, Miss, did I overhear you correctly? Did you see the security guard last night?"

"Yes," Heather sobbed.

"I'm Detective Dayton with The New York City Police Department's Homicide Division," he addressed her as he pulled out a badge and I.D. card. "I'll have to ask you some questions if you don't mind."

"She's far too upset to talk to anyone right now," Niall responded.

"It's all right, Niall. I want to help if I can." Heather pushed herself away from Niall's embrace.

"I take it you were a close friend of the deceased?" the officer asked.

"Yes, I was. And his name was Ned Williamson." Heather spoke harshly through her tears. Ned wasn't just a lifeless body, a *deceased.* He was a human being.

"Could you tell us when you last saw him?"

"I left late last night. Ned walked me to my car. It was about 9:30."

"Did you notice anything unusual or hear any strange noises before you left the building?"

"No. Everything was like it always was. Ned walked me to my car, which was parked right over there." Heather pointed toward a large oak tree. "He stood right there and said good night and told me he'd see me in the..." Heather's voice trailed away.

"If I can get your name, address and phone number, we'll contact you when you're more able to talk. We might need to get a statement from you." Dayton proceeded to write down the requisite information Heather gave, then continued. "Right now, I'll be working inside the building. Sorry about the inconvenience, but it's necessary if we're going to find out what happened last night. Let me know later if there's anything valuable missing. As yet, we don't have a motive for his death."

"We'll be in touch if anything's missing," Niall responded for Heather.

Heather would have normally resented Niall's answering for her. But all she could think of was the friend she had lost. Why should such a thing happen to a kindly old man who had never hurt anyone?

***

Three days later, Niall and Heather were unpacking crates when he paused, looked up and caught sight of Heather's face. There were dark circles under her eyes, and she seemed unusually distracted. "Honey, if you don't mind my saying so, you look like hell. Haven't you been sleeping well?"

"No," was all Heather could say. She looked around at the musty boxes she'd spent all morning unpacking. Excelsior and foam packing material lay everywhere, and a faint odor of peat and earth pervaded the shipping and receiving room. The flourescent lighting in her work area made the Celtic artifacts look hideously grey. Just like her mood.

"It was a good thing Professor McPherson asked the Board of Directors to close the museum for a few days. Our new Celtic exhibit will be opening soon, and the publicity from this murder won't sit well with our investors and the Board of Directors." Niall idly picked up a small Celtic cross which had been chiseled from marble.

Heather audibly gasped. "Is that all you can think about? *A man is dead, Niall*!"

"Darling, I'm well aware of that," Niall spoke to her as if she were stupid. "But there's nothing anyone can do about the murder. The man is dead and life has to go on. Williamson would have wanted it that way. He loved working at the museum and wouldn't have wanted to see our work hindered." He patted her arm in a condescending manner. "By closing for a few days, the police have more time to investigate the crime scene, and we have more time to defuse the situation with the people who make our work possible. Remember, without the big bucks, none of us does any research nor do we acquire any new artifacts."

"You know, Niall, sometimes you can be the biggest ass!" Heather declared.

"I'm going to ignore that in light of your emotional condition over Williamson's death. You'll see reason soon enough when you get back into your research."

"Ned. His name was Ned!" Heather insisted. "And where were the people with the big bucks when the coroner released his body for the funeral? Ned worked here for years. Did they even send flowers or contact the family?"

"Sweetheart, it's late, you're overwrought and you should go home and get some rest."

"You're right, Niall, I'm overwrought and I'm going home. But do me a favor."

"Yes?"

"Don't ever call me sweetheart again. I've just about had it with the possessive crap!"

"Again, I'm going to make allowances for your behavior because of your emotions," Niall patronizingly soothed. "You've worked too hard today on Angus's latest shipments. You should have knocked off earlier and let me finish the inventory."

"That detective told me that Ned was killed upstairs where we were working. I don't know how anyone could have gotten inside that area. The police found the outside doors locked."

"You're dwelling on this too much, Heather. You're going to make yourself ill over it. From now on, we'll work together if we have to stay late. Hopefully, the new security people will be able to take care of the situation. Don't worry about anything. Williamson, that is, *Ned*, wouldn't have wanted that."

"McPherson hasn't had much to say about all of this," Heather muttered.

"He's as shocked as you are, darling. Now, go home and get some sleep."

Heather put down the piece of stone she'd been holding, grabbed her coat off a nearby rack and walked out of the building. Niall followed her to the parking lot, talking the entire time. As she got in her car and drove away, she thought of the many women in every department of the museum who would give years off their lives if Niall would glance their way. His tall, Nordic looks made women drool, but Heather was finding his personality cloying and obnoxious.

***

From the night shadows beneath the trees, Gryph watched thc blond man walk back into the museum. He'd heard enough to know he'd come to the right place. Gryph was dismayed to find that the headlines in the newspapers had neither shocked nor frightened the hard city dwellers around him. The news reported that a man had been slain and insinuated the murder was animalistic. People commented on the death as if it were just one more breakfast topic before starting another day filled with plodding sameness. The only voice of humanity came from the woman in the parking lot. She spoke softly of her dead friend, and her voice lingered on the night air. Her long brown hair drifted with the autumn breeze. She wasn't as tall as most of the women he knew. Despite the bulky coat she wore, he could see she was slender and walked with a grace Fairies would envy. She lifted her face to the sky, and he saw her profile. It looked like one he'd once seen on a cameo. A small, slightly turned up nose wrinkled when she smelled cooking from a nearby diner. Her lips were pink and full. But when he heard her mention McPherson, all these thoughts fled. That name prompted him to action.

He couldn't go into the museum without knowing where to look. The building was monstrously large. According to her conversation, the woman had been performing an inventory of McPherson's latest shipments, so Gryph would seek her out. Stepping deeper into the darkness, he quickly stripped off his clothing and placed his things into the large leather bag he carried. This he tied loosely around his neck. He then fell to one knee and willed the *change*. As always, he saw the familiar glittering lights before his eyes and felt his body go numb. Then his flesh altered and grew. His limbs became thick enough to hold the massive weight of his new form, and feathers took the place of flesh. Fur melded to him where feathers would not. Wings unfolded between his shoulder blades, and the call of a bird of prey took the place of his voice. He spread his wings to the night sky, but was unconcerned about catching the car the woman drove. No matter how fast a car could be driven, a mythical beast could fly faster.

THREE

Heather stepped into a hot shower and tried to relax. She was more tired than she could ever remember being. Besides mourning the loss of her friend, she'd thrown herself into classifying the artifacts Professor McPherson and Niall had helped dig out of their various crates. It amazed her how much Angus had been able to obtain. Some of the pieces were very old and brittle. All of them were listed as having been recovered from approved sites within Britain, Scotland and Ireland.

After the shower turned cold, she towel dried her hair, turned out the lights and slipped into bed. The familiar site of filled bookshelves, Celtic figurines and neat stacks of papers comforted her. The apartment was a small duplication of her office space but, with a few vases of chrysanthemums and some pictures of famous European ruins hanging on the walls, it was home. She only had to take a few steps to enter the utilitarian kitchenette and living room. The main attraction to the place had been a patio with a wonderful view of the New York skyline.

A warm cup of tea would be wonderful, but she was simply too tired to throw off the cozy blanket and turn on the tiny gas stove. The autumn wind must have picked up. Just before she fell asleep, she heard what she took to be a branch from the nearby trees scrape against the roof.

Gryph waited on the gravel roof for some time. He changed back into human form, untied the leather bag from around his neck and, except for his shirt, quickly redressed. The sight of him needed to be impressive enough to frighten information out of his prey. And there was nothing he could think of that might frighten her more than awakening to a half-clothed intruder. It would leave her thinking the rest of his clothing would come off if she didn't cooperate. Something deep inside him abhorred treating anyone so vilely, but he wanted this thing done and over.

Leaving the bag on the rooftop, he lightly pounced onto the patio. The lights from within went out. Again, he waited. He had made sure the woman had entered this particular apartment. Years of honing his skills would never let him make the mistake of entering the wrong place, especially not when his survival depended on such stealth. Creeping silently through the tiny living room and into the bedroom, he made his way through the clutter. The lilliputian space directly contrasted to the cavernous abbey ruin and lush forest he inhabited. Books were everywhere. Small Celtic objects littered spaces not reserved for books. Despite the darkness, he could see the furnishings were mismatched pieces better suited to comfort than appearance. He wondered if any of the things displayed were the stolen artifacts from the burial mound. As he approached the bed where the woman slept, his vision adjusted, and he found the outline of her slender form. Quietly, he knelt by the bed and very slowly and deliberately placed his hand over her mouth.

Heather felt warmth close over the lower portion of her face. She instantly came awake, tried to fight, but found herself pulled against an enormous warm body. The first thoughts to careen through her startled brain were those of being raped and murdered.

"Don't fight," a deep voice whispered into her ear. "I won't harm you. All I want is information. Answer my questions, and I'll leave as quickly as I came."

The low, lilting accent frightened Heather more than anything else in her life. She remained frozen, her back against her attacker's form. Her heart pounded so loudly that it threatened to drown out the sound of that deep, masculine voice. Sweat suddenly beaded on her body, and her hands shook so much she knew he had to feel it.

"If you promise not to cry out," he spoke, "I'll take my hand away. If you make any sound other than in answer to my questions, you'll regret it. Do you understand?"

She had heard that sometimes it was best to humor an attacker to give yourself time. She would do her best to see his face so she could tell the police later. If she were fortunate enough to have a later.

Heather nodded. The man slowly lowered his hand, but only to cradle her jaw with it.

"Now, tell me where Angus McPherson placed the items he took from Ireland."

When Heather didn't speak right away, the man pulled her closer to him. The back of her head rested against his left shoulder.

"Talk!" he commanded. "I don't have time for any histrionics."

Her fresh, clean scent drifted up to Gryphon as he held her. He could feel her trembling and attempted to discard himself of pity and of the warmth her body radiated. *I must stick to the task at hand. She's nothing but an outsider.*

"He... he...put the crates on the top floor of the museum...the west wing," Heather whispered.

"There are guards?"

"Yes. But, you know that. You killed Ned, didn't you?" Having foolishly said the words, Heather was sure he would kill her as well. This man wouldn't leave any more witnesses than had been present when Ned died.

"If I had killed the guard, why would I promise not to harm you? Why wouldn't I just break your neck and have done with it?"

"Maybe...m-maybe you murdered him because he couldn't tell you what you want to know. Whatever it is you want, you think I can help you get it. Then, you'll k-kill me, too."

"I did not kill the guard, little fool. And I would never harm a woman!" Contempt colored his voice. Why was he even wasting time justifying his actions? That angered him. He didn't owe this woman anything. Still, he had to have her help. Even if that meant terrorizing her into giving it."It's my guess that whoever stole the ancient belongings from my people committed the murder."

"Stole?" Heather's breath was coming in gasps.

"McPherson took objects he had no right to. Among those things he stole were a set of three large rune stones. They're Irish ancestral symbols and don't belong here. They must be returned."

"Are you accusing Professor McPherson of murder?" Heather's eyes grew wide.

"Why not? I know he's a thief."

"As far as I know, there are no rune stones in the crates." Panic and increasing terror made her start to babble. "I've told you everything I know. I-I haven't seen your face, so it would be impossible for me to tell the police what you look like. D-Don't kill me!"

Slowly, he dropped his hands from her shoulder and jaw and turned her to face him. "I'll say it again, I *killed no one*! I'm here to recover stolen pieces of history, objects that were taken through the desecration of burial sites. McPherson didn't have permission to do what he did. Because of him, your friend died. Others may be hurt or killed if the items aren't returned."

The massive hands holding her belonged to the biggest man Heather had ever seen. His chest was bare and, even in the moonlight from the window, she had no trouble discerning every muscle in his well-formed body. He had on dark leather pants, and his black hair fell well below his shoulders. His jawline was square and strong. There was no spare flesh stretched across his bare torso, which looked as if it would be deeply tanned if she could see it in the light.

As if he could read her thoughts, he reached beside the bed and boldly switched on the lamp. She gasped, turning her head from the sudden brightness. Once her eyes adjusted to the light, she looked toward her captor. His eyes were the darkest onyx she had ever seen. Small strands of his hair had been braided along both sides of his face. Her academic mind immediately registered the significance. *Celtic warrior braids.* Heather could see lines of what she knew were Celtic knots tattooed around the biceps of his herculean arms. His face was perfection. He had features like those she'd seen carved into Grecian statues. His nose was straight over brooding, full lips. She only had a glimpse of straight white teeth. But his eyes were what captured her. It was as if they were filled with magic. They compelled her to look into their black depths and tell him everything he wanted to know. He spoke again, but the words didn't register. Muscle loomed from every plane and angle. This was a man who could kill with very little effort. There was no pity, no mercy in his expression.

Gryphon felt stunned. What he'd seen of this woman in the museum parking lot did not do her justice up close. She had the most beautiful silver-blue eyes he had ever seen. Even the lovely, ethereal Sylphs, with their ice-colored stares, couldn't match this color. It riveted him into looking deep within her gaze. Her skin was clear and glowed with health. A hint of freckles scattered across her straight nose, and her lips were soft and trembling. Her long, nut-brown hair fell from a side part to just past her shoulders. Golden highlights captured the glow from the lamp. The ends curled temptingly close to the tips of small but full breasts. And the bed clothing revealed she wore nothing more than the blanket separating them.

"I won't harm you, Heather," he spoke slowly. "I didn't kill your friend. I only want your help."

"How do you...h-how do you know my name?" she stuttered."And how did you know Ned was my friend?"

"The night listens."

"That's a pretty cryptic answer, Mister. Why have you come here? You could have come to the museum to see me. If you believe someone has stolen something that belongs to you, you can go to the law..."

"No," he interrupted, "I can't draw attention to myself or the items I seek. They belong to my people, not to me. The person who killed the guard will kill again to keep the stones."

"What makes you think Ned's death has anything at all to do with Professor McPherson's acquisitions?"

"If your newspapers are to be believed, I know the manner of his death. Such a demise can only come from someone who's misusing an ancient power. More than this, I can't explain."

"Who are you?"

"To you, I'm but a dream in the night. To those who do wrong by my people and harm others through deceit, I'm a nightmare."

"I don't understand..."

"Help me recover what was stolen. No harm will come to you or anyone else if I can quickly take back those stones."

"And if you can't find what you're looking for?" Heather asked.

"I *will* accomplish what I came to do. One way or another."

"We have laws..."

"Your laws can't hold a myth. They don't protect me, so they don't apply to me. They can't control an ancient power."

"A *what*? What myth? Which power? I don't understand," Heather blurted.

Gryph switched the bedside lamp back off. "Sleep. And be careful, Heather. Don't act in haste tomorrow and ask the wrong questions of McPherson." He stood and allowed himself the luxury of sliding his hands gently off her soft shoulders. "If he knows someone has become aware of his thievery, he may panic and hurt you. That may have been what happened to your friend. The guard may have been in the wrong place at the wrong time."

"If you knew the Professor, you'd know he couldn't hurt *anyone*," Heather declared loyally.

"Be that as it may, take precautions." He didn't want his mission jeopardized by this woman's behavior. He wished for the umpteenth time that he hadn't had to approach her at all. It only added complications to an already monumental task.

He vanished as suddenly as he had appeared. Heather began to shake violently. Petrified, she waited in the darkness for what seemed an eternity. Then, carefully standing, she made her way to the living room without turning on any lights and checked around. The front door was still dead bolted from the inside. The French door to the balcony was also secure. She was turning away from the door when something caught her eye. She thought she saw a distant, indiscernible shape fly across the moon. Heather began to doubt her sanity. Maybe she was more tired and upset about Ned's death than she realized.

Backing away, she ran to the telephone, stared at the receiver for several moments and wondered what she'd tell the 911 operator. *'Help, my apartment was just invaded by some kind of drop-dead gorgeous, Gaelic accented, tattooed warrior who didn't do anything to me, take anything or cause any damage*!' Any police officer who responded would insist on a drug test or give her a lift to the nearest psychiatric facility. Heather put the receiver down. She went to the bathroom, threw cold water on her face and looked at herself in the mirror. Nothing in the apartment looked different, but somehow she knew nothing would ever be the same again.

***

"Where have you been, Son?" As Gryph walked in from the balcony, James could tell that he was brooding over something. The younger man's eyes were downcast and his expression stern.

"Looking for the stones, Father." Gryph slowly walked through the Victorian-style room. He watched his father's eyes light up. A sign of his sire's anticipation to end this mission.

"You have news?"

"No, but I've met with someone. I did a little questioning, and this person told me where McPherson put the crates."

"Then, all we have to do is find a way to look in them." James grinned, certain that his son's mission would soon be over.

"It's not that simple, Father. I don't think McPherson is foolish enough to keep the stones where anyone working in the museum can find them easily. A thief doesn't want to get caught with stolen goods." He paused before continuing. "Tonight I questioned this person I've met about what she's seen in the shipments."

"*She*?" James asked, pretending to appear nonchalant about his son's activities. He picked up an apple from a crystal bowl and examined it.

"Yes. This woman works with the professor. She's seen nothing resembling the stones."

James watched his son closely as he casually tossed the apple up and down in one hand. "You believe she's telling you the truth?"

"Yes, for some reason, I do." Gryph walked to the bar to

pour himself some whiskey. The house where his parents were staying belonged to old family friends. These friends, more of his parents' Druid acquaintances, were currently gone on vacation. They often loaned the place to the elder O'Connors when they traveled to the States. They were aware of Gryph's condition, and he felt safe enough staying there. Shayla had made it clear to all who knew of him that the penalty for revealing his ability to outsiders was death. Gryph gazed out the open balcony windows and wondered how the lovely Heather would react if she knew she had been held in the arms of a myth. He could still smell the faint scent of some floral shampoo she used, could still feel her soft warmth. He could count on one hand the number of times he'd been that close to a woman. The difference was, none of those other women had been frightened half to death. Just sexually curious about his abilities. It hadn't felt good to intimidate her. Whatever else he might be, Gryphon knew he wasn't a damned savage.

James interrupted his musings. "It's late, lad. The museum will have been closed for hours."

"Your *point*, Father?" Gryph studied the glass he held.

"Where did you meet this woman?"

Gryph's guard went up immediately. His actions—following Heather to her apartment, breaking in and frightening her—wouldn't sit well with his parents. Even if they innocently mentioned to Shayla he'd done such a thing, the woman might be suspected of knowing more about him than she should. Heather could be subjected to some close scrutiny by members of the Order, or *worse*. And *he* would most certainly be punished for such rash actions.

"What difference does it make, Father?" Gryph shrugged.

"Well, by approaching someone and asking questions, you bring attention to yourself. Suppose this person calls the law?" his father asked with concern.

"There's no law against asking someone about ancient artifacts. And I've told you before. I'm the one who's responsible for finding the rune stones. I believe this person might be persuaded to help." Gryph pretended to have an interest in the parkland surrounding the sprawling house.

"Can you trust her, Son?" Fear colored his voice as James moved to stand behind Gryphon.

"To some small extent, I have to trust someone. I can't just burst into the museum and search every square inch of it. That would cause a little attention, wouldn't it?"

"There's no reason for sarcasm, Gryphon. I'm just concerned about your safety. If the papers are reporting the truth, the way the security guard was murdered indicates someone has released the stones' power, " James warned. "If that's happened, you have no idea what you'll be up against."

"I know. But this woman has nothing to do with the theft of the stones."

"How do you *know* that?"

"The man who was killed was a close friend of hers. She mourns his loss. She's not involved in his death." Gryphon's instincts were certain of that.

"Who is she? What's her name?"

"You're asking a lot of questions, Father."

"And you're being very evasive, which causes me some concern," James growled.

"No harm will befall the Order because of anything I do. It never has." Gryph looked into the night sky, wanting the conversation to end.

"I never insinuated any such thing, Gryph. All I asked for was the woman's name."

"All that matters is retrieving the stones. The woman isn't an issue. She doesn't even know *my* name."

"That's of little comfort. You're not in this country legally and you certainly didn't get here by any conventional means. And you're not exactly inconspicuous." James turned away, angry.

"If I'm not, Father, ask yourself why?" Gryph responded before he could stop himself. He quickly threw back another swallow of whiskey.

James bowed his head.

Gryphon watched as guilt etched itself into every line of the older man's handsome face. He felt immediate shame. "I'm sorry. I shouldn't have said that. I didn't mean it, Da." Gryph slipped into the Irish name for *father* that he hadn't used since he was a small boy.

"I just don't want you hurt anymore than you've already been, Son," James spoke softly.

"I have a decent life, Da. I can control the *change*. You're worrying too much. This woman is just a means to an end. She's given me the location of the crates, that's all. I'll find a way to locate the rune stones, and we'll head home."

"All right, all right. You're in charge. Just be very careful. You don't know what you could be facing. Shayla was clear on that, and I don't want anything to happen to you. Your mother and I love you very much."

"Yes, I know, and I love you, too." Gryph smiled. He controlled his features so that his father wouldn't see his sorrow.

FOUR

Heather awoke with a start. *A dream.* That's what it must have been. She quickly got out of bed and ran into the living room. The doors and windows were still secure, though the lock on the French door was the worse for wear. That didn't mean someone had been inside her apartment. Shaking her head, she made coffee and dressed.

***

She was going through the second box of artifacts on her list when Niall came into the small inventory room. Every object that wasn't being researched went into the little pantry just off the larger receiving area. Here, all the tags and labels to identify the artifacts were kept in neat order. She was trying to make sense out of the mess caused by lists that didn't match with the artifact locations. It was a frustrating experience made more so by Niall's appearance.

"Hi, babe. How's everything going?" He leaned over and kissed her neck.

Heather sighed in irritation."Fine, Niall. Where's Professor McPherson? I'd have thought he'd want to oversee the unpacking of these things himself. Some of them are quite rare and extremely breakable."

"He's playing kiss-up to the Board of Directors. He'll be here soon." He grabbed her around her wool-skirted waist and pulled her to him. "How about playing kiss-up with me?"

"Niall, stop! I have to get these things categorized. Some of them aren't fitting into any profile I'm familiar with."

"Come on, honey. You know what they say about all work and no..."

"I'm not kidding, Niall. I'm here to work." She pushed his

wandering hands away. "Why don't you give me a hand?"

"Man, what's eating at you this morning? I thought I told you to get some rest."

"You *did.* Only it just isn't that easy for me. I don't seem to have your ability to shrug off what happened to Ned. He was *brutalized.* Who knows why anyone did such a thing. And whether the killer might try something like this again."

"We have a new security staff and a new alarm system being installed, Heather. And whether you want to accept it or not, life *does* have a way of going on." He stopped speaking when Professor McPherson entered the room.

"Having any luck with these pieces, Heather?" McPherson asked. His gaze wandered around the room, checking her progress. He occasionally fidgeted with the bifocals in his left shirt pocket.

She watched the older man as his brown eyes focused on the work she'd done, and his thin, frail body stooped so he could get a better look at some of the smaller artifacts. Heather tried not to smile as his weathered hands lovingly touched everything. It was clear he was checking on her without wanting to look as if he were doing so.

"As a matter of fact, I was just telling Niall that some of these objects are rather obscure. I was wondering whether I could look at the paperwork on where some of this stuff was found?" she asked, and put down a piece of pottery before tagging it.

The Professor stared and didn't respond for a moment. But before he had a chance to say anything, Niall interrupted.

"Heather, if I might remind you, your job is to categorize acquisitions," Niall said, "not plot their dig locations. Asking to see the site charts is rather like a recalcitrant eighth grader asking her teacher if he's sure the lesson plan is being properly taught."

"*Excuse me, Niall.* I wasn't aware that I was offending anyone," Heather snapped. "Some of these items were badly packed. Others look as if they were never properly cleaned and labeled at the site. That's why we've got Irish peat all over everything. But I *was* talking to Professor McPherson. *Not you*!"

"Please, please." McPherson tried to calm them. "I'm sure Heather just wants to get a feel for what she's doing here. After all, a good assistant is interested in *all* phases of the work. Not just the proper displaying and categorizing of the artifacts." He pulled his glasses out of his pocket and placed them on the bridge of his nose as he spoke.

Niall glared at her. "You have to forgive her, Professor. Heather hasn't been herself since the murder. She just doesn't seem to be able to get past it, and I'm afraid her behavior is a reflection of her emotional state."

"I don't need you justifying my emotional state or patronizing me, Niall. I'm doing my job, and I suggest you do the same. If you paid half as much attention to your work as you do to me, all this might have been done by now." She nodded toward the boxes of work before her.

"That's enough, both of you," McPherson admonished. "We're all on edge because of what's happened. I suggest we get to our work and calm down."

Niall stalked out of the room. Heather was glad he was gone. Lately, he was becoming a big, pain-in-the-butt, chauvinistic bastard. He acted as though he owned her. But if Niall thought she was going to fall all over herself fawning over him, he had another think coming. Knowing him, he'd head straight to the secretarial pool where his bruised little ego could be bandaged.

Returning her attention to the packing crate she was searching through, Heather found a small gray statue made of marble. It was definitely Irish, probably from somewhere near the time period of one thousand years before Christ. The arms of the stylized man had some kind of design etched into their surface. Wiping away the dirt which still clung to the little figure, she could see Celtic knots winding around its biceps. Just like the man from her dreams.

"Professor?"

"Yes, Heather?" He examined some of the objects she had already laid aside for displaying.

"Did you happen to run across any ancient rune stones on

this trip?" Heather pretended to be studying the statue she held, but found herself watching the professor closely.

"Why do you ask?" he replied and quickly looked up.

"Oh, it's nothing, really. It's just that sometimes you come back with them, and you know how interested I am in prophetic items from that part of the world." She tried to convince herself his response to her query wasn't a little too sharp and the anxiety on his face to her simple question was her imagination. *Is he forcing that calm response*?

"Yes. Yes, you've always had that fascination." He sighed with relief. "I'm sorry. There was nothing like that in any of the acquisitions I sent back this time. I'll tell you what. I'll keep my eye out on the next trip to Britain. If I find some stones worthy of the collection, I'll bring them home and let you have first chance at researching the markings." He walked out of the room.

"Thanks, Professor. That would be great," she called after him. "Well," she spoke to the little stone man, "that dream of mine is certainly causing me to ask some accusing questions. Maybe I saw you yesterday while I was digging through these boxes, and you caused me to dream up that babe magnet in my room last night. *Babe magnet*? That sounds like something Niall would say. And why in the world am I asking McPherson about rune stones? I don't believe he would actually steal anything. His reputation is impeccable. Last night was just a dream. No one really came into my apartment." She smiled at having poured out her thoughts aloud to a Celtic figurine, then continued, "Well, little man, it's off to the display section for you and back to work for me."

***

"Gryph, you shouldn't have approached anyone." Gwyneth paced the room, biting at her lower lip in agitation.

"Mother, I can't search the museum or the crates holding the stolen objects without knowing something about the inside of the building. To do that, I had to make contact with someone. You and Father are going to have to trust me to know what to do. If you can't, I'll have to ask you to go back to Ireland and wait for me there. You're both making far too much out of my having made contact with her."

"Of course we trust you, Gryph. But we're your parents. We worry," James placated.

"There's one other thing I want you both to do for me." Gryph stopped his mother's pacing by placing his hands on her shoulders. "I want your promise that you won't mention to Shayla my having contacted this woman."

"Why?" James asked.

"As I've told you both, this person is someone who works with McPherson. She's an unwitting accomplice and knows nothing about me. But Shayla may not see it that way. In her zeal to protect the Order and guard my identity, the Sorceress may send others to harass or do harm to the woman. The taking of the stones has already cost one innocent man his life. I won't have anyone else hurt or involved insofar as I am able to prevent it. Within days, I'll have the stones and we'll be on our way home. No one here will see me again, and there'll be no proof I ever really existed. The woman will never know who or what I really am. The Order will be safe."

"I understand, Son. We won't tell Shayla you've approached anyone here unless something happens which threatens our safety."

"That's all I ask, Father. Now, I consider this discussion closed."

Gryph sternly nodded as he left the room. He should have realized that his father would tell his mother about contacting an outsider for help. He'd heard nothing all afternoon except his mother's complaints to stay away from Heather. He wouldn't stay away. Somehow he knew that he couldn't. The woman had direct access to every place he needed to search. At least, that's what he kept telling himself.

Gryph walked outside toward the woods. The scents of autumn surrounded him. Somewhere a fireplace burned, and colorful leaves whirled in small circles. It reminded him of the night he had first approached Heather. He tried to force his thoughts to other subjects, but it was impossible. He had never touched a woman from outside. She'd been so afraid of him. Despite that fear, she had still managed to summon the courage to question his motives. Goddess only knew what she'd believed would happen to her. He didn't believe some of the things he'd been told about women from the outside. Members of the Order said they were cold and cruel, that they hurt their children and cheated on their men. Maybe some did. *Herne's antlers*! There were some within the Shire that did that and more. But Heather had shown concern for an old man who'd been her friend, belying the tales of callousness he'd heard. She'd even shown loyalty for McPherson, though it was misplaced. He found himself wishing he could know more. How warm it would be to lie by the firelight with such a woman and...but that could never be. *Never*.

***

Heather pulled on her coat and stepped outside the museum entrance. The tall young man who walked her to her car was friendly and professional, but she missed Ned. Having lost her parents in an automobile accident several years before, Heather had allowed the old man to assume a position in her life much like that of a loved uncle. She missed him dearly and had never felt so utterly alone.

"Thanks for walking me to the parking lot, uh...I'm sorry, but I don't know your name."

"Simmons, Miss," the red-haired man responded. His posture was straight, the leather shoes polished. His neat navy uniform and shiny badge looked very official. He wore a police-type cap upon his head instead of the battered baseball cap Ned had always worn.

"Just, *Simmons*?"

"Yes, ma'am," the guard answered, abruptly. "It doesn't pay to get too close to folks. We may be working here one night, then someplace else another. Our supervisor switches us around to keep us from getting too bored with what we're doing."

Heather got the message. This security guard was strictly by the book. There would be no friendly banter while walking her to the car or gossip in the lunch room. No sharing a cup of coffee while working late at night. There would be no birthday or Christmas gifts exchanged. Nothing personal. It made her want to cry.

"Would you like for me to wait until you're in your car before I leave, Miss?" he asked. He kept his posture professionally stiff.

"No, Simmons. I'll be fine. My car is just over there under that tree. You'd better get back to your rounds." *I wouldn't want you to go out of your way...be friendly or anything.*

"Yes, ma'am." He nodded, then turned and left. He didn't bother to say goodbye.

She stared after him with tears in her eyes. Ned would never have let her walk alone to her car this late at night. No matter how insistent she might be. And he had always wished her good night. She slowly turned and walked the few remaining yards to her car. She was putting the key into the door when some instinct made her turn. Out of the shadows walked a man well over six feet tall. Like Atlas, his shoulders looked wide enough to balance the weight of the world. Heather froze. Everything in her said *go*. But she couldn't seem to get her body to respond fast enough.

"That young fool should know his job better, and you should have been more insistent that he stay in the area until you'd left."

Heather recognized the man who had been in her apartment. "My God," she whispered, "you're *real*!" She dropped her briefcase and keys and backed against her car. Had the guard walked too far away to hear her scream?

He tilted his head slightly, then he slowly smiled. "Ah, you did think I was a dream."

Heather backed as far down the side of the car as she could. A tree stopped further retreat. "If you don't leave *right now*, I'll scream so loud half of New York will hear!"

"Use your head, woman. Had I wanted to harm you, I'd have already done it."

"Then, what do you want?" Heather stared up into his face. It was, if anything, more handsome than before. Some part of her brain registered this even as she felt she should be running for her life.

"I told you. I want what rightfully belongs elsewhere.

You've seen the objects which were sent here from Ireland?"

Heather didn't speak. If she told this obviously crazed man that she had seen the artifacts, he might force her to take him to where they were stored. Having no more use for her, he might do to her what had been done to Ned. If she lied and said she'd never seen any of the artifacts, she was afraid the guy would go ballistic and kill her. Either way, she knew she had to try to find a way to get back to the guard station on the museum's first floor.

Gryphon moved forward until Heather was pinned against the tree. "Have you seen the three rune stones?" he asked again.

Heather tried to run, but he held her wrists together with one hand and covered her mouth with the other. "Please listen, lass." He pressed his body to hers and tried to make his voice sound sincere. "Those stones are sacred. If something valuable had been wrongfully taken from your family or friends, wouldn't you try to return those items if you were given the chance?"

Heather stared into his eyes, and her fear temporarily receded. The man removed his large hand from her mouth. "I still don't know why you won't go to the police. What do you want with me? Why did you follow me to my home and *who in hell are you*? You know, breaking into somebody's apartment doesn't exactly encourage cooperation or instill trust."

He almost smiled at her outburst of brave temper. Considering the differences in their sizes and weight, she was exhibiting some real brass. "I'm sorry about that, but I had to act quickly, and the less you know, the safer you'll stay. Now, I'll ask again. Have you seen the rune stones or not?"

"No," Heather replied, "I haven't seen them. There were none sent with the shipments."

"So, you checked?"

"Yes. I asked Professor McPherson if he'd acquired any rune stones on his trip."

Gryph shook his head. "You shouldn't have done that. The man may suspect you know something about them. You could have endangered yourself."

"Look, if you'd tell me what all of this is about and who

you are, I might be able to make some sense of this and get you the help you need." Mental or otherwise.

"Have you called the law about me?"

"No. Like you guessed...I thought you weren't real, that I'd dreamed you up."

"Lass, take me to the place where McPherson stored the crates. Time is against me now, and the sooner I find what I came for, the sooner you and others will be out of danger." Gryphon gazed into her beautiful eyes. "It was a mistake to have involved you in this. I should've broken into the museum and searched alone."

Heather stared hard at the muscular, flannel-clad chest in front of her. He wore jeans, hiking boots and had left his hair beautifully loose. It flowed over his shoulders in black sheets. Any modeling agency in New York would have signed him to a contract on the spot. He seemed more masculine and less murderous. "You really didn't kill Ned, did you? You really believe Professor McPherson took artifacts illegally and is somehow involved in the murder?"

"It's just as I've told you. I *must* find those stones. Please, help me to stop this before more harm comes to anyone. And I'm certain I can prove to you that the things I'm talking about were stolen."

"How?" Heather's guard began to drop. He allowed her to ease slightly away from his huge body.

"You work in acquisitions, don't you?"

"Yes. Professor McPherson is my mentor."

"Have you noticed anything wrong with the objects you've seen so far?"

Heather thought to remain silent, but this man knew too much. "There were discrepancies in some of the paperwork. That can happen with a shipment of this size."

"There were items taken from County Donegal. Were they listed?"

"No. Everything in the collection from Ireland is tagged as having been found in the southern part of the country, County Cork. That was where the professor and his team were looking. They had complete sanction and assistance from the local government to excavate some sites there."

"An ancient burial site was sacked. Up north near Creeslough, County Donegal. The objects McPherson took were from that site. There are people in Donegal who remember that Angus McPherson and some of his team were in the northern counties just weeks ago. You can check on all I've told you, Heather, but time is running out. I have to bring the rune stones back to Ireland."

"I don't understand why you can't go to the police. Why the hurry? If you truly believe something illegal is going on, then . . ."

"I can't, lass! I know what I'm telling you is difficult to understand, but there must be as little public knowledge of this as possible. You've no reason to trust me, I know. But that's exactly what I'm asking you to do. Please, take me to where the crates are stored."

"A man was murdered, and you've told me that it has something to do with this shipment from Ireland. If that's true, then that's all the more reason to go to the police. Ned Williamson was a good man. He didn't deserve to die. If there's a reason for his death and you know it, then you should help put the person responsible in jail."

"If I can prove what I say is true, will you help me look for the stones? Will you set right what's been done, for your friend's sake?"

"I've told you, there are no stones in those boxes, and I can't take you to them. I don't know anything about you. You won't even tell me your name."

Gryph released a heavy sigh. The stones were in that building, though whether they were still in the crates was uncertain. He needed her help. Without her, he would have to break in to search. Even if he succeeded in getting past the staff, there were the alarms to consider. If he was caught, someone could get hurt, including himself. And what if the stones had been removed from the crates? The museum was four stories above ground and probably had a basement. He simply couldn't search the whole place, and the Order couldn't afford his capture. Against common sense and his parents' pleas, he relented. "My name is Gryphon O'Connor."

"Well, Mr. O'Connor, if I find anything that indicates you're telling the truth, I'll notify the proper authorities. Until then, I suggest that this be the last, and I mean the *very last* time we see each other. None of this makes any sense to me at all. Professor McPherson would never steal anything, let alone hurt anyone. Now, please go, or I swear to God I'll scream my head off!"

"*Fine*," Gryphon angrily responded. "By the time you find out what I've told you is the truth, it may be too late. No human law is a match for the power connected with the stones. I should have known better than to contact an outsider with no comprehension of Celtic ways. If the rune stones are still within the walls of the museum, I'll find them without your help. Justice demands they be returned." He stopped, moved closer and gazed into her eyes. "It surprises me that you can have so little knowledge of what you profess to study. The artifacts you display are thousands of years old and represent a culture which existed before recorded history. Magic and wonder are connected with each piece. But like the rest of your kind, you perceive only the analytical, the tangible. There's no room for myth, magic or tradition. Only the monetary value you can assign to an object." He paused. "Not everything comes with an admission price such as those charged by your museum, Heather. There are things in this world best left alone. Those stones are sacred. *They will be returned*." He turned and walked into the darkness.

Heather stared after him and muttered to herself, "What's all *that* supposed to mean...power...outsider? And what in hell is my *kind*? That man isn't right!" She took a deep breath, picked up her belongings and drove away as fast as she could.

FIVE

The next morning, the doorbell rang. Heather looked through the peephole of her apartment door, recognized Detective Dayton and let him in.

"Hello, Ms. Green. I was in the neighborhood and took a chance on you being home. I hope you don't mind. I was wondering if we could talk?"

Despite the friendly tone, Heather knew his request to speak with her wasn't a question. "If it's about Ned Williamson, I'm afraid I don't know what else I can add," she said as she ushered him into her living room. She offered him coffee which he refused.

"There are one or two questions I'd like to ask you concerning Mr. Williamson's relationship with you. Then I'll be on my way."

"How can I help?" Heather sat down, pushing her hair back from her face. She settled herself on the sofa while Detective Dayton sat in a matching arm chair across from her.

"According to some of the staff who work at the museum, you two were very close. I was wondering if you ever heard of Mr. Williamson having any enemies?"

"No, of course not. Ned was liked by everyone who knew him."

"There are indications Mr. Williamson may have known his killer. Of course, I'm telling you this in confidence. I'd like you to keep this information to yourself for the time being."

"You think someone at the museum may have...Oh, God," Heather whispered.

"Ms. Green, this is just a hunch. I'm only telling you this because you seem to be the one person closest to the victim.

At first, we thought the murder may have been random. One theory we had was that a junky had hidden in the museum looking for something to steal to get money for drugs. Nothing's missing from the displays. And the more we investigate, the more it appears that the guard walked in on someone familiar to him."

Heather nervously pushed her hair back again. She remembered Gryph O'Connor's words about Ned being in the wrong place at the wrong time.

"Ms. Green, are you all right?" Dayton asked, staring at her.

Heather knew she must look pale. She could almost feel the blood draining from her face. "I can't believe this. I want the person responsible for Ned's death brought to justice."

"I was hoping you'd feel that way. I need to ask you for a favor."

"Of course. I'll do anything to help."

"If you hear of anything unusual, or find out anything that doesn't fit in with the normal pattern of operations there, will you let me know?"

"I'm not sure I know what that means, Detective, but I'll keep my eyes and ears open."

"Thank you, and Ms. Green...? A word of caution. Until now everyone was considered a suspect. I've contacted you because I'm personally and professionally certain you had no hand in Mr. Williamson's murder. But there are others about whom I'm not so certain. For your own safety, please keep this conversation to yourself."

"I understand."

Heather escorted the detective back to the door, closed it, then stared into space. She had heard the same words of warning from Gryph O'Connor. *Why didn't I tell him about O'Connor or call the police last night?* Shaking her head in confusion, she gripped the back of a chair. Her mind searched for reasons why. There simply was no excuse. Perhaps it was because no one would believe her, or a small part of her thought O'Connor was sincerely trying to do what he considered right. That didn't give him a reason to break into her apartment or follow her around like some crazed stalker. Still, he'd had two chances to hurt her and hadn't. Maybe some deep Freudian thing in her wanted the attention of a man so devastatingly masculine and dangerous. Someone so like the Irish heroes she'd dreamed about when she was younger. The mythic image of Finn Mac Cool immediately came to mind. One of the most famous of Irish heroes, he was supposedly the source of many Arthurian legends. Heather had always imagined a man like that would look like Gryphon O'Connor.

"Man, I'm a mess," she mumbled. "That guy is dangerous. I should call the cops." But she knew she wouldn't. At least not for the time being. The reason why escaped her, but her mind raced back to what the detective had said.

Maybe she hadn't taken O'Connor seriously enough because she had believed he was half crazy. But hadn't the detective confirmed some of what Gryphon had claimed? The man surmised that Ned had known his killer. Now, Heather didn't know *what* to think. Pouring her unfinished coffee down the drain, she walked into her bedroom to change. If Gryphon was to be believed, all of this was linked to the shipment of artifacts from Ireland.

Half an hour later, she was running up the steps to the museum. She wanted a chance to look through the crates one more time before anyone else showed up for work. Entering the labeling room where some of the crates had been placed, she threw off her jacket and began to examine everything without leaving evidence that she had done so. She thoroughly searched through each wooden box.

"Dammit," she muttered to herself, "there's got to be something here. That crazy Irishman knew all along what the police are only just finding out. Stones. He said there were three of them."

She continued to search, torn between helping find her friend's murderer and the possibility of implicating Professor McPherson. She looked until it was almost eight o'clock and time for Niall and Professor MacPherson to come to work. She was turning to pick up her jacket when she tripped on the corner of one of the crates and fell to her knees. As she pulled herself up, something caught her attention. A board at the bottom of the crate had been loosened when she hit it with her foot. Wiping her hands on her blue jeans, Heather pulled at the loose piece of wood. It came off easily. As though it had been removed before. She stared at the bottom of the crate then compared it with others in the room. Because the crates were so deep and so close to one another, it would have been impossible to detect the false bottom had she not tripped over the loose corner. Wiping off her sweating palms, she carefully reached inside the narrow space.

Her hands felt smooth, cool stone. She pulled out an object about the size of her own palm, and about an inch thick. It was a marble rune stone with Celtic emblems chiseled into its surface. One of the marks was that of Ceridwen, supposedly a female deity of regeneration. The other markings were unfamiliar. Heather's heart began to race. She quickly reached back into the narrow space and found two more stones the same size as the first. The only difference were the markings each bore. They were like nothing she'd ever come across in her studies, but they were very definitely Celtic.

"My God," she breathed, "O'Connor was telling the *truth*."

A door closing at the end of the outer hallway warned her of someone's entrance into the collection department. Heather panicked and shoved the stones back into the space in what she hoped was the same position. She grabbed the wooden plank and forced it back onto the bottom of the crate. The last thing in the world she wanted was to have anyone catch her with them.

Staying low, she maneuvered around the large boxes to the other side of the room, out the far door and into the stairwell. Breathing hard, she raced to the first floor and out to her car. She had no idea where to go. She thought about Detective Dayton, but wasn't sure what she'd found was connected to Ned's death. It was almost a certainty someone on McPherson's...not the professor himself, had stolen the stones. No one would go to the trouble of building a false bottom into a crate if the objects they were shipping had been legally obtained. Then there were the discrepancies she'd noticed in the shipping and packaging of the artifacts. She pulled into a convenience store and dialed the telephone number to the antiquities division.

"Antiquities and collections, Niall Alexander speaking."

"Niall, this is Heather. I called to say that I might be late today. I wasn't feeling too well when I got up this morning." She was surprised how easily she could lie to him.

"Sweetheart, what's wrong?"

"It's nothing, really. It's a woman thing, if you know what I mean."

"Oh, uh, I see. Uh...well...maybe you should stay home and get some rest."

"I'll see how I'm feeling later. I just wanted to touch base and let you and the Professor know why I'm not at work."

"Don't worry about a thing, babe. I'll make up an excuse for Angus. You just take care, okay?"

"Sure. And thanks, Niall." She hung up, certain he wouldn't question her absence further. The more she thought about it, the more she wondered what she'd ever seen in him. It occurred to her how cold their relationship had always been. He was supposed to care about her, yet he'd always immaturely found the subject of her period a major embarrassment. If he knew it was "that time of the month," he stayed away from her apartment as if she were contagious.

Right now, she didn't want to have anything to do with him or anyone. A few hours alone would help her decide whether to wait or go to the police about the stones. Gryphon had told her he couldn't go to the police about them, that the fewer people who knew about them, the better. *What's the deal with the damn stones*? Why had someone risked his professional reputation by smuggling them into the United States, jeopardizing the museum's acquisition program in the process?

***

"The woman was killed the same way as the security guard at the museum." Gryph shook out the afternoon newspaper his father handed to him and reread the grim headlines. "In fact, the park where her body was found is only a short distance from the museum's main entrance."

James nodded. "Someone has used the stones again.

Whoever it is seems to have tried out their newly found powers on an unsuspecting victim. The guard may have been an accident, but this was definitely deliberate."

Gryph looked at his parents. "I have no choice. I have to go to the museum. This has to stop!"

"Gryph, if you're caught..." Gwyneth's voice faded away.

"What else can I do? The stones must still be there. Someone has deciphered their meaning and is abusing their power." Gryphon leaned against a desktop.

James voiced his concern. "What can we do to help?"

"If anything should go wrong, contact Shayla. She'll know what to do. Today, I'll try one more time to convince that stubborn woman to listen to reason. If she still won't help me, then I'll have to get inside the building tonight and search alone," Gryph told them and noted the look of concern on their faces.

"Gryphon, from what you've told us, this woman can't be trusted. She doesn't believe you. Please don't contact her again. She'll only call the police," Gwyneth pleaded and placed her hands on her son's arms.

"For some reason, Mother, she's had that opportunity and hasn't called the police yet. I'd be a suspect and there would be news of the authorities looking for someone matching my description. Every reporter in the city seems to be covering this. That makes it imperative that I try once more. Perhaps the stories of this latest murder will convince her I'm telling the truth."

***

Heather walked back into her apartment as her phone was ringing. "Hello?"

"Ms. Green, this is Detective Dayton. I tried to discreetly reach you at work several hours after I spoke with you, but was told that you weren't feeling well."

Heather didn't want to tell him about the stones just yet. Some instinct warned her to keep that information to herself. "That's right. I was feeling a little under the weather."

"Have you read the afternoon newspapers or listened to the television?"

"No, I haven't. Why?" The man's tone of voice had

immediately alerted her.

"There's been another murder. This time it was a prostitute found in the park near the museum. Joggers found her body shortly after I spoke with you. The evidence leads us to believe the killing was committed in the same way as Ned Williamson's murder. I tried to keep it under wraps, but the press was all over the area before one of our investigators could get to the scene and contain it."

"God, no!" Heather gasped and felt her skin grow cold. "Detective, there were some horrible rumors at work about the...about Ned's death and how he was killed. Now you're saying someone else was murdered, and that Ned and this person were both attacked in the same way. What *exactly* does that mean?"

"Without being too graphic, Ms. Green, both of the victims were...well, you'll read about it in the newspapers anyway. Both of them were attacked by someone with enough physical strength to dismember a body. That's another reason why I ruled you out as a suspect, along with a few dozen other people."

Heather almost retched. The thought of someone hurting people in such a way—of hurting *Ned* like that— was too much. "Oh, Ned," she murmured before she began to cry.

"Ms. Green, I called to tell you not to stay late at work. The security guards tell me you have a habit of doing that almost every night. Now, they're doing the best they can to keep the area safe. But they're understaffed and underpaid. It's my advice that you don't hang around there too long after hours."

"I won't, Detective. I can promise you that." Heather tried to speak coherently through her tears.

Dayton said his good byes and hung up, but Heather leaned against the wall a long time before placing the telephone receiver down. Gryph O'Connor was a powerful-looking man. Was he or anyone capable of tearing a human being apart, of dismembering them as Detective Dayton had described? No. She couldn't believe that O'Connor had anything to do with the murders. Her mind kept grasping at the fact that he'd had more than one opportunity to hurt her and had never done so. In fact, he'd warned her that all of this would happen if the stones he sought weren't returned. Heather felt she had no choice.

After finding out about this second murder, Gryphon O'Connor would come to the museum for what he thought was the cause. The rune stones. When he did, she'd be there. He was damned well going to explain what in hell was going on, even if she had to risk her own life getting to the truth. Ned deserved it.

***

Heather waited in her usual spot in the parking lot. The cool fall air did nothing to ease her tattered nerves. The sun had just set, everyone had gone home. It was about this same time of night that she'd seen him there before. Leaves fell, eerily, from the nearby trees, and she imagined she could hear strange noises. One of those she imagined was like the wings of a large bird flying in the distance. She leaned against the car hood and waited. She didn't wait long.

"Are you *insane*, woman?" came a deep, resonant brogue from behind her. "What are you doing here by yourself?"

Heather turned to see him standing in the dim light. "I knew you'd show up tonight. You've heard about the woman who was killed in the park, haven't you?" she asked as Gryph moved out of the shadows toward her.

"Yes. More will die if I don't take back those damnable stones!"

"Were you planning on breaking into the museum?"

"If I had to, yes. But I'm glad you haven't left for the day. I wanted to ask you once more to take me to the artifacts and give me a chance to prove what I'm saying is true."

"I'm not leaving for the day. The truth is, I just got here and was waiting for you. Like I said, I knew you'd show up."

Gryph tilted his head quizzically. "You just got here?"

"Yes." Heather paused. "Today, a police detective who trusts me told me some things. He said he suspects Ned was killed by someone he may have known, possibly someone who works at the museum. I didn't want to believe it, but some of the things you'd said started to make some sense. You've believed all along that Ned's death was connected to the Celtic artifacts. You tried to tell me, but I guess I wasn't ready to listen. Now it seems the police believe we have a murderer employed at the museum, though they know nothing about a possible connection to McPherson's shipments from Ireland. You *and* the police are working from opposite ends toward the same conclusion. And I've found something I wasn't meant to."

"What have you found?" He could hear the excitement in his own voice. The prospect of good news rallied him.

"After I spoke with the detective, I came in to work early. I tore into every box, crate and container I could get my hands on and didn't find anything. I was ready to give up and then, by accident, I found that one of the crates had a false bottom installed. Your rune stones are there. Professor McPherson or someone on his team took special pains to hide them. I don't know who's lying, but Ned was killed near the room where the crates are now located. From everything you and the Detective have told me, and because I've found the stones so deviously hidden, I think Ned was killed because he knew too much or saw something he shouldn't have. I don't understand why the woman in the park was killed, but the police are connecting her death to Ned's."

"Heather, what I'm about to tell you is the absolute truth. You won't want to believe it any more than anything else I've told you, but you *must* listen. Those stones are the source of an unspeakable magic. It's said that if they're correctly deciphered, they can give great power to whoever possesses them. While I believe McPherson took the stones, I'm not sure if he's the one abusing their gifts. Whoever killed the woman in the park and your friend did so with the help of the stones."

"You're speaking of the Rune Stones of the Tuatha De! Danann."

Gryph stared at her in absolute shock. "You *know* of them?"

"I know about the *legend.* Celtic studies are my specialty. But those stones are a myth. They don't really exist. I can't believe all of this is over a folktale!"

"Did you touch the stones?"

"Yes," she said, remembering their cool, grey-green surfaces.

"Then you believe that what you physically held in your hands was a *myth*?"

"Mr. O'Connor, I quit believing in things that go bump in the night a long time ago. These were rune stones like hundreds of others that have been found in that part of the world, albeit a bit larger."

Gryph slowly shook his head. "Someone believes in them enough to have stolen them and to have killed innocent people by acquiring the stones' power."

"Well, I guess we'll find out about them soon enough." Heather sighed as she pulled out a set of keys from her coat pocket. "I'll take you to the room where the artifacts are kept. The guards are making their rounds. The outer doors are locked, but a keyed access won't alert them to anything. Should be easy enough for an employee to get past them right now. There aren't enough of them on duty anyway."

Whether the guards posed a problem or not, he had to get in. But her inaction in alerting the local authorities was puzzling. "Why didn't you call the police when you found the stones? Thievery is a motive for murder, after all," Gryph told her.

"I've thought about that all afternoon. That's why I didn't come to work today. I don't really know *what* to think, or what to do anymore. That's why I left the damned things there .The only thing I'm certain of is that you haven't lied to me yet."

Gryph followed her as she walked around a side entrance, avoiding the security guards and the museum's security cameras. He believed she was confused, hurt and afraid. But she had enough strength of character to want to get to the truth, even at considerable risk to her own safety.

"You should leave. You're getting yourself far too involved in all of this."

"No, I'm not leaving. Ned was my friend. I want to know why he was killed and who did it. And would you *please* tell me how the hell you know my name and where I live? That's really been bugging me."

Gryph smiled. "I overheard you and the blond man talking in the parking lot. He called you by name. When you left, I followed you to your apartment."

"Crafty," Heather murmured.

"Survival,"Gryph responded.

"You see what you did as *surviving*?" she asked in surprise.

Gryph didn't answer. If she knew who and more importantly *what* he was, she would never question why he maintained a low profile. She would run in horror.

They went up the back stairwell to the upper floors where the archives and new collections were kept. Gryph made very sure they weren't discovered by any of the security guards. She unlocked the last door and turned the dead bolt behind them.

"Even the security people aren't allowed in here," she explained. "The artifacts are too valuable and fragile for anyone but the professor, Niall and some of our staff to be around."

"Niall?" Gryph asked, looking around the room at the large boxes scattered about.

"He was the blond man you saw me talking to in the parking lot. I'm surprised you didn't remember his name, too. You've remembered everything else," Heather said sarcastically.

"He's of no concern to me," Gryph remarked, shrugging his shoulders with disdain.

Heather led the way to a large shipping crate at the center of the room. She knelt down to the floor, pulled off the wooden slat that had come loose earlier and reached inside the space. She reached even farther inside until she touched wood. "They're not here!"

"That doesn't surprise me. Whoever has them will probably hide them separately from now on. Especially if that person thinks the law is too close. They may have been taken from the crate so they can be used again tonight. According to legend, their power can be addicting."

"What do you mean by *used*?" Heather spoke as she stood up and looked at Gryph.

"I thought you knew about the Rune Stones of the Tuatha De! Danann." Gryphon's gaze moved up and down her jean-clad figure. Inappropriately, he imagined her wearing a soft gown of Fairy gauze, then tried to pull his mind back to the business at hand.

"I know they're a legend, and that's all."

Gryph looked at her for several more moments, wondering how much more he should say. Finally, he explained. "The stones have the power to give their possessor the ability to shape shift. Deciphering the symbols on all three stones and chanting their meaning out loud is all that's necessary for the magic to work. After the initial enchantment takes place, the stones are no longer required. That person may change at will."

"That's the *myth*, right?"

"If it makes you feel better to believe that, then think what you must." He turned to look at some of the artifacts that had been placed on a nearby table. He picked up the small figure of the man Heather had been studying earlier. "This was taken from somewhere near Galway," Gryph declared.

"Professor McPherson has it listed as coming from Cork," she responded and wondered how he knew so much. It occurred to her that Gryphon O'Connor might be an antiquities expert as well. He certainly spoke about the subject matter with authority. It further piqued her curiosity about the man.

"These aren't from Cork. McPherson's a liar. In fact, none of these items should have left Ireland. The man has no business with them." He paused, then turned to her. "How many places has this professor been sent to obtain pieces for the museum?"

Heather was still stunned over hearing what she had been suspecting was the truth. Angus McPherson was stealing ancient artifacts. "He goes all over the world. He's been to Peru, Central America, Africa," she listed the countries, then stopped when his meaning became clear. "He may have done this in other countries. Is that what you're implying?"

"If he's done it once and has the cunning to alter his paperwork to fool the authorities, what do *you* think?"

Heather shook her head, not wanting to believe what she was hearing. "The man has been my mentor for five years. I had just graduated from college when I got this job, and considered myself unbelievably fortunate to have been chosen to work here." Now, his reasons in hiring her became crystal clear. "I guess a novice like me didn't pose much of a threat to what he was doing. I've never been allowed on a trip with him and always assumed the inventories and manifests he gave me to work with were accurate. God, I may have even helped him get away with it."

Gryph placed a hand on her shoulder. "It isn't your fault. You trusted him. This is his responsibility, not yours."

"I'm afraid that doesn't make me feel much better. Despite your earlier opinion of me, I'm not in this line of work for the monetary value of the artifacts. I happen to love Celtic history and what the objects represent. Especially the things from Ireland."

"I believe that now, lass. I apologize for what I said." He moved the hand he had placed on her shoulder to her face and gently cradled it. The expression in her silver eyes showed the truth of her words. A door opening in the hallway made them suddenly look up.

"No one but Niall, the Professor or me can come through that door at these hours. It's got a specially coded lock," Heather whispered, alarmed by the disturbance.

Gryph quickly dragged her to the far side of the room where the crates were stacked on top of one another. There was enough room between the boxes and the wall for him to step out of sight, pulling her with him. Instinctively, he shoved her into the space ahead of him to protect her. They heard someone maneuvering one of the wooden boxes. Silence followed. Gryph felt Heather's heart pounding. He held her close, telling himself he was protecting her. She looked up into his face, and he could see the fear in her lovely eyes. To calm her, he caressed her back and shoulders. She responded and leaned into his chest. He could smell her crisp, clean scent. It was like the cool air outside, inviting and haunting. It seemed an unbelievably long time before whoever was in the room went back down the hall. Gryph didn't move. He waited, holding her a little longer only to be sure no one would come back. Eventually, he ventured far enough to see around the boxes.

"Whoever it was is gone, but they may come back. We should leave," he murmured.

Heather swallowed hard and followed him as he walked carefully back to where they had been standing. Gryph stopped by the crate with the false bottom, stooped and placed his hand inside the space. Then he smiled. When he stood, he had one of the stones in his hand.

"Whoever was here left this. But the Luck o' the Irish is with us, and they didn't know we were here." He shoved the stone inside the leather jacket he was wearing.

"Why would someone put one back in the same place?"

"It's as good a hiding place as any. And if I were the thief, I wouldn't hide them together. But this means the others are close by." He grinned.

Heather was still shaking, but not so much she didn't notice what she thought was the most beautiful smile she had ever seen on a man. As they'd hidden, she remembered responding to the warmth of his embrace, and his muscular legs and torso enveloping her. At that moment, she wanted nothing more than to be held again. To not feel so alone.

Gryph grabbed her hand. "Come on. We'd better not push our luck. Whoever that was might come back for this stone. Because of where we were, I couldn't get a look at the bastard." He pulled Heather with him. It was all she could do to keep up with his long legs, even though she was wearing comfortable jeans and hiking boots.

They had almost made it outside to the first floor when Gryph suddenly stopped and turned. "Go, Heather! Take the stone and run!" He shoved the stone at her and looked up.

"What's wrong, why are you..." Heather stopped in mid-sentence when she saw a strange green light heading down the stairwell toward them. She couldn't see what was causing it, just the light itself.

"*I said go*!" Gryph shouted.

SIX

Heather moved faster than she had ever moved in her entire life. She reached the parking lot, undetected by the guards. She turned, looking for Gryphon, but he wasn't there. Something had alerted him to trouble. It may have been the same thing that obviously had lured the guards away. Having heard Gryph shout, they should have been all over the place, watching every entrance and exit, and calling the police. Either the new guards weren't as adept as they appeared, or someone else might know their routine, and that there were too few of them. Maybe the same someone Gryph stayed behind to confront.

Only God knew what Gryphon had seen. *What was the green light*? She looked at the stone he had given her, but didn't know what to do with it. *Where was he*? Panting, she scanned the darkness for his huge frame, but saw nothing. Time passed. It seemed like hours, but she knew it was probably only a very few minutes. Something was wrong. It *had* to be, or he would have followed. The stone meant too much to him to just shove it at her and leave.

Slowly, Heather made her way back to the door. She couldn't hear anything coming from inside the stairwell. Pulling the door slightly open, she paused to listen. "Gryphon?" she whispered.

Taking a deep breath, she moved back up the stairs. There was no sign of the strange green light or Gryphon O'Connor. She rounded the corner to the upper level stairwell, and saw Gryphon kneeling, holding on to the rail. Heather ran forward.

"What happened?"she gasped. Gryph stood to his full height. She could see blood oozing from a wound in his left side. The left thigh of his jeans had been shredded. She could only imagine the damage done to his leg. "My God, we have to get you to a hospital!"

"You have to leave here. It isn't safe to stay. Hurry, Heather!" If the guards didn't show up and catch them, what had been in the stairwell just might.

Gryph began to descend the stairs with surprising strength for a man who had just been attacked. Heather followed. They quickly made it to the parking lot. She grabbed Gryphon's arm.

"We can get security to call an ambulance and the police. You can tell me what happened while we wait for them."

"No! No hospital, and no police either. Don't worry about me. *You're* the one who's in danger. You must leave. Now!"

"Are you *mental*? I'm not letting you stay here like this." She pointed toward his injuries. "Those wounds are bad, and what in hell do you mean about me being in danger? Tell me what happened."

He glanced back toward the building, then grabbed her by the arm. "Woman, by all that's sacred, *leave*!"

"No! I'm not going anywhere without you." She looked into his dark eyes and could see a faint glimmer of admiration there even as Gryph dropped to his knees. The loss of blood kept him from being able to stand. She knelt beside him. "Why won't you let me call the paramedics, or at least let me take you to an emergency room?"

"Because, I'm not in your country legally," he replied.

Heather looked at him as though he were crazy. "Why doesn't that surprise me? But it doesn't make any difference. You have to have medical attention. How far do you think you'll get like this?"

"You're a damn stubborn woman." Gryph paused. "All right, if you won't leave because of me, then I'll let you take me somewhere safe. The address is 1301 Embercross Road."

She helped him to his feet and to her car. It was no small task considering how large he was. Heather drove according to the directions Gryphon gave her and watched him closely the entire time. He was fighting to stay conscious, and losing more blood by the minute. Twenty minutes later, they pulled up outside a Victorian-style home in the suburbs. Heather opened her car door, but Gryph placed a strong hand on her arm to stop her.

"No. This is as far as you go. I can make it into the house by myself." He paused, bowed his head and tried to fight off the pain. "You mustn't go home, lass. It isn't safe for you there right now." When he saw her about to interrupt him with more questions, he quickly opened the car door and got out. He took several steps, then sank to the ground again.

Heather was at his side in an instant."Gryph, dammit! I'm calling an ambulance. We can worry about your legal status later."

"I said NO," Gryph shouted at her. He tried to stand and would have fallen again, but Heather stubbornly stayed by him, letting him rest some of his weight against her until they got inside the house. He made it to the living room before collapsing onto a sofa and sinking into unconsciousness.

"Well, I can call the ambulance now, can't I, you big jerk." Heather spoke to herself. Looking around, she saw no sign of a telephone. "Is anyone home?" she called out. There was no response. Gryph was growing more pale by the moment. She had two choices. She could either search for a telephone, or stop the bleeding. She *knew* she had a first aid kit in the trunk of her car. Gryph's still form and pallor made her go for the first aid kit. It only took her a few minutes before she was back and kneeling beside him.

The shirt would have to go. Using the scissors in the kit, Heather slowly cut away enough of the shirt to reveal massive, clawlike gashes in his left side. They weren't very deep, but the bleeding was severe. Gryph's handsome face was so still, his breathing uneven. She was so busy cleaning the wounds and trying to stem the flow of blood that she never heard the front door open and close.

"In the name of the Goddess, *what's happened*?"

Heather turned her head when she heard the deep voice. She saw an older, very handsome version of Gryphon hurry into the room. And she anxiously tried to explain what was happening. "He's badly hurt. He gave me this address and..."

"*Gryph*!"

Heather halted her explanation when she saw a second person barge into the room. This woman's long dark hair fell over one shoulder, and her face paled when she saw the bleeding and unconscious figure on the sofa. The older man knelt beside Heather and continued what she had started.

"I'm his father, James O' Connor, and this is his mother, Gwyneth," he explained. "What happened?"

"He wouldn't tell me. He wouldn't let me call anyone or let me take him to an emergency room. If you'll show me where a telephone is, I'll dial 911."

"No!" Both of Gryph's parents spoke in unison.

Heather was shocked into speechlessness, but only for a moment. "Look, he told me he's an illegal alien. I don't give a damn about that. The man needs medical attention, and he needs it quickly."

"I thank you for what you've done, Miss..." James stopped when he realized he didn't know her name.

"Heather Green," she supplied.

"Miss Green. We'll take care of him now. And we thank you again. You've done the right thing."

Heather felt completely dismissed. Gryph's parents began to dress his wounds, but he didn't look any better. She didn't want to just leave. Aside from wanting to know if he'd be all right without medical help, she wanted to know how he had been so badly attacked. What had made the animal-like marks on his body? Gryph wasn't a small man by anyone's standards. He looked like he spent half his life in a gym. What kind of creature could do this to him with such apparent ease? How had some animal found its way inside the museum? Was it the same thing that had attacked Ned and the woman in the park? There were so many questions to be answered.

"Easy, son! You're with us now and safe. We'll see to these wounds and get you upstairs."

"Father," he whispered, "is Heather still here?"

Gryph's father glanced back over his shoulder. "Yes."

"She can't go home, Da! She has one of the stones. The creature that attacked me will miss it and come after her. She can't go." Gryph's voice faded as he lost consciousness again.

Gryph's mother turned to her. "He's concerned about your safety, Miss Green. Perhaps, in light of what's happened, it might be best if you stayed."

"Gwyn, are you *crazy*?" James asked.

"James!" Gwyneth chastised. "This woman has brought our son to us and has done as he requested by not calling an ambulance. The least we can do is make sure she's safe. Gryph wants that."

"Well, of course. I didn't mean to imply that I didn't care about your being safe, Miss Green. It's just that this situation is a bit *complicated*," James remarked.

"Please, call me Heather. I understand. You don't even know who I am. I can explain what I know about Gryph's injuries later and how we met. Right now, I only want to make sure he's going to be all right. I'd like to stay at least long enough to help."

"Good, that's settled then. It will take all of us to get Gryph upstairs anyway," Gwyneth said as she gazed down at her son.

Heather saw all of the concern in the world in her expression. His mother was frightened beyond reason, but managed to maintain composure. She could see where Gryph's strength of character originated.

Half an hour later, Gryph was finally in a bed on the second floor. Some of the color had come back into his tanned face, but Heather still feared for the blood he had already lost and the possibility of infection. As his parents helped him, she was able to study them more closely. Gryph's father was a tall man with broad shoulders like his son. His hair was white, thick and shoulder length. His face was, despite his fifty-odd years, still uncannily handsome. Gryph's mother could only be described as beguiling. Her hair was long, black and braided. There was a wonderful streak of silver in it which ran from her forehead to the very end of the braid. She was tall, but very slender. Both of them spoke with the same odd accent as Gryph. It wasn't exactly Irish, but not Scottish either. Heather could see both of them in their devastatingly handsome son. He was lucky to have a family, especially when she could see how much they obviously loved him.

"Come, Heather." Gryph's father led her from the room. "Gwyneth is quite skilled at tending wounds. She'll know what to do. I thank you from the bottom of my heart for bringing our son safely to us. Please...can you tell me how this happened?"

"I'm not sure I know where to begin." She paused for a moment to gather her composure. "I'm an assistant at the Manhattan Museum of Antiquities. My job is to help research, catalog, and display objects which are part of our permanent collections. My specialty is Celtic studies. Gryph, uh, *introduced* himself to me recently and had some questions about some acquisitions from Ireland. In particular, there were three Celtic rune stones that he wanted information about. Tonight, I was showing him something I'd found in the collection." Heather stopped not sure how to explain. Then she plunged ahead.

"We were leaving the museum together when something happened. I'm not really sure what. We were going down a back stairway when Gryph became frightened by something I couldn't see. He made me leave while he stayed behind. I got to the parking lot and waited, but he didn't come out. I got worried, went back into the museum to look for him and found him in the stairwell. It looked like he'd been attacked by some kind of wild animal. I really don't know how to explain all of this any better," Heather finished, pushing her hair away from her face.

James seemed to weigh her words and watch her closely. "Gryph told you that the stones as well as other objects have been stolen from Ireland, didn't he?"

"Yes." Heather nodded, with a sigh.

"Do you believe what he's told you is the truth?"

"At first I didn't," she admitted. "But now I do. The rune stones he seemed so interested in were meticulously hidden in one of the crates shipped from County Cork. Many of the objects shipped from Ireland have been mislabeled and tagged improperly to make them appear to have come from approved archeological digs. Gryph said the artifacts were actually taken from unapproved burial sites. Someone was graverobbing."

James nodded. "Exactly. But why are you helping my son?"

His gaze seemed to pierce right through her. It reminded

her of that first night when Gryph had broken into her apartment. Their eyes were so alike. "To be quite honest, I don't know. Except he's the only person who's been telling me the truth lately. I don't even know why any of this is his concern. Is he some kind of cop or something? He told me he was here to retrieve what's been stolen. But, if he's working within the law, why won't he go to the local police for help, and why is he here illegally? There's so much I don't understand, so much he won't tell me." Heather glanced back toward the room where Gryph was lying.

"He's trying to protect you. For that same reason, we can't tell you any more than he can," Gwyneth said as she entered the hallway outside Gryph's room. "He's asking to see you."

Heather nodded and quietly entered the room. Gryph was awake, but any fool with eyes could see he was in a great deal of pain. Muscles in the side of his jaw seemed to clench, as did his hands. "Why are you so stubborn?" Heather asked.

"Why are *you*?" Gryph responded with a hint of a smile, trying to belie the pain he felt.

"Your mother said you wanted to see me." She pushed a stray lock of black hair off his forehead as she sat next to him.

"I want you to give the stone to my parents. I know you don't know much about any of us, Heather, but you have to trust someone. If you go to the local authorities, they'll take the stone, and it may never be returned to its rightful place. It could be locked away indefinitely." Gryph closed his eyes, fighting unconsciousness.

"It's evidence in a murder case, Gryph."

He needed to make her understand, without telling her too much, that the stones couldn't remain in the outside world. "The rune stones have to be where no one can get their hands on them. They've got to go back, Heather. Back to where they came from."

"That's all you've said you've ever wanted, isn't it? For the things that were taken to be returned?" She studied him.

"Yes. And I'll make a bargain with you. I'll let you do what you think is best about the other artifacts. There are more than enough stolen objects to use as evidence in a murder. But I've got to retrieve the other two rune stones and take them back to Ireland. When I've done that, I promise, you'll not be troubled by me again."

"You won't be lurking about parking lots anymore?" She tried to smile and raised her eyebrows in disbelief.

Gryph returned her smile with one of his own."I promise you, lass. And I always keep my word."

"How will you keep it if you're dead, Gryph? Tonight we only took one stone. What's going to happen when you try to retrieve the other two? And why won't you tell me what happened to you?" Heather persisted.

"Heather..." Gryph began with a warning note in his voice. He didn't want her to know what would have to be done to secure the other stones. She'd done more than enough.

"I know, I know. You're not going to tell me. God, I'm getting sick of hearing that." Her gaze softened when she felt how hot his skin was. She traced his face with her hands and knew he was desperately ill.

"Trust me, Heather. You don't really *want* to know." Gryph placed one of his hands over hers to keep it on his cheek.

"Stubborn," Heather muttered, referring to his nature.

"Tenacious," Gryph replied. He laid back, sighed and closed his eyes.

From the tortured expression on his face, his pain looked like it was increasing. Heather gently placed one hand on his chest where his shirt had been torn open. It was an automatic gesture of comfort. Gryph's response was spontaneous. Without opening his eyes, he turned his face toward her other palm, which still rested on his cheek.

Gwyneth and James watched from the doorway in amazement. They had never seen their son interact this way with another soul. His way was to guard his every action, to have no real connection of any permanence to anyone. They carefully left the room and closed the door behind them.

"Gwyn, what's happening in there can't be allowed. The Sorceress would never approve," James admonished.

"Approve or not, it *is* happening, and I won't stop it. Neither will you," Gwyn replied, staring at her husband.

"You know our law, and so does Gryphon. He can't..."

"James," she interrupted, "*he's dying*!"

James looked at his wife and felt absolute horror flood his gut. "What are you talking about? The wounds are serious, but Gryphon is unbelievably strong."

"It isn't the wounds themselves, it's the poison that's now in Gryph's system," Gwyneth whispered, lowering her head. Tears fell down her cheeks.

"*Poison*! What poison?" James took her in his arms and stared into her face. Fear made him punctuate his words.

"The creature he fought was a creation brought about through the evil use of the stones. Its talons were poisonous. I don't know how to save him. And unless the Sorceress does, he'll see two, possibly three more sunrises. Then, he'll die." Gwyneth turned away slowly.

James' face fell in misery. "You didn't tell him?"

"He knows. He told the woman what he wanted her to hear. He doesn't want her to suffer. Apparently, he feels a deep connection to her."

"Is there nothing that can be done?" James asked softly. "He can't just die. He *can't*."

"I'll send for the Sorceress. That's all that *can* be done. But the poison is very strong. It spread quickly."

"I'll retrieve the other stones myself, " James promised.

"No," Gwyneth insisted, "I'll not lose the both of you. The creature will have to be destroyed, but it should be left to the Sorceress. The beast no longer needs the stones. According to Gryphon, it can change at will without them. All it needed was the original enchantment from the stones' surface. Gryphon said that each time he struck the beast, it adapted and overcame the force of his attack. He didn't have time to induce his *own* change for protection. The only reason he wants the stones is to keep this from happening again. To keep anyone *else* in the outside world from interpreting them and abusing their powers. Our son knows someone else will have to stop the beast if he can't. He might just die having tried to do what the Sorceress commanded." Gwyneth began to cry in earnest.

James pulled her to him again and held her close as his

own tears fell.

***

Heather leaned forward and placed the cool cloth against Gryph's forehead. He wasn't responding to her voice any longer. "Please, let me take him to a hospital. I'm *begging* you. He isn't getting any better here."

"There are reasons why he can't go, Heather. Gryph understands this," Gwyneth sadly responded.

Heather turned back to Gryph, got out of the chair by the bed and sat next to him. "He's in so much pain. I *know* it. I wish there were more I could do." She crossed her arms and gripped her own shoulders in frustration.

"You're doing more than you can ever imagine. Gryph doesn't make a habit out of getting close to people. In the short time he's known you, he's become closer to you than to anyone else in his life besides his father and me," Gwyneth told her, watching how carefully Heather reached out to touch him.

"Why? What's made him that way?" Heather looked at Gwyneth, wanting to know why a man like him would be so alone. His character led her to believe he'd have a great many friendships. Many of those would probably be relationships with beautiful, seductive women.

"It's a long story. Maybe I'll ask Gryph to tell you one day." Gwyneth left the room.

Heather saw tears and abject sorrow in the woman's eyes. If she was that afraid for her son, then why wouldn't she let him have proper medical care? Why wouldn't Gryph let her call the damn ambulance? It was crazy. The man was getting progressively worse. Even Heather's limited first aid experience told her so. She looked at him lying so still. Occasionally he would moan softly, unable to suppress the pain.

The night went on. Gryph's parents stayed in the room with him. They would touch him and talk to him, give what words of comfort they could hoping he could hear them. By the next morning, Heather knew he would die if the situation persisted. Pleading with Gwyneth and James had done no good. She was almost hoarse with her efforts and was surprised they didn't send her away. Perhaps they realized that she wouldn't go if they tried.

By mid-morning, Heather was beside herself with fear. Gryph had gone even more pale than he had been from the loss of blood. She tried to cool his heated chest by placing wet compresses against his flesh. Having no care for the liberties she was taking, Heather stroked his shoulders, arms, and legs. She ran her fingers through his long hair, speaking softly to him as his parents had. She talked about her life as a child, her schools and friends. She told him about her job and the death of her parents. Anything, just to give him something to listen to and to keep him from drifting away for good. Afraid and exhausted, she finally began to cry.

"Gryph, why is this happening? Why does everyone I care about have to die? First, it was my parents then Ned, now..." her voice trailed away as the realization struck her. *When did I get so obsessed with him*? Why couldn't she just walk away? After all, Gryphon was a complete and total mystery, a stranger really. Yet, in her heart, Heather knew he was a kind and decent man. He was losing his life because he had tried to do an honorable thing. How many people were noble enough or had enough courage to give so much? At first, he'd frightened her beyond reason. But Gryph had never hurt her, had even tried to protect her. And he'd *always* been gentle. There was something so lonely about him. So lost. But he had more dignity and gallantry than anyone she'd ever known. He believed in what he was doing and wanted to keep people from being harmed. She'd never met anyone like him. Heather looked at him and stroked his cheek before she leaned into his shoulder, crying. Heroes shouldn't have to die, and that's what he had become to her. No book image. No myth.

SEVEN

The door opened behind her. Gryph's parents and a beautiful, strangely dressed woman entered the room. Her long white hair was braided and fell down her back. She wore robes a Druid might wear. Heather recognized the clothing from her studies. Had she been less frightened for Gryph and more coherent, she may have guarded her behavior. The woman emanated some kind of power. Tall and stately, she embodied mysticism and magic. Gwyneth and James moved forward at the same time. They gently pulled Heather away from Gryph, though she tried to fight them.

"Come, Heather," James implored. "Someone is here who may be able to help. She needs to see Gryph alone. Come along." He walked Heather toward the door and into the hallway. Gwyneth followed.

"She's exhausted, James," Gwyneth said as she pulled Heather into her arms and held her.

"Yes. We all are. But we should know soon enough. One way or another." James ran a weary hand over his face.

Heather let herself fall into Gwyneth's arms. All she wanted was not to be afraid for Gryph any longer. His parents could help ease her pain.

They waited for only a few moments. The door opened and the strange woman walked out. The look she gave Heather could only be described as threatening. Ice-grey eyes pierced through her.

"I've determined how I can best treat the injuries. There's a poultice I have which may draw out enough poison to allow Gryphon a chance." She turned to James. "You said that one of the stones was found?"

"Yes," James nodded. "Heather has it."

The woman turned to Heather and glared at her hard for several moments. "What do you know of the stones?"

"She's just a friend, Shayla. She only wants to help," James said.

Heather could hear a kind of desperation in his voice. It was as if he spoke quickly before she could respond and utter something that would condemn her.

Shayla looked at Heather again. "You appear to be too young to be involved in this. How old are you, girl?"

"If it makes any difference, I'm twenty-six. And I'm old enough to know that if Gryph doesn't get medical help soon, he'll die. Why won't any of you understand that?" Heather cried out, angrily.

"You *are* young. You know *nothing* of ancient ways. Gryph knew the possible consequences of his actions. He has acted accordingly, as far as I have been able to determine." Shayla stared at Gryph's parents as she spoke the last part of the sentence.

"Heather knows nothing," Gwyneth insisted. "Gryph has told her *nothing*."

"We'll see." The Sorceress spoke cryptically. "I'll get the poultice. Bring me the stone and meet me in Gryphon's room, girl."

Heather wasted no time running down the stairs to get her jacket. It was still lying in the living room where Gryph had collapsed. She grabbed the stone out of the pocket and ran back upstairs. Who had the stone, whom it belonged to and what should be done with it weren't issues she cared anything about at the moment. All she wanted to do was help Gryph. If his parents and the cryptic old woman upstairs wouldn't call an ambulance soon, then she'd do so against all of their wishes.

"Here's your damned stone, now what about Gryph?" Heather glared at the older woman as she handed her the rune stone. She heard Gryph's parents gasp and had the strange feeling she'd just stepped over some kind of invisible line best left uncrossed.

"Take this and place it on the wounds. Leave the bandages

off," Shayla commanded as she passed Heather a green glass jar. "Gwyneth, you and James come with me. I must speak to you."

As the others left, Heather walked to the bed where Gryph lay. As ill as he was, he was magnificent. She sank next to him and lifted the bedcover away from his chest. The angry, red claw marks scored into his beautiful body made her want to weep all over again, but he needed her. She opened the top of the jar and smelled herbs that reminded her of a mountain meadow. Dipping her fingers into the concoction, she found that it was cool and tingled. She began to carefully spread it on the wounds on Gryphon's chest. As she did so, he moaned softly. Whether it was in pain or relief, Heather couldn't tell.

When she was through with his chest, she looked toward the lower part of his body where the bedcover still concealed him. Now wasn't the time to suffer an attack of Puritan prudishness. Gryph's parents had undressed him earlier. Heather knew he wore nothing under the covers. Without worrying over it another instant, she lowered the covers to his knees and swallowed very hard. Gryph O'Connor was the most exquisitely well-built man she had ever seen. His body was perfectly and muscularly proportioned. Bulk muscle met taut sinew in a combination of raw strength. Whatever attacked him had to have been unworldly. Celtic knot designs had been tattooed on his inner thighs matching those on his arms. Heather shook her head to get her mind back on the business at hand. If the ointment didn't seem to bring Gryph some relief within a short time, she'd find a phone and dial for help. She feared his parents would refuse to let him be treated. If that happened, Gryph could die while the authorities hassled over their right to administer medical aid.

Spreading some of the herbal medicine onto her hands, she rubbed them together to warm them. Then, carefully, she applied the salve to the cuts on his thigh and hip. Gryph moaned again. But it was accompanied by a deep sigh. Heather was almost certain that he knew what was being done and that it *was* having a positive effect.

She pulled the covers gently back over him and put the lid

back on the jar. A large chair had been placed by the bed. She climbed into it and curled her legs under her to make herself more comfortable. Within minutes, she was fighting a war against the exhaustion trying to claim her. It was a battle she lost. Her head fell against the wing of the chair, and her eyes closed.

***

The pain had been worse than anything he could remember. Gryph could almost feel the claws shredding his flesh, and their poison burning into his veins all over again. Because of it, he could hear his parents and Heather's anxious comments and fear, but had been unable to respond to them. The intensity of the pain had seemed to go on forever. Then he felt small, warm hands cooling the burning of the wounds. The relief had been instantaneous. Sleep, unhindered by the burning poison, aided him.

But now he was awake. The morning sun streamed through a nearby window and landed in shining rays on Heather's light brown hair. In her sleep, it had been gently tossed around her shoulders. Gryph knew he'd never seen anything so lovely. Her small form was curled into the huge chair. Her head rested gracefully against one side. He couldn't remember ever waking to anything that had enchanted him so. He rested and watched her as she slept. If only his world and hers weren't so different. His imagination took him to a place where they could spend time alone. Time learning about one another and sharing the things all men and women who were attracted to one another share. Weakly, he lifted his hand toward her and was able to touch his fingertips to hers. Such small contact was still electrifying. That she'd stayed with him touched his hard heart the way nothing else had ever done. He wanted to hold her, but his injuries wouldn't allow much movement. He had to be content just to watch her sleep. Occasionally, she'd moan and shake her head slightly. It was as if bad dreams tormented her exhausted sleep. It made him want to pull her into his arms that much more. Even though his life had been devoid of such warm and meaningful contact, he knew nothing else would ever come near the feeling of holding her as she slept. He wanted to believe he could chase away her demons. From that flight of fancy, his imagination went to other possibilities. All of them wonderful, yet impossible.

Slowly, hours later, she awoke. Gryph watched as her eyes, gray as the sheen off a full moon, focused on her surroundings. When she saw he was conscious, she quickly left the chair to sit on the bed.

"Gryph," she whispered as she touched his cheek with one gently placed hand. "I thought you might not make it. I was going to ignore what you'd said and call an ambulance. How are you feeling? Are you in a great deal of pain?"

Gryph felt the icy wall he'd spent a lifetime erecting begin to melt. She seemed to truly care. Before he could analyze it further, he shored up the wall around his heart to keep from hoping. That way lay pain. There could be nothing between him and this woman.

"I'll be fine. It was good that you did as I asked." There was nothing a doctor could have done that Shayla Gallagher couldn't. He'd been aware of the Sorceress' presence. "I'm glad you stayed. It was too dangerous for you to go back to your apartment."

"I know it's going to be pointless to ask, but *why*?"

"If there's any way you can leave the city for a short time, do so. The rest of my business here shouldn't take very long. In a few weeks, it'll be over," he lied. For him, nothing would ever be over or be the same. He would never be able to forget the beautiful, irritating American woman before him who asked too many questions and who didn't have the sense to know when to be afraid.

"I *can't*. I have to know what all of this is about. Sooner or later I'll find out, with or without you telling me."

Gryph sighed in frustration. He feared for her safety if she stayed. Those who had stolen the stone might harm her. Or Shayla would, thinking the girl knew too much. Either way he had to protect her. It was his fault she was involved at all. He reached for a strand of hair that had fallen against her cheek. The door to the room opened. He immediately dropped his hand when he saw Shayla and his parents standing there watching him. There was an accusatory look in the Sorceress' gaze, fear in his parents'. His mother rushed past his father and Shayla to sit on the other side of the bed.

"Gryph, you're awake! We thought we'd lose you. I was so afraid," his mother spoke softly.

Gryph touched her cheek and smiled. "I'll be well again, Mother. Don't worry."

At his words, Gryph's father moved quickly forward and touched his son on the shoulder. Honest, open love gleamed in his parents' eyes. Heather knew she didn't belong in the picture. His parents' tears of relief prompted her to leave the room, as slowly and unobtrusively as possible.

Shayla watched the girl rise and leave. She followed her into the hallway, slowly closing the door to the room behind her. "I would like to speak with you." She used a commanding voice to get Heather's attention.

Heather, unused to being spoken to in such a way, turned with an angry expression and resorted to sarcasm. "I'm grateful that you were able to help Gryph. Whatever that stuff in the jar was, it seems to have worked wonders. You should bottle it and sell it. I'm sure the medical community would beat a path to your door."

"Don't be impertinent with me, girl. My name is Shayla Gallagher. You don't know who you're dealing with. It wasn't just the herbal medicine that helped rid Gryph of the infection, it was his will to live that aided the cure. *That* and *you.*"

"What are you talking about? I barely know the man." Heather's instincts told her not to say too much about her real feelings. Besides, they were too new, too precious to share with this imperial-looking, Druid-dressed harridan.

"Perhaps, but the heart has a way of choosing its own path. Be warned, there can be nothing between you and Gryph O'Connor. He belongs with his own kind."

"Oh, *great,*" Heather muttered, "another cryptic little message I'm supposed to decipher. Look, I'm sorry if I'm being rude. I'm not usually like this. It's just that over the past few weeks, ever since that damned shipment from Ireland came into my life, everything's been a circus, and I'm getting tired of it. You people can keep your little secrets to your hearts' content, but don't tell me who to choose as my friends, where I can go or what I can do. Now, I'm going back in to see Gryph."

"*You will not.*" Shayla stepped in her way, her voice echoing off the walls. "None of us needs or wants you here. *Go*, girl! Go before you wish you had never heard of Gryphon O'Connor. If you had not distracted him, he'd have done what was necessary by now and would never have come to harm. He almost died trying to protect you."

Heather stared at the older woman. The last statement had been true. Something had attacked Gryph in the stairwell of the museum, and he'd stood between it and her. Without another word, she turned and left. She went downstairs, picked up her jacket, walked outside to her car and drove away. She wouldn't endanger *anyone* any more. Gryph O'Connor was a grown man and could live his life as he saw fit. From now on, she'd do what her instincts told her and stay clear of him. New York was full of weirdos. Why she had to have romantic feelings for one of them was something she was going to have to deal with on her own. She was more sure than ever that she should have called the police when the man had first shown up. God only knew what craziness she'd gotten herself into.

Tears stung her eyes as she drove. The old woman was right about another thing. Gryph didn't want her in his life. Except for the information he thought he could glean from her, he'd done everything he could to distance himself. Hadn't he told her he'd be leaving? Hadn't he been as tight-lipped as a Pentagon employee about his activities? What she knew of him and this whole affair had been dragged out of the man, or circumstances had forced him into talking to her. Well, *she'd* be the one doing the distancing from now on. She hadn't asked to become involved in any of this. For her own peace of mind, Heather knew she had to stay away from him. Gryph was a man with too many secrets. Most of them very dangerous.

***

A week later, Gryph stood on the balcony staring at the setting sun. His parents and Shayla sat at a nearby table, discussing alternatives to the problem of retrieving the stones.

"The other two stones *must* be found," Shayla declared. "While the creature can now change at will, the stones must by retrieved to keep anyone else from obtaining the same power. And the being that has evolved through their use must be destroyed. This is Gryphon's task. He'll be immune to the poison the beast wields now."

Everyone looked at Gryph. He kept his gaze on the sunset as night descended.

"Gryph, have you heard anything we've said?" his father asked, concern making him lower his voice to a soft inquiry.

Without turning to look at them, he responded. "Yes, Father, I've heard it all. A million times. Retrieve the stones and kill the beast. It's my task to complete. Then, afterward, I can retreat to the abbey." *Back where I belong*, was the unspoken thought hanging in the air.

His parents stared at one another.

James stood and moved to stand beside his son. "Gryphon, what troubles you? Are you still unwell? Perhaps you need a little more time. The poison was strong. A day or so more won't..."

"Have you ever wondered what you'll do tomorrow, Da?" Gryph interrupted and paused as he saw the confusion on his parents' faces. "Of course, you don't. You and Mother travel. You have each other. Together, you see the world and all the miracles it holds. I never wonder about the next day. *Never*. Each one is just like the last and always..." he stopped and dropped his head in disgust at the self-pity and bitterness in his tone. The depth of his responsibilities swamped him like never before.

"I'll kill the damned thing and get back the stones, Father. I'm healed. The Sorceress, in her infinite wisdom, saw to that. Never let it be said that we didn't honor the pact. That *cursed, damned* promise!" With that he leapt off the balcony and gracefully landed on the lawn below. He shed his clothing, put it in his ever-present bag, and lowered himself to one knee. Without any effort, he willed the *change* to happen. He felt his wings unfurl to the night sky and flew toward the waning light.

***

Heather had said nothing about her brief absence from work except that her *female* problems were worse than she had first thought. Neither Niall nor the professor wanted to question her about something so personal and were glad to let the matter drop. Ignoring advice not to, she was working later than usual when she noticed the security guards staring at her. They were getting tired of waiting and were anxious to get their rounds over with so the alarms and cameras could be set for the evening. Whatever danger Gryph was concerned about hadn't reappeared at the museum. But she had heard something occurred which caused the guards to be severely reprimanded. They were a great deal more attentive. At least most of the time.

But Heather had been careful not to work *too* late just in case. She grabbed her coat from the rack by the door and walked down the stairwell with the security guard. Habitually, he went his own way as soon as they reached the boundaries of the parking lot. Except for Ned's death, everything might have been the same as always. Only Heather knew that nothing was the same. She was now more than passingly familiar with the false paperwork McPherson was filing. She'd copied enough to go to the police with her findings. But she couldn't really prove anything, and going to the law could cost her the job she'd come to love. But she didn't see any other way to stop what the professor was doing. He was stealing a people's culture and heritage. To her, only a violent crime could be worse. A crime like murder.

She was about to put the key into her car door when a hand grasped her shoulder from behind. Crying out, she turned to find Niall Alexander standing behind her.

"God, Niall, you scared the hell out of me!" Heather moistened her dry lips with the tip of tongue.

"Sorry, babe. I thought I was making enough noise to wake the dead." He grinned, oblivious to her fear.

Heather drew her jacket closer. "You probably were. I was just a bit preoccupied, that's all."

"You've been in a daze a lot lately. I've been wondering what the deal was." Niall leaned carelessly against her car.

"It's nothing. I guess I'm just tired," she lied, not wanting to reveal anything about what was going on with the artifacts. For all she knew, Niall might leak something of her suspicions to McPherson.

"You should be more careful, honey. Whoever was attacking people might try again."

She watched as an odd expression covered Niall's face. "Yeah, you're right. I guess I *should* pay more attention to what's going on around me," Heather nodded. Maybe if she had, McPherson wouldn't have been able to smuggle artifacts into the country, Ned might still be alive, and a god-like Irishman with midnight eyes wouldn't have come into her life and catapulted her emotions out of control.

"Look, I'm free for the rest of the evening. Why don't we pick up a pizza and make a late night of it?"

"No, thanks. I'm anxious to get home to bed."

"That's exactly what I had in mind..." Niall put his arms around her.

"Maybe some other time." As she spoke she turned to open the car door. He couldn't have said anything *less* appealing. But Niall pulled her around to him again.

"Heather, I know things between us haven't been exactly kosher lately. Let me make it up to you?"

"It's all right, no big deal. Maybe we've all been on edge."

He tried to kiss her, but she pushed him away. "Niall, I'm really not in the mood. All I want to do is get home and get some sleep."

"Well, you know what they say, baby. There's no better way to get to sleep than after hot sex," Niall said as he tried to kiss her again.

"No. I *mean* it. I want to go home *alone*," Heather insisted, feeling anger rise at his persistence.

"Oh, come on, honey! You've made your point. I've been ignoring you lately, and you're in a snit over it. But this hard-to-get game is doing nothing but giving you the reputation of being a prick tease." He tried to kiss her again.

Heather pushed him away, hard. "I don't give a damn what you or anyone else thinks about me, Niall. Now let me go!"

She tried to get into her car again, only to be roughly pulled around and shoved into the side of the door.

"I thought we had a good thing going, baby. But maybe you like things the hard way. Is that it, Heather? You want it the *hard* way? I can oblige. Oh yeah, I can give it to you *real hard.*"

He crushed his mouth down on hers. Heather slapped him with all the force she could muster, and the strength of it knocked him back a short distance. In his rage, his boyish good looks turned disgustingly ugly. He raised his hand and backhanded her once across the jaw, knocking her back over the hood of her car. She struggled with him, tried to scream for help, but he forced his mouth on hers again. Her knee came up and caught him dead in the groin. His eyes widened in pain and he dropped to the ground, both hands grasping his crotch as he writhed. Before he could recover, she had her car door open and the engine started. She was pulling out of the parking lot when she saw, through the rearview mirror, that he was able to sit up.

My God, what in the name of heaven did I ever see in that bastard? She drove away and felt blood dripping from the corner of her mouth where he'd hit her. It had been a small price to pay for putting Niall where he belonged. Tomorrow, when she could stop shaking so much, and the nausea wouldn't overwhelm her, she was going straight to the police. Her instincts told her to file a report with them now. Go straight to the police station and start pressing charges. But her body was telling her something else. She felt defiled and dirty. And it might come down to his word against hers that the entire incident had ever taken place. Disbelief began to mingle with rage and pain that a man she once cared for could treat her in such a way. Doubts and self-loathing about her involvement with him filtered into her brain. And whatever she did or said would certainly affect her job. Still, she didn't give a damn about the rumors that would surface among the museum staff. Nobody was going to hit her and get away with it. But getting Niall's repulsive touch scrubbed from her body was an overwhelming need that just couldn't wait.

EIGHT

Heather ran up the six flights of stairs to her apartment, closed the door behind her and locked it. She tore off her clothes, stepped into the shower and almost scraped herself raw from head to toe. All to rid herself of Niall's abhorrent touch. *Castrating would be too good for him.* She hastily towel-dried her hair. Looking in the mirror only provided evidence of what she was feeling. There would be a nasty bruise on the left side of her jaw by morning and her lip was cut. If nothing else, *that* should provide proof that she'd been attacked. Filling a small towel with ice, she sat on her sofa with her head in her hands trying to reduce the pain. Her entire body still trembled with fear and shock. The last thing she wanted was police questioning her about the incident so soon after it happened. And she didn't want a doctor probing at her like a science experiment. Not yet. Tomorrow would be soon enough to file her charges. Her mind would clear, and the sickness would pass. Things would fall into perspective, and her intellect could outweigh her shattered emotions.

***

Gryph glided aimlessly through the ink-black sky. Tomorrow night he'd break into the museum and take it apart, piece by piece, until he found the rune stones. Afterward, he'd take care of the beast, return to Europe and hope to never hear of the stones again. Whoever had abused them was keeping them at the museum. He was sure that was why the murders had been committed there. More people would die if the creature which attacked him wasn't destroyed. Next time, he'd be ready. He would change quickly and not give the demon a chance. As Shayla had pointed out, he'd now be immune to its poison. In the middle of all the turmoil surrounding the stones, he prayed Heather was safe. In the short time he had known her, the woman had managed to fill his head with thoughts, impossible dreams that made his pain all the worse. She reminded him all too vividly of what he could never have. And his actions had placed her in danger. That was another reason why he needed to act swiftly. She was innocent of any wrongdoing. Because of what he was, the instinctive need to protect her was strong. It was the way of his kind. Every waking moment his thoughts had been filled with her. If she knew what he really was, her horror would know no bounds. Yet he still had to protect her.

Before he realized where his thoughts had taken him, Gryph landed lightly on the roof of her apartment building. He cursed himself for being a fool. This was the last place on Earth he should be. The darkness hid his form well enough, but he still had no business at her apartment. He should leave her alone and get on with the business at hand. Still, he couldn't resist making sure she was safe. There should be no harm in quietly checking on her as she slept. She would never know he had been there, such was his stealth.

Changing into human form, he climbed onto her balcony and walked to the French doors. He pulled his clothing out of his leather bag and quickly dressed. Only one light was on in the living room. Forcing open the door as he had before, he crept forward. He sensed her presence just before he saw her. She was dressed only in a towel, leaning forward with her head in her hands. He sensed pain and immediately drew near to help. All thoughts of keeping his distance fled.

"Heather," he spoke quietly, "what's happened?"

Startled, she jumped up. Fear darkened her silver eyes. "Gryph, you scared me! What are you doing here?"

"I'm sorry I frightened you. But I..." He stopped, then immediately held out one hand and pointed at her face. "What happened? Who's done this?" His hand came forward to gently caress her jaw.

Heather saw his eyes darken with a horrible anger. She sank back onto the sofa. "It's not as bad as it looks. I'm going to report it tomorrow. What are you doing here? Breaking into people's homes is a felony, you know. I shouldn't have to keep reminding you." Her tremulous voice indicated she wasn't quite as angry as the words were meant to sound.

"Dammit, Heather! *What's happened*?" He gripped her by the shoulders.

She pushed him away, stood up and quickly backed toward the bedroom. "Stay away from me. *No one touches me unless I say so. No one!*"

"Heather, lass, be calm. I won't hurt you, and I won't let anyone else hurt you, either." Gryph stood, but made no move toward her. The last thing he wanted to do was corner an injured woman. And, by Herne, someone was going to pay for the injury done to her.

"I've heard that before. Just stay away."

The look in her eyes frightened him. Someone had placed his hands on her against her will. Had she been raped? He could see bruises on her arms, and his anger grew proportionally as the seconds passed.

Heather backed against the wall and her head fell forward. "I just...I don't understand why any of this is happening. There's no one I can trust." She sobbed.

Gryph recognized exhaustion, pain and fear in her voice. She had been through too much lately, and it was taking its toll. Part of her dilemma was due to him, but whatever had happened tonight was the act of a coward. He'd avenge her by drawing blood. He silently swore it.

"Heather, give me your hand," he softly pleaded and offered his own. "I won't hurt you. I couldn't. In your heart, you know this to be true. That's why you never called the police about me. Let me help you. You can trust me. I swear."

Heather pushed her hair back with one hand, continuing to move away. Not wanting to frighten her more, Gryph let her have some space. She wrapped her arms around herself, her beautiful hair a tangled mass about her shoulders. Even bruised and disheveled, she was exquisite. Her eyes were like those of a trapped doe he'd once freed from a poacher's snare. She turned, stopped, and looked straight into his face. He didn't move. Those lovely eyes held him to the spot.

"Can I trust you?" she whispered. "Can I?"

"With all Creation as my witness, Heather, I swear I'll never hurt you. Not ever!"

She unwrapped her arms from her body. It had been a defensive posture Gryph instinctively recognized. Her breathing grew deeper, and her eyes took on a pleading look that almost broke his heart. She was so alone. He knew what she felt because he'd been in that empty place before.

Suddenly, she ran to him, and he gently embraced and cradled her as if she were more precious than anything else in life. A gift of trust so given was a precious and rare thing. His heart swelled, and a large lump formed in his throat. It took a moment for the emotion to settle and he could speak.

"Heather," he whispered, "it's all right. Don't be afraid anymore. Please, don't be afraid."

She raised her head, looked into his face, and Gryph knew he was irrevocably lost. He lowered his mouth to hers, and her kiss was the sweetest thing he'd ever known. It was soft and gentle at first. But, as their tongues met, a fire ignited within him that no magic could ever extinguish. A thousand voices of reason screamed in his brain. This shouldn't happen. It *couldn't*. She trusted him not to hurt her. That's why she had run into his arms so willingly. But he would hurt both of them if he didn't stop. Worse, he could get them both killed.

"Heather, you don't know what you're doing. You're confused and hurt," he told her as he gently pushed her away.

"Gryph, for some reason, I know we can't have a normal relationship. You and everyone around you has made that clear. All I want is one night. Just one before you go back to where you came from, and I have to go on with my life. All I'm asking for is one *memory*."

"Lass, you've been through too much tonight to make that kind of decision," he said as he pulled her close.

"It's *my* choice," she insisted.

He touched her jaw and ran a finger sensuously across her injured bottom lip. "You may need to see a doctor about this," he murmured, trying to change the subject.

Heather smiled, then laughed. "Does this sound like a role

reversal? Only, now *I'm* the one who's refusing to be treated."

"If you won't let a doctor look at you, tell me where there's some more ice."

"Kitchen," she sighed as she ran a hand through her hair and nodded toward her small refrigerator.

Gryph returned moments later with more ice in the towel. He carefully placed the towel over her jaw and tried to keep his voice and demeanor calm when all he wanted to do was kill the person responsible for hurting her.

"Now, tell me what happened."

"Niall Alexander decided he wanted something I didn't want him to have," she explained.

"And what was that?" Gryph asked in a nonchalant fashion. He massaged one shoulder until he felt her relax a little. Alexander was a dead man.

"Me!"

"He's the blond man I've seen before in the parking lot, isn't he?"

"Yes." Heather sighed contentedly as she leaned into Gryph's shoulder.

"And he forced himself on you?" Gryph's voice lowered perceptibly, though he tried not to show too much anger. That wasn't what she needed at the moment.

"He *tried,* but I incapacitated him with a knee shot to the groin." She gamely tried to smile.

"Good! That's my lass. The bastard won't go near you again, Heather. I swear!"

"Am I your lass?" she asked, holding her breath and waiting for his response.

Gryph looked at her for a very long time before he spoke. "As sure as time, if you're not mine, I'm certainly yours."

Heather wrapped her arms around his neck and began to kiss him, slow and deep. Gryph felt every word of warning he'd ever been given echo into his being. If anyone ever found out he'd even been in her apartment, the assumption would be made that they'd loved, and she would be in danger because of him. He knew he should leave. But the same need that fueled her drove him. Still, his conscience called to him.

"Heather..." he tried to pull away.

"Gryph, shut up! Just one night. I'm not asking for you to reveal your deep, dark secrets. I want just a few hours. That's all," she said as she nuzzled his neck and kissed the corner of his mouth.

He moaned as she slid her hands inside his jerkin, stroked her hands over the wounds healing there. She seemed oblivious to the fact that his clothing was different from anything she'd seen him wear before. He was dressed in the medieval-like garb of the Order. When he had flown away, he hadn't intended on seeing her or anyone. His clothing was comfortable and kept him from feeling as if his connection to the Shire weren't completely broken. He had only wanted some space away from his parents and Shayla's ever-demanding presence. Now, he found himself in the very last place he should be, holding her small, soft form in his arms. The black leather jerkin, pants and boots didn't seem to concern her at all. Her academic mind might recognize it as the garb of a Celtic warrior. But at the moment, he just didn't give a damn. He *had* to hold her. Just for a while. The feel of her was intoxicating. Her body molded to his so exquisitely. It was worth any amount of punishment the Sorceress could administer. Later, he could think of this time and remember. But he didn't have the right to risk her.

"You don't know the consequences of what you're doing," he spoke softly, longingly. His hands slowly moved over her.

"Then, tell me," she entreated. All she wanted was to lay within his arms. Safety, peace, friendship and ecstasy were there.

"I can't, little one. It would cost both of us our lives," he softly uttered.

She pushed away from him so she could look into his eyes. "You wanted me to trust you. Why can't you do the same?"

Her eyes seemed to capture the starlight filtering through the windows. "My life is very...complicated."

"Are you some kind of agent from your country? Are you wanted by the police for some crime? If you tell me what it is, I swear I'll try to understand, Gryph. I know enough about you to know you would never hurt anyone unless it was in self-defense. You're too strong, too caring." Her gaze drifted to his clothing.

If you only knew, he thought. Her keen brain was overcoming the emotional upheaval so recently inflicted upon her. She was beginning to assess the difference in his attire. It was a major mistake to have let her see him dressed so unusually. The Order would never understand such a breach of ancient law. Including himself, beings in the Order could be deadly. Any of them would see them both destroyed for what he had done, and what he was doing. He held her to him, breathed in her clean scent, then he rose.

"I have to leave now. It's for the best, Heather."

She stood with him. Her gaze held a hurt and lost look. "All right. I won't ask you to do something that's wrong for you. But if you're using my safety as an excuse, don't do me any favors, Gryph. I can look after myself. I've been doing that for a very long time." She turned away.

"Heather, lass," he grabbed her arm and pulled her back around to face him, "It's not an excuse. It's reality."

"It's okay. Go your way and do whatever it is you came to do. I'll never understand, and you won't explain. I won't ask any more questions. Just know that I want you. It isn't something I can help. It just happened. If you could tell me that you don't have feelings for me, it would make it easier."

"I..." his voice faltered. He could turn her away from him forever and save them both by telling her he didn't care. But he couldn't. "By *Merlin's balls*," he muttered, "I can't tell you something you know is a lie, woman."

Heather's response was to wrap her arms around his neck and kiss him passionately. Gryph tried not to respond, but his arms enveloped her and his sense left.

"We'll both be damned," he murmured against her lips.

"Then, we'll both be damned," she replied.

Gryph picked her up and walked into the bedroom, cradling her against his massive chest. Lowering her until she stood, he pulled the towel away from her. His breath left his body. She was the most enchanting creature he had ever seen. He had watched seductive Forest Fairies in England whose beauty was beyond description. They were known for their ability to sensuously lure men into their domain, leading them into another reality. But nothing in the world had prepared him for the slender shoulders, narrow hips and small waist his hands caressed. Her long legs were made to be stroked, made to be wrapped around a man's body as he plunged into her. Her breasts fit perfectly into his palms—so soft and yielding. If he could spend one night resting his head against such soft flesh—*her* flesh...

She caressed his arms and shoulders, slowly learning his body and watching for his reaction. Soon he was unclothed as well, falling into the softness of the moonlit bed and pulling her with him. She reveled in the feeling of power as he moaned. Her hands stroked the outside of his hips, then made soft sweeping circles inward. His head dropped back, and his chest heaved with gasping breaths.

Her long, graceful fingers closed around him, and a million nerve endings screamed at once. "I'm lost to you, lass. So lost..."

Thousands of lonely days and nights had burned themselves into Gryph's memory. For this one night, he wouldn't be alone. In his arms, he held the golden warmth of the sun and a silver-eyed memory to keep. He plunged his hands into her hair, kissed her until she moaned. The small sound was so inviting, he feared he might hurt her with his uncontrolled passion. He wished for more experience in the art of making slow, tender love instead of joining in quick lust. So, he watched her face, learning from her expression and her soft, breathless sighs what she wanted. Needed.

"Easy, little one, we've all night and I don't want to hurt you," he whispered into her shoulder. Loving the way she touched him, stroked him, he almost lost the very power to breathe.

"You won't hurt me, Gryph," she whispered as she kissed his neck and jaw line, "I *know* you won't. It's like you said. I know it in my heart."

He pulled her body even closer to his, wanting every inch of them to touch. He lowered his head to taste her breasts and stroked her thighs open with his palms. One of Heather's hands dug into his shoulder while the other brushed the rapidly healing injury to his left hip. The feel of her hands on him was almost more than he could stand. The evidence of his full and uncontrolled arousal lay throbbing expectantly against her abdomen. She reached between them and gently cupped his swollen member. Gryph growled in pleasure. He felt her rotate her small, firm hips against him, telling him she was ready. He wasted no time maneuvering over her. His fingers tested and parted the delicate folds of her woman's flesh before he entered. Heather cried out in satisfaction at his thrusting finger. He stroked her and let his fingers enter her over and over, until her soft moans became louder. She was so close to finding release. Gryph quickly pulled his fingers away and replaced them with his erection. He pushed partially into her and stopped, trying to control himself.

"Please," she begged, "Gryph, *now*!"

He plunged forward in one long, straight thrust and thought he would die with the pleasure of sheathing himself within her. His own cry of deep pleasure joined hers. Soon, they were moving together as one. She leaned back into his arms, letting his mouth caress every inch of her within reach.

"One long memory to take into the night, lass. One sweet..." he lost his voice as he felt himself losing all control.

Heather felt her climax nearing, then it burst upon her with the brilliance of a comet. Her cry brought Gryph to his own release, and she heard him roar out her name over and over. He pulsed within her, and her second climax followed the first. She heard his voice encouraging her from a distant, starry world.

Coming back to reality took a long time. But he was there, holding her, stroking her back and calling her name. How could she have ever imagined being frightened of this sweet, gentle warrior? She lifted one of his hands from her breast and kissed his palm.

He stroked a tear away and buried his head in her shoulder so his own would not come. She held him close, rocking him, stroking his hair. What fools they were. What a memory they would have. If he survived this quest, he would be far away in Ireland or wherever the Sorceress chose to send him next.

This woman would be here, and he would love her for touching his soul as no one ever would. She was so precious to him. Brave and intelligent. The little fool had even stood up to Shayla. If she only knew...if only...

Gryph cuddled her against him. They caressed each other, finding no words to speak, sensing the profound depth of emotion in one other. Finally, he found his voice. “Heather...”

“Don’t, Gryph. Don’t say anything,” she told him as she placed her fingers over his lips.

He kissed her fingertips, then placed them on his chest, loving the feel of her touch. His hands stroked her silken flesh, and he wondered what it would feel like to take her on a windswept moor or in a sheltered forest glen. He mentally shook the images from his mind. Those things could never happen. They were only fantasies he could carry with him. Heather ran her hands down his arms, stopping to examine the Celtic designs on his biceps.

“These are ancient markings. I never thought much of men wearing tattoos until I saw them on you. They’re beautiful. And they suit you.”

“From the beginnings of our race, they’ve been present.”

“But what about these? Why are they here?” she asked, playfully running her hand down his chest to the tattoos on his inner thighs.

Gryph was unable to answer, and his quick intake of breath made Heather continue to caress him there. No one had *ever* touched him as she did. Soon, they were making love again with all the passion born of desperation. They both knew their time was short.

In the early hours before dawn, Gryph awoke but didn’t bother dressing. Heather was lying on her side, facing away from him. He allowed himself the luxury of watching her sleep and stroking her hair as it lay against her creamy back. She had been intoxicating. For all his life, he knew he’d remember each splendid moment with her. But the ugly reality was that she didn’t even know *what* she’d chosen to lie with. He made sure the blanket was securely tucked around her before he left. He gathered his clothing, went to the balcony and looked up into the waning night sky. And, for the first time in ages, Gryphon O'Connor literally cursed who he was. He let himself shape shift. The strength of his wings effortlessly lifted him toward his temporary home, his parents and Shayla. He had to find the cursed stones, stop the beast, and leave New York. The unending days and cold nights at the abbey awaited him. Such was his fate. But the warmth of Heather's sweet heart would be his. No one could ever take that away.

***

Dawn was soon approaching. Gwyneth paced the floor in panic. Shayla and James still slept, thankfully unaware of the fact that Gryph hadn't returned home the previous night. After his recent close call, Gwyneth feared that he'd gone alone to retrieve the remaining stones. Perhaps he'd fought the beast again and was hurt, or worse. She was almost ready to awaken James and the Sorceress when she heard the familiar beat of strong wings. Gwyn breathed a deep sigh of relief when she saw her son alight on the outside patio. Dawn was soon approaching. She ran to him as soon as he changed back to human form and dressed.

"Gryph!" She embraced him.

Relief was evident on her still lovely features. He let her enfold him, then pushed her gently away. "Mother, you look like you're going to have a panic attack. What's wrong? You should be asleep."

"How can you ask me what's wrong after you left so angry, telling no one where you went?"

"I had to clear my mind." He looked away, not wanting to reveal anything.

Gwyneth cocked her head and studied him. "You're lying," she accused. "When you were very small, you'd sometimes lie, and I would always know. You have that same look about you now, and I haven't seen it in all these many years. Gryphon, what have you done?"

"Mother, I'm not a child. Must I explain away or justify everything I do? Do I ask you and Father to tell me where you are every hour of the day?" He sighed, shaking his thick mane off his shoulders.

"You've never been secretive before," his mother accused and looked at him with a deliberately piercing gaze.

"I'm tired, Mother." He turned toward the hallway. "Tonight, I intend to take back what we came here for. I'll find a way to stop the demon, and then we can leave. First, I need to get some rest." Sleep was the furthest thing from his mind. All he really wanted was more time alone with memories of Heather. Time to imagine her waking up, imagine he was with her. Holding her so very close.

He tried to move past Gwyneth, but she blocked his way by putting her hand upon his chest.

"You've been with that girl, haven't you?" she asked as her eyes searched his face.

Gryph didn't respond. He stoically stared over her shoulder.

"If Shayla finds out, you'll die!" She began to shake and put her hands to her face.

"Mother," Gryph spoke calmly as he pulled her to him, "Heather doesn't know who I am or anything about the Order. My part in the pact doesn't dictate that I remain celibate. It was one night, that's all."

"Is that all it was, Son? Just one night? You won't ever be with that outsider again?" Gwyneth looked at him searchingly.

"Yes, that's all. Now go inside, Mother. You've worried all night for no good reason, and we both need to rest."

They went upstairs together. Gryph cursed himself for his earlier weakness. He should have left Heather alone. He could lie to others, and they might believe him. He could never lie to himself. What he'd shared with Heather was unlike anything he could ever imagine, unlike the meaningless trysts he'd had in the past. If he got the chance to be with her again, he'd *have* to take it. His better judgement was swept aside with the realization that she was all he'd ever wanted. Nothing else mattered without her. He couldn't go back to living his life the way he had. Far better to be dead than live in the emotionless prison he'd built for himself. The problem was, he feared his weakness would see her dead too.

NINE

When Heather awoke, she found herself cocooned in a warm blanket and knew Gryph was gone. She really hadn't expected him to be there, but was still disappointed. There wasn't anything to indicate he'd ever been present except the disappearing warmth of his body heat. And the soreness of her own body.

After a quick breakfast and repairing her injured face with makeup, she went to the police department to report Niall for assaulting her. Even though he was a homicide cop, Detective Dayton was the person she asked to see. She remembered he'd instructed her to come to him with any unusual happenings. She assumed that Niall hitting her qualified as unusual enough. He didn't quiz her much on why she hadn't come in immediately, but accepted her excuse that she was just too upset by the incident. And it was easier talking to a policemen she knew. Better him than some complete stranger.

"We have your statement, Ms. Green, but we'll need to take pictures of your injuries so we can prosecute," the detective told her.

"I understand. Just put the bastard away so he doesn't do this to someone else," she begged. She stayed at the police department for another hour, then went to work. The police called ahead so the security guard would meet her in the parking lot and escort her to the acquisitions department in case Niall was on the premises. She wasn't surprised to learn that he hadn't shown up for work. Cowards didn't take responsibility for their actions.

"I just don't believe this, Heather!" Professor McPherson shook his head. "Niall has always been rather full of himself.

But to deliberately attack another employee, to attack *you*. Well, it's unthinkable, that's all. Are you sure you're going to be well enough to work?"

"Yes, Professor. I'll be fine. Besides, what he did to me was nothing compared to what I did to *him*. He'll be lucky if he walks right or fathers children."

After patting her on the shoulder, McPherson walked away, still shaking his head in apparent disbelief over the situation. Heather threw herself into her work so she wouldn't think about Gryph or the night they'd shared. The man was right. They didn't belong together. She tried not to think about who he really might be and the sinister nature of his actions. It was all too strange for her academic, logical mind to grasp. Still, she couldn't help wanting him. He was a combination of all of the men she had ever envisaged loving, strong and drop-dead gorgeous with the heart of a knight. There would never be anyone else like him. At least not for her.

***

It was almost quitting time when she found the second of the three rune stones. Apparently, whoever had taken the things had separated them, as Gryph had suggested they might, in an effort to keep them all from being found. She had picked up a Peruvian vase and was moving it to another room when she heard the distinct sound of a moderately heavy object move within its wide bottom. She put her hand inside the vase and pulled out the stone. A quick look around to see if anyone had noticed told her there was no one in the work area near enough to see around the assorted crates and boxes. She hastily placed the stone into her jacket pocket and continued to work, hoping the thief wouldn't notice its absence. Heather didn't want to believe it could be Professor McPherson. There were, after all, others who had gathered artifacts on his team. Any of them may have been motivated by the bribe of a private collector to illegally obtain rare antiquities. The museum had a longstanding reputation for properly locating and acquiring its collections. What would happen when that reputation crumbled? The reputable dealers of the world would have nothing to do with the museum, and the legitimacy of all of their current acquisitions would be questioned.

By the time she was ready to leave for the day, Heather was confused by what she should do. If she went to the police and gave them the stone, it would probably take forever to return it to its rightful place in Ireland. There was still no way of knowing who'd taken it.

She couldn't keep it. That would amount to stealing it herself. And she couldn't go to anyone at the museum without knowing who'd been involved. She might hand the stone right back to the very people who had taken it in the first place, endangering herself.

It only took her a few seconds to decide. Whatever else he was, Heather's instincts told her Gryph O'Connor wasn't lying about wanting to return the stolen items to their rightful places. He'd risked his life trying to recover them. His parents and that odd woman, Shayla, seemed to be seeking their safe return as well. Perhaps she could even save the museum's reputation by letting him take the things away before anyone discovered them and linked the rest of the shipments with other illegally obtained objects. Later, she might find a tactful way of returning things that hadn't been accepted into the museum's inventory. But if McPherson was involved in Ned's death, he needed to be punished. Her options were confusing, which added to the entire dilemma.

She let the security guard walk her as far as the end of the sidewalk then quickly continued to her car. She was opening the door when a sound like a stick breaking made her look over her shoulder. There seemed to be nothing there and the knowledge that the security guard wasn't too far away calmed her. *Steady girl. Don't let Niall rattle you into jumping at every sound.* As she turned to leave, she saw a green light approaching her in the reflection of her driver's door mirror. The night Gryphon had been attacked there had been a green light coming from the upper stairwell levels toward them. He had almost died trying to fight off whatever had been there. Heather wasn't stupid. Whatever had been killing people had something to do with that light. Were it not for his physical strength, stubborn determination and that old woman's ointment,

Gryph would be dead too. She wasn't waiting to find out what the light meant.

Heather jumped into the car, turned on the ignition and stepped on the gas. The exit out of the parking lot was only a few hundred yards away, and she would be going too fast for anything or anyone to catch her. At least that's what she thought. She had almost made it to the parking lot exit when some huge form suddenly leapt in front of the car. She instinctively slammed on the brakes, hoping to stop in time to keep from killing someone.

It was the wrong move. There in front of her stood a nightmare. A nude, man-like beast with glowing green eyes and grayish skin, it stood a full eight feet tall and had long talons at the ends of its massive hands. Horns like those of a bull protruded from its forehead, and fangs rivaling those of a tiger replaced what should have been incisors in its upper jaw. Long pale hair flowed like a river down its humped back and shoulders. The headlights on the car illuminated every feature of its naked male body. Heather was petrified. She couldn't move or scream. Nothing in her life had ever prepared her for the existence, much less attack, of such a creature. It threw back its gargoyle-like shoulders, shook its huge head and laughed deeply. Drool from its gruesome mouth spattered across the hood and windshield of her car.

"What's the matter, Heather? Playing hard to get again?" the demon spoke loudly as it glared at her.

"*Oh, my God...Niall?*" Heather whispered.

The beast quickly stalked around the car to the driver's side. She locked the door, but she knew he would get to her one way or another. When he saw what she'd done, he smiled sickeningly. Greyish foam dripped from his jaw.

"Locks won't keep us apart, bitch," Niall sneered. "You've got two things I want. One is the stone, the other is between your legs. Before the night is over, I'll have both."

Heather plunged the gas pedal to the floor, but Niall's strength was so great the car would only lurch forward, wheels spinning on the pavement. She clawed her way to the opposite door. There was a horrible sound of tearing metal as Niall neatly ripped the driver side door off the car frame. Like a can opener peeling the lid from a soup can. In an instant, she was out the passenger side door and running for her very life. She could hear him roar with rage and knew he would be upon her in seconds if she couldn't get to help quickly. She ran toward the park, toward an all-night diner on the other side. If she could get to a phone, to where there were people congregated, surely Niall wouldn't follow. It was her only chance.

She could hear heavy, fast footsteps coming from behind. Heather turned into a stand of trees and hoped the thick undergrowth beneath them would help hide her. She stopped behind the trunk of a large oak to catch her breath. She couldn't run forever. Though the night was cold, sweat poured from her body. It ran into her eyes and burned. She swiped at them with the back of one forearm.

"Come out, Heather," his deep voice crooned. "Maybe I'll decide to spare your sorry little life. If you please me, that is. I have the power of the ages at my fingertips. The stones have given me that power. I no longer need them to make the change, but possessing them keeps anyone else from obtaining their spell and stopping me. One of them is gone, but I'm sure you know where it is. Don't you, Heather? I want it back. Come out, and maybe I'll share the secrets of the stones with you. We could be invincible, have anything we desire. We could rule together."

The sound of his eerie voice made her skin crawl. It was like hearing him speak through an amplifier. He was *insane,* and knowing he'd do worse than kill her, she stayed hidden. More than ever, she knew she had to get the stone in her pocket to Gryph. If what Niall said was true, no one must ever have any of them. Gryph had been right about everything. Her trust in him hadn't been misplaced.

"I said come out, you little whore. Your Irish friend isn't here to stop me now. I killed him just the way I killed that old fool in the museum, the same way I killed that harlot in the park. She was like you. Thought she was too good for me. Well, what do you think of me now, Heather?" he asked as his eyes began to glow green again. "I'm four times the size of any man. *All* of me. That should please even *you.* Little Miss Prude. Little Miss Tease!"

Heather thought she would vomit. Niall had killed Ned and the prostitute. He *thought* he'd killed Gryph. But she believed he wouldn't kill her until he could get back the stone Shayla now had. She didn't want to think about what he'd do to make her tell him where it was. Lowering her stance, she quietly crawled forward into some nearby shrubbery. Thorns, brambles and assorted vines tore into the soft skin of her lower arms and hands. She could hear him lumbering about, looking for her. And the glow from his eyes lit the bushes nearby. She heard him roar in anger when he couldn't find her and she wouldn't respond to his demands. She kept crawling forward. Her heart beat a drumming sound she was sure would give her away. Niall would grab her at any moment. Her mouth had gone dry, and she was shaking so hard it was difficult to move quietly.

When she neared a clearing about fifty yards wide, she knew she'd have to make the best run of her life. He'd see her in the waning light for sure. But the major street where the diner was situated lay beyond the trees, on the other side of that clearing. It was now or never, and Heather wasn't about to give up. It wasn't in her nature. If Niall wanted her, he was going to have to run hard to catch his prey. She thanked God for the miles of jogging that had seemed such an ordeal.

Taking a deep breath, she bolted. Niall saw her and propelled his gargantuan form forward, but Heather had too much of a head start. She was into the stand of trees on the other side of the clearing and heading toward a row of park lamps. Several couples and some homeless people moved about beneath the lights. Heather kept running until she had crossed the street where the glass doors of the diner welcomed her like the entrance to a fortress. Panting, she navigated through the tables to the counter. No one seemed to notice. *This is New York for you.* She was bleeding from cuts, wore brambles in her hair and had been obviously running. But no one even questioned her.

"Is there a phone I could use?" she gasped out at the employee behind the counter.

"In the corner," he replied, without looking up from his newspaper.

Heather searched through her torn jeans pockets and found some change. She couldn't call the police. They'd think she was crazy. She didn't have a phone number to call Gryph, so she picked up the remnant of a telephone book and looked up a taxi company. Ten minutes later, the cab pulled up outside the diner and Heather gave the driver the address to the house where Gryph and his parents were staying. As the car pulled away, she looked out the rear window. There was no sign of anyone or any*thing* on the street. That wasn't surprising. Niall would never show himself in the form of that demon. He was insane, not stupid.

***

Twenty minutes passed before the cab pulled up in front of the house. The cab driver, like the employee at the diner, hadn't seemed to notice her appearance. The man seemed more intent on listening to the radio. Besides, he'd probably seen people in much worse condition. In the time the drive had taken, Heather had pulled what was left of her sense together, but the situation was catching up with her emotions. She pulled the money to pay the cab driver out of her pockets, ran to the front door and pounded on the heavy oak with her fists.

Gryph, barefoot, dressed in jeans and a flannel shirt with the sleeves rolled to his elbows, opened the door. *Funny.* That was the first thing that came to her mind. Aside from being as handsome as sin, he looked completely normal. He wore none of the strange, black leather clothing she'd previously seen, and he made none of his usually cryptic remarks. Just stood there staring.

Heather began to laugh. Her hands covered her face, and she fell to her knees in front of him. Her laughter turned hysterical. Gryph knelt and pulled her to him.

"What's happened?" he asked as he lifted her into his arms and closed the door with the heel of one foot. Her arms went about his neck, and she clung to him. Gryph took her into the living room, gently deposited her on the sofa and placed both of his hands on either side of her face.

"Now, tell me, little one. What's happened?" he asked, softly.

Heather began to cry. Her tears fell into some of the scratches on her face, stinging the sensitive flesh. The pain was enough to help her gain some control.

"I know I shouldn't be here, and that your family and Shayla don't want me near you. But there just wasn't anyplace else to go." She tried to continue speaking. But her minimal control left. "Niall...h-hh...he..." she tried to talk.

"My parents and Shayla are away for a few days. To me, it doesn't matter what they would think of your coming to me. You need help and I'm here for you." He took a deep breath to control his panic over her condition. "Did that son of a bitch try to force himself on you again, lass? If he did, I'll rip his heart out!" Gryph cupped her cheek with one hand.

"You don't understand, Gryph. He's *not h-h-human*!" Heather stammered as she tried to speak.

"Take a deep breath, Heather, and tell me what he's done." Gryph lowered his voice, trying to calm her.

Heather did as he suggested, pushed her hair away from her face and began. "I was leaving the museum." She stopped, closed her eyes and tried to gain more control.

Gryph waited patiently, searching her face to gauge her injuries.

"I saw this green light. Like the one in the stairwell the night you were hurt."

Gryph gripped her shoulders carefully. "What else did you see, lass?"

"I tried to get out of the parking lot but *it*...I mean, *Niall*, blocked my way. Gryph, he literally tore the door off my car. He's insane, and he's turned into this...this *thing*," her wavering voice drifted away.

"So, it *is* him. I suspected as much, but I wasn't sure until now. He was the demon I fought in the museum," Gryph said as he massaged Heather's shoulders and pushed loose strands of her ponytail off her face. He searched her features for other injuries. The woman's hands were practically in shreds. Drops of blood stained her shirt and torn jeans.

"He spoke to you?" Gryph asked, trying to sound calm. *I'll rip his cowardly spine out!*

"Yes," Heather nodded. "He wants the stone we took. And when he finds it's gone, he'll want this one, too." She pulled the second stone from her pocket and gave it to him.

"By all of the...*Heather*, where did you get this?" Gryph looked at her in amazement.

"I found it in a Peruvian vase by accident."

Gryph continued looking at her in complete wonder. She had managed to retrieve yet another stone and escape a demon. He'd never met anyone like her. She had more courage than any three men he knew. Outsiders were not as weak as he'd been led to believe. Certainly Heather wasn't.

"You can't go back to the museum, and you can't go to your apartment. It's as I've suspected. This man knows where you'll go and won't hesitate coming for you. Especially, since you know what he is." He cursed himself for not trying to get her to leave town. She hadn't been safe since he'd approached her. What she'd been through was his fault, and the guilt almost crushed him.

"Gryph, *please...please*, tell me what in hell is going on? Who are you? What kind of power do these stones have, and why won't you tell me everything?"

He pulled her into his arms and held her close, stroking her hair. "First, let's clean these wounds before they become infected. The beast didn't make any of these marks on you, did he?"

"No, I had to run into the park to get away from him—*it.* I got caught in some thorns."

"That's good, because his claws contain a powerful poison. That's what almost killed me. Now, we'll get you taken care of. Then we'll talk about what happened."

His low, deep voice was like a soothing ointment to Heather's shattered nerves. Gryph led her upstairs to his bedroom. "Here, use this robe." He handed her a dark green, terrycloth robe from the closet. "There are fresh towels and a first aid kit in the cupboard. I want you to make sure you clean those wounds well. I'll be back in half an hour. All right?" he questioned as he watched her movements.

Heather nodded. He walked over to her, kissed her gently on her forehead then left. She was already beginning to feel more calm. But she would never be able to rid herself of the monstrous vision she'd seen earlier. How could such a thing exist? What Niall had become defied every known law of physics and nature. Fighting off pain and the shock of what had happened, Heather's intellectual brain began to put pieces of things together. Gryph was trying to stop all this. That was why he was here. Of course, he couldn't go to the police. They'd never have believed anything and, in light of a murder investigation, he might have become a suspect. Exactly who he was didn't matter quite as much, though her curiosity would keep her asking questions. He was doing the right thing, trying to stop anyone else from being hurt. In her book, that made him a *hero.* No legend she'd ever read about could equal what he'd already done. Men like him were rare and wonderful. She slowly walked into the bathroom, trying to sort her feelings.

She scrubbed herself under a hot shower and washed her hair, then entered the bedroom and was tying the robe when Gryph knocked on the door and joined her. Heather ran to him and he held her. There was no doubt in her mind that was exactly where she belonged. She snuggled into his chest and almost cried with the need to be there.

"Easy, lass. I've made some hot tea. It will help you feel better." He handed her a steaming mug. When she took it, he began to adjust the sleeves of the robe she wore. It was sizes too large, but she looked so adorable in it. So precious. If anything had happened to her...

"Gryph, you once told me those stones held a special power. I thought it was just a legend. Now I know it isn't. We *have* to find that other rune stone. Niall doesn't need them to change into that devil thing anymore, but he wants to keep the stones so that no one else has the power. He thinks he's killed you. And he admitted killing Ned and the prostitute in the park." She paused and sipped her tea, her hands visibly shaking as she did so. "I feel like I'm in the middle of someone's bad dream."

"It's not a dream, little one. It's real enough. It's to my

advantage if he thinks he's killed me. I can use it against him. As for *us* finding the last stone, you can forget it. You're not leaving this house until I get the damned thing myself. Understand?" He stroked her drying hair, tucked a bit of it behind one ear, and adjusted the belt of the robe to fit her tiny waist.

"You'll never get in the museum without setting off an alarm, and there are thousands of places where the stone could be hidden. What I don't understand is how Niall got his hands on them, how he found out what they were and why he's keeping them at the museum." She walked away from him and started pacing.

"Heather, come here," he gently commanded.

"I've wondered if McPherson was in on this too. Although I can't believe he'd be capable of murder."

"Heather," Gryph calmly spoke louder, trying to her attention again.

"How did Niall invoke this kind of power unless he translated the symbols on the stones? He'd need help to do that. Outside the professor's realm of knowledge, I'm the only one with that kind of expertise and I can *assure* you I didn't translate any such thing. And what can anyone do about Niall now that he has this ability to change himself into this horrible *thing*?"

"Heather, *stop*!" Gryph took her by the arm, walked to the bed, sat down and pulled her into his lap. "You need to calm down. You've been through too much." He paused to put the cup of tea on the night stand and to make sure he had her attention. Then, he waited until she was comfortably within his arms. He searched her face, noted the scratches and saw the trust in her eyes. How he'd love to hold her there forever. Just make the world go away and leave the two of them alone. He sighed, knowing she'd hate him for being a creature, too. Though he wasn't like the one who had just tried to kill her, that lovely look of trust would die and turn to horrifying disgust. His heart felt like marble, even as she felt so soft and inviting. He took a deep breath and tried to keep the bitterness out of his voice. To stay calm for her sake.

"First, I suspect that when McPherson took the stones from

Ireland, this Niall fellow found out about them from the professor himself. Second, McPherson had probably heard of the stones' legend and allowed them to be translated thinking no harm would come of it. Once translated, I'm told the spell is easy to invoke. Third, I don't think this man wanted to move the stones from the museum because it gives him a quiet, isolated place to practice the powers he's so recently acquired. They become stronger the more they're used. Your friend the security guard probably walked in on something he wasn't meant to see and was slain for it. And lastly, Niall will have to be destroyed. It's the only way to stop him now."

Heather stared at him as she searched her battered senses for the proper words. "You've been sent to recover the stones and, more importantly, kill Niall. That's was this is all about, isn't it?"

Gryph could only look at her. He neither denied nor confirmed anything. He'd already told her too much. His mission had involved her in his world and had almost cost her life. As it was, he'd never forgive himself for what she'd already been through.

"You *can't* kill him, Gryph. You've seen what he is. No insult intended, but you and five like you would be no match for him. Besides, even if they don't believe it, we should go to the police. They can deal with this."

"Like you said, they won't believe any of it. So, what would you tell them? Would you say that a man has invoked an ancient Celtic spell from the stolen Rune Stones of the Tuatha De! Danann and that he's now walking the streets of New York killing at will? What do you think they'd do?"

Heather listened to his words and realized how impossible it sounded, but she wanted to keep Gryph from being slaughtered like Ned. "If I said it like *that*, the police would probably lock me away and say I was crazy. But I could tell them only that he attacked me a second time and that he told me he committed the murders. Maybe they'd find him and get a confession out of him. I've already reported him once. They're looking for him now to press assault charges."

"Maybe they *would* go after him and maybe they'd even

find him. But at what cost? He might kill one or more of *them* by turning into that creature. He would surely escape then disappear someplace, taking the one remaining stone. Then, he'd surface again and hunt you to get back the other two stones so that only he would have their power. I'm trying to keep anyone from knowing about the damned things, Heather. If this man got desperate enough, there's no telling how many people might be exposed to all this. That can't happen. Not *ever*."

"But to send you to take a life, even an *evil* one, isn't justice. And it isn't fair to you."

"It's what has to be done." Gryph shrugged. It's what he'd always done. Only this time his mission was a thousand times more lethal.

"He'll kill you," she whispered, finally admitting out loud what was worrying her most.

He sighed. "I've been sent to stop him. It's a chance I'll have to take." He smiled when he saw the concern in her eyes. No one but his parents had ever looked at him like that. "Besides, I've got a few surprises for him. He caught me unprepared before. That won't happen again."

Heather shook her head, then wrapped her arms around his neck and held on tight. He hugged her back, desperate to assure her that he would be all right. Even if the truth was that he didn't know *what* the outcome would be. Knowing Niall would come after her gave him incentive he never knew he'd have.

Heather pulled slightly away, and her eyes widened as a thought occurred to her. "Gryph, if the professor knows the translation, what's to keep him from using it or telling it to someone else who will?"

"To invoke the stones' power, one must have physical contact with all three stones the first time the spell is uttered. Thereafter, the stones are no longer needed. Remember, I told you about the legend. If McPherson didn't take advantage of using the spell when he had all three stones together, it's too late now. Telling someone the translation wouldn't do any good. It would be like wishing on a star. One *must* touch them all at once."

"Why did Niall turn into such an awful creature, and why would the stones have been endowed with that kind of power in the first place? Someone must have realized that they could fall into the wrong hands. I mean, what if someone like Hitler had gotten hold of thc things?"

Heather looked at him with such confusion that Gryph held her close and rocked her gently. "Long ago, the power of the stones was used by ancient Celts to defend, protect and render justice. There was a particular clan chosen to protect them and hold their power secret. When the last members of that clan died, the stones were buried with their remains. They weren't ever supposed to be found or used again. Their origin is steeped in legend. No one really knows exactly why they were first created or how. McPherson found them by looting that same clan's ancient burial site. He probably didn't know what he had, but the damage is done now. If the stones' power is invoked for evil intent, the user becomes the reflection of his soul. In Niall's case, his soul is that of a demon."

"But..."

"Hush, now," Gryph interrupted, placing gentle fingers over her lips. "I've already told you all I can and more than you needed to know. You mustn't ever repeat what I've told you to anyone. Now, rest and drink the tea I brought you."

"Don't worry. All this is too unbelievable," Heather murmured. "Nobody would ever listen to me." She reached for the mug, drained it, and snuggled deeper into the warmth and security offered against his broad chest.

That was true, Gryph thought as he held her a moment longer then took her empty tea mug before laying her upon the bed. She looked up at him with all the trust in the world in her eyes. She would never look at him like that again if she knew that Niall wasn't the only beast in her life.

It didn't take long before the Fairy herbs began to work. Her eyes closed, and her breathing began to slow. Gryph hated to drug her, but she wouldn't have slept otherwise, and she desperately needed the rest. His fingers lightly brushed her hair back. It was all he could do to keep from lying next to her and pulling her close. He could smell her clean body and feel his own respond.

If he made it back to the Shire alive, Gryph knew he'd spend a thousand sleepless nights wondering about her and *wanting*.

"Why couldn't I have been like anyone else in the world? Why couldn't you and I have met and..." He stopped. There was no sense torturing himself. He couldn't have her. End of subject. He sat on the edge of the bed. The only thing he could do was make sure she was safe before he left. That bastard would pay dearly for hurting her. With every feeling of retribution attributed to his kind, he'd make sure of it. Gryph's hand closed around the mug, and he had the satisfaction of feeling the pottery yield and break into several large pieces. He had every intention of doing the same thing to Niall Alexander's neck. That savage would never get the chance to touch Heather again. *Never.*

TEN

Gryph stayed with Heather until she finally slept without tossing. With all she had seen, she had maintained not only most of her composure but her sanity as well. The woman had even more courage than he had originally credited to her. Most people would not have been able to deal with what she'd been through. Gryph knew she'd have made a fine Celtic warrior with the resourcefulness she'd shown. He looked down at Heather as she rested. How he would explain her presence in the house, especially to Shayla, would pose an even bigger problem. But if things worked as he planned, perhaps all of this would be over, and she could safely leave.

He held the second stone in his hand and then hid it in a safe place until his parents and Shayla returned. They'd decided to travel to Salem, Massachusetts to confer with some of the Order about matters in New York. The identity of the beast had been one of the mysteries surrounding the stones. He now *knew* the demon was Niall Alexander.

One of the other problems had been locating the remaining two stones. Again, Heather had solved part of that problem by bringing the second one straight to him. The last concern was how to find the remaining rune stone and destroy the creature. Gryph would handle that by himself.

He'd lure the beast out to some remote place by offering to do battle. The prize would be the sum of all three rune stones. In its zeal and false sense of omnipotence, the beast would gladly come forward. Niall didn't know that he'd be meeting a creature of equal size and strength. *That* was Gryph's trump card.

***

Heather kept running. But no matter how fast she ran, the horror chasing her pursued and closed the distance. She'd been in the museum trying to hide in a vase that was physically too small to contain her. When that didn't work, she ran through a room of crates and boxes only to have oak trees on the other side of the room bend their massive branches to capture her. She held the last stone in her hand. There had to be a place to hide it so the creature chasing her would never find it. She looked around knowing she only had moments before the beast would pounce. Suddenly, she was outside. In a nearby maple tree, she noticed a large knothole. Heather shoved the stone into the hole and ran. She could feel hot breath upon her neck. The beast grabbed her and spun her around, but instead of seeing the demon form of Niall Alexander, Heather saw a creature of gargantuan proportions with an eagle's wings and a lion's hindquarters. This new beast was dark, and its wingspan was at least twenty feet from tip to tip. "Heather, lass," a voice rumbled from deep within the thing, "Don't be afraid of me...please, I need you."

"Easy, shhhh, lass. Don't cry," the same deep voice pulled her back into reality.

Heather opened her eyes to find Gryph cradling her. "W-what happened?" She tried to sit up, but he held her close to his chest.

"You were having a nightmare. I shouldn't have left you alone. I was only gone for a few minutes when you screamed."

"I'm sorry, Gryph. I guess everything's just catching up with me."

"You've no need to apologize. In fact, maybe it's for the best if you'll be able to sleep calmly from now on. Tell me what the nightmare was about."

"I really can't. It didn't make any sense," Heather responded, slowly. "It was one of those scenes where you're being chased and can't run fast enough. Everything was in slow motion."

"Here now," he crooned as he brushed the tears from her face with his thumbs, "lean back against me. I'll not leave you again tonight."

"Do you promise, Gryph? Do you promise not to try to go after Niall alone?" she asked as his arms encircled her.

"I'll stay with you tonight so that you can rest. That's my promise."

Heather sighed in resignation and leaned her full weight back against him. It was the most inviting, safe place she'd ever been. She knew there was nothing she wouldn't do to remain there for the rest of her life. His strength and the scent of pine woods surrounded her. How warm he was. That was the feeling that calmed her before she slipped into a deep sleep.

Gryph held her close and breathed in her floral scent. She was light to his darkness, logic to his turmoil. He knew he was inviting tortuous nights of loneliness by letting their strange relationship continue, but he couldn't help it. He'd never met anyone like her. If only...No. To think there might be a chance for them would yield an unhappy, disastrous end. If his own people couldn't accept his alter ego, this woman *never* would. Even if he was as normal as any other Druid and Heather could come to accept him, the Order would never allow an *outsider* into the Shire. He frowned. For two worlds to be so different but share some of the same intolerance didn't bode well for civilization in general. That was the way of her people and his. Some things never changed.

He reached toward the bedside lamp and switched it off. Starlight drifted through the open window and a soft, autumn breeze blew into the room. Heather snuggled closer into his chest. The desire to protect and possess flooded through him. Soon, her soft breathing and warm, gentle presence lulled him to sleep. Holding her was like wrapping a warm blanket around his lonely heart.

***

Gwyneth felt disappointment that the trip to Salem had yielded nothing fruitful. James and Shayla would be coming back to New York soon, but she had booked an earlier flight. Her excuse was an avid dislike of crowded planes, which James knew to be true.

The *real* reason for leaving Massachusetts early was

Gryphon. Her son hadn't been acting normal lately. Perhaps some of his injuries still plagued him. Gwyn walked quietly up the stairs and stopped by the door to his room. The hallway light was dim and, as she had so many times when he was a child, she opened the door a crack to check on him. He would laugh to think she was doing such a thing for a grown man, but she was still his mother. Even as her acute senses told her Gryph wasn't alone, the pale light from the hallway fell across the sleeping forms of her son and the woman. Gwyn quickly brought her hand to her mouth to keep from gasping aloud.

What in the name of the Goddess was Gryph doing? If Shayla knew of this, the Sorceress would pass judgement on them both. Closing the door as quietly as possible, Gwyn backed away. Her son had been holding Heather so tenderly. Gryph had been lying about his relationship with her. It was obvious that the two of them were lovers and would take foolish chances for a tryst. Shayla mustn't find out, or Gryph's life could be endangered. She rushed to her bedroom, withdrew her crane bag from a closet and used herbs, essential oils and charms to pray for guidance and the strength to confront the Sorceress.

***

Gryph came down the stairs quickly, rolling up the sleeves of his clean shirt as he did so. He walked into the kitchen to fix himself some coffee and found his mother sitting at the table. He stood, evaluating her glare, and knew that she was aware of Heather's presence.

"Good morning, Mother." He sighed ruefully, awaiting the inevitable outburst.

"I suppose its a *very* good morning for you," she replied sarcastically.

Gryph ignored her comment, turned and poured himself a cup of coffee. He walked to the table with the pot to offer her another cup.

"No, thank you," she responded. "I'm much too upset with you to have more caffeine in my system."

"Maybe you should consider de-caff?" Gryph attempted to lighten the mood, but his mother's expression darkened. He pulled out a chair, seating himself so that he was facing her.

"All right, you know she's here. What of it?"

"Are you *widdershins*, Gryphon? Do you know what Shayla will do to the both of you if she finds out you've been lovers? She'll assume the worst."

"Mother, you don't even know why Heather is here, and you're already passing judgement."

"A moron could see why she's here, Son. She *wants* you. And while I know you've a right to your own life, a permanent involvement with anyone outside the Order is impossible. You *know* that."

"Yes, I know. I know it all *too well.* Heather came to me out of desperation, and I wasn't going to turn her away." How could he?

"Of course, she's desperate, Gryph. She's in love with you."

"Mother, I love you dearly, but you're *daft.* If you'll let me explain what happened, you'll know she had no other place to go."

"Your *daft* Mother is listening," she replied, raising one eyebrow and crossing her arms across her chest.

Gryphon let his breath out in a slow release and inwardly prayed for patience. "Last night, the beast confronted Heather and almost killed her. She found the second stone and was leaving the museum when she was attacked. But for her ingenuity, she would have died like the other victims. Heather came straight here with the stone and told me what happened. The woman has no other place to go. The demon is a man by the name of Niall Alexander. He works with her and McPherson. Since he knows where she lives and that Heather knows *what* he is, he'll undoubtedly come after her."

"*Goddess*!" Gwyneth gasped. "It actually came after her at the museum?"

"It'll do anything to keep the stones with it. But it thinks that I'm dead. That may give me an edge."

Gwyneth leaned forward. "You have a plan, then?"

"Yes. I'll surprise the beast and lure it out to fight by telling it that I have the stones. It knows nothing of my ability to shape shift."

"That may work. How dangerous will it be?" Gwyneth

leaned forward, her hands wrapped around Gryph's.

"I intend it to be deadly for Niall Alexander," Gryph promised, remembering the way Niall had hurt Heather and how frightened she'd been.

"I was speaking of the danger to *you*, Son."

"The element of surprise gives me all the advantage I'll need."

"What about Heather?" Gwyneth asked.

Gryph remained silent for a moment. "You don't need to worry on that account. As soon as I have what I want, we'll head back to Ireland."

"You still say you have no feelings for her?"

"I know what my duty is and where my loyalties lie, Mother. As always, the Sorceress will get what she wants." Bitterness colored his words, and he shoved his coffee mug toward the middle of the table.

"And if Shayla finds her here?" Gwyneth asked, ignoring Gryph's angry gesture. "Do you fully understand what the penalty would be for dallying with an outsider?"

"Shayla didn't return with you and Father?"

"No. I came home early. Their flight won't leave Massachusetts until this morning."

"And what prompted you to come back to New York so soon?" Gryph asked as he leaned back in his chair and wearily passed his hand across his face.

"To be honest, Gryphon, you've been worrying me lately. You haven't been acting...well, your temper hasn't been in check."

"Everything will be back to normal soon." He sarcastically smirked. *I'll be the same, introverted man I was. The Order will take pains to stay away from me, and everything will bloody well go back to the same damned way it's been for years.*

"Will it go back to normal, Son?" She reached across the table and placed a gentle hand on her son's face.

Gryph grabbed his coffee cup, refilled it and didn't respond. His mother knew him better than any soul except for one. What he wanted or didn't want wasn't pertinent to the business at hand. He had a job to do. It was part of the pact that had been made. Since no one had ever asked him how he felt about what Shayla ordered him to do, he'd always assumed it didn't matter. Until now. Part of the damned deal was that he was supposed to have a semblance of a normal life. Someone had obviously forgotten to define the term *semblance*. If that meant shutting himself off from almost everyone and living in dark abbey libraries the rest of his life, then maybe the pact wasn't worth keeping any more. If he denied Shayla's wishes and refused to do her bidding, he'd no longer be able to control the change. He'd shape shift at random intervals. But could it be any worse than life as he knew it? The Order couldn't possibly shun his presence any more than it did.

"What are you thinking, Gryph?" Gwyneth asked, breaking into his thoughts.

"I was just wondering if the monks at the abbey would let me join their order. You know...I could be, *Brother Gryph*, the silent friar of Glen Rowan. Vowed to obedience and celibacy."

"Gryphon!" she gasped, standing up in shock.

"It was a joke, Mother." Gryphon smiled and tried to look as if it was amusing.

"Well, it isn't funny. Whoever heard of one of the Order doing such a thing? And I'm quite sure you aren't celibate." She stalked off to start breakfast.

***

Heather woke slowly, confused by her surroundings. Then everything that had happened came to her like a bomb being dropped. She got out of bed gingerly, wondering what to do. Her clothes were no longer in the bathroom where she'd hung them the night before. She was retying Gryph's robe when the room's door slowly opened.

"Ah, good. You're awake." Gwyneth nodded as she walked into the room carrying a mug of coffee.

Heather pushed her long hair back and gratefully took the drink. "Thank you. Would you happen to know what time it is?"

"It's early in the afternoon. Gryphon told me what happened, and we decided to let you sleep. The attack last night must have been terrifying for you."

Heather nodded in confirmation. "So, you know about what I saw?"

"Yes. It's why we're here. Come and sit." She patted the side of the bed. "We need to talk."

"Where is Gryphon?" Heather asked.

"He's out preparing for what he must do tonight. Shayla and James aren't here. They've been away for a while, but they'll return before long."

"From what Shayla has said to me, I don't feel I'm very welcome. Maybe I should find someplace else to go before she shows up."

"Please understand, Heather. It isn't her way to be uncaring. She has her reasons. It's those same reasons that I've come to discuss with you."

"You mean, someone is *actually* going to tell me what's going on?"

"Yes. I will. But this is mortally important. You must swear you will never tell another living soul what I'm about to tell you, Heather. It's a long story, and one which has been protected at all costs. I'm telling you now because you must understand why there can never be anything between you and my son."

Heather's heart grew cold. "What makes you think there's anything between us but a mutual desire to see all of this over?"

"I've seen the way you look at Gryph and heard the way he speaks of you. Men are slower at realizing these things than women. I know you're in love with him. I'm counting on your love for him to listen and do as I ask."

"All right, I'm listening." Heather didn't bother to deny anything. She squared her shoulders and prepared to hear the woman out.

"Almost thirty-three years ago, when I was carrying Gryph, I realized he would be the only child I would ever have. Like all parents, James and I wanted the best for him. For some parents that means the best education or opportunities. For us, it meant giving him what he would need to survive. You see, James, Gryph and I belong to an ancient Order of creatures who have banded together to insure each other's survival."

"*Creatures*? What *kind* of creatures," Heather asked in trepidation. After the previous evening's occurrences, she wanted to be sure she understood the definition of the term.

"To be specific in our case, Druids. Others are members of factions long thought extinct or mythological. Creatures of legend."

"Legend?" Heather whispered, remembering Gryph had once used that word to define himself.

"Yes. Some are Gnomes, Fairies, the list goes on—"

Heather stood up abruptly. "I don't think I want to hear any more."

"Please, you *must* listen. Gryphon's life depends upon your doing as I ask."

Sitting back down, Heather looked at her in alarm. "What do you mean?"

"Shayla is the supreme power among all of the factions of the Order. It's her job to uphold law and dispense punishment for breaking our rules. Chief among these rules is that no *outsider* must ever learn of our existence. Your world barely tolerates some of your *own* kind. Can you imagine what would happen to the Sprites in England or the Little People of Ireland were the world to know of them? They would be hunted down, feared and destroyed as they almost were centuries ago. And there are many others who hide with us."

Heather shook her head in disbelief. She didn't want to know any of this, but couldn't turn away. Especially not after what she'd seen the night before. "Go on," she choked out.

"The penalty for telling an outsider or in any way leading them to know of our existence is death for both the one who told and the outsider who finds out. If Shayla believes Gryph is too close to you, she'll never believe you don't know or won't find out about us. You and my son will be hunted by the creatures she sends. Gryph, although by accident, is the only one of his kind left. It was mine and my husband's tampering with unknown forces before his birth that made him what he is."

"What *is* he?" Heather blurted.

"First, let me tell you *why* he exists the way he is. As I said, it was our intent to give him the ability to protect himself, to *survive* should something happen to us. Before his birth, James and I found a very old tome in an abbey. It was accompanied by a crystal ball. Although we'll never be sure, we believe the spell we invoked with them originated in some ancient part of Asia. It seemed to be *exactly* what we'd been searching for. It would give our unborn son the ability to protect himself and others. But something went terribly wrong."

Heather began to tremble. She could feel an iciness creep over her skin.

"We performed a ceremony to endow our unborn baby with the powers written in the manuscript. During the ceremony, the crystal exploded, and the pages from which we read burst into flames. At the time, we thought it was part of the spell. But after Gryphon was born, we soon learned what we'd done. The spell self destructed, never to be used twice." Gwyneth bowed her head.

"*Tell* me," Heather insisted when the older woman stopped.

"Gryphon began to change uncontrollably. One day he would be a beautiful baby, lying in our arms. The next, he would turn into a creature many of our Order fear. We were unable to control when, where or how he would change. You can imagine how difficult life would be for him, and us, under the circumstances. We became desperate for a way to reverse the spell. So, we took Gryphon to Shayla. We believed that if anyone could help him she could. Her powers are legendary. However, the best she could do was to give Gryph the ability to control *when* he changes. Much the way the rune stones work, once a power of that kind is invoked, it can never be undone altogether. Not even by someone as powerful as Shayla Gallagher, Sorceress of the Ancients. There was a price for her help, though. We promised her that whenever she called him to help, whenever the Order was threatened by the outside world, Gryph would come forward and use his *abilities* as she commanded."

"When he was old enough to understand, he reaffirmed the pact with Shayla himself, proving he understood what was expected of him in exchange for the ability to control his changing into the creature. That's when he received the marks of the ancient Celts he wears upon his body. It was a right of passage for him. Half of him, the Druid part, is as human as you. The other half is as otherworldly as many in the Order. So, you see, it's impossible for him to be with you. Even if he weren't a creature of myth, he belongs to the Order both as a Druid and a warrior. He may never stay or have a relationship with anyone outside our ways and laws."

"You still haven't told me what he is," Heather said as tears formed in her eyes. She wasn't sure who she was sorrier for, herself or Gryph.

"Tonight, Gryphon will change so that he can get to the museum undetected. He'll force the beast to fight for the last remaining stone. My son intends to let the beast think it can win the two stones we've recovered if it will fight him. The demon beast doesn't know of my son's ability to change into a creature of great strength and power. Gryph means to destroy the abuser of the Rune Stones of the Tuatha De! Danann. He hopes to recover the one remaining stone." Gwyneth took Heather's hand in her own."When he leaves from this place tonight, I want you to be present to see what you've loved. I believe I owe you that for the help you've given and the risks you've taken. But, and I warn you, if Shayla finds out what I've told you, she'll send her minions for you and the rest of us as well. On Gryphon's life, Heather, you must swear that you will never tell anyone what you know."

"How could I? Who would believe me any more than they would believe me about Niall?" she whispered as her tears fell.

"Shayla won't take that into account. She'll never let you live if she finds out you know."

"I understand. I swear, on my love for your son, I'll never tell another soul," Heather promised.

"I believe you. My son would never care for someone who wasn't true to him." Gwyneth patted her shoulder consolingly.

"May I be alone for a while," Heather asked quietly.

"Of course, my dear. You have a lot to think about." Gwyneth nodded, feeling the younger woman's pain.

The older woman rose and left with a grace defying her age. Heather fell on the bed. Crying wasn't something she normally did, and she abhorred women who easily succumbed to tears. But she believed it was all that was left to her. If Gryph had been in love with another woman, Heather would have left him to his happiness. The way it was, neither of them would ever know peace. She knew he cared for her. And his pain would hurt her far more than her own.

ELEVEN

Gwyneth and Heather agreed that she should be out of the house before the others returned. When darkness approached and Gryph's mother left to meet her husband and Shayla, Heather hid in the nearby woods. It was a place of safety from which Gwyneth had said she could see for herself the truth of Gryph's circumstance.

Heather had no idea what Gryph would think of her absence from the house, but suspected that his mother would make the excuse that she needed to get her away from Shayla. She settled herself as comfortably as possible behind an old log. Gwyneth had mended and cleaned her torn clothing, and the older woman had thoughtfully given her an old coat of Gryph's with which to keep warm. As darkness approached, she waited. She was as frightened as she had been the night before when Niall had attacked, although for different reasons. What would she see? Whatever it was, it couldn't be as repulsive as Niall.

The balcony door to the house opened, and Heather knew she wouldn't have much longer to wait. Four figures emerged from the house. Three of them were clothed in traditional, white Druid robes. The fourth, a tall, muscular man was shirtless. Gryphon! He wore leather pants and boots and carried himself with the pride of a warrior ready to do battle. His dark hair drifted about his shoulders in the evening breeze, and the setting sun gilded his tanned, honed physique. Heather held her breath at the sight of him. He was truly magnificent. Her heart began to beat wildly at the thought of witnessing something ordinary people had never been allowed to view. According to Gwyneth, those who had even dared were dead.

As the three white-clad figures backed away, Gryph took

off his clothing and placed it into what looked like a leather bag. He placed the bag around his neck and dropped down to one knee. Heather leaned forward as much as she dared. Gryph's body was surrounded by a strange rippling, much like what happens on the surface of a pond when a stone is tossed and breaks the surface. Within moments, the rippling effect expanded, and the shape within grew. Heather gasped at the size of the thing developing. It was about ten feet tall with wings spanning twice that distance. As the rippling stopped, she watched in awe. *Of course...his name was Gryphon*! That's what he was. A creature of inexact mythological origin, the gryphon was a beast which appeared to be half bird, half lion. The head was thickly feathered, and there was a beak where his mouth would normally be found. Except for his upright, feline-like ears, Gryph's head and upper torso looked exactly like an eagle's. His two front legs ended in clawlike feet, also like that bird of prey. His wings glittered, blue green, in the sunset. The rest of the hind part of the body was decidedly leonine. A long, forked tail whipped to and fro as if the beast was anxious to be about its business. Gryph's entire body, except for the shimmering, strong wings, was black as death. Even from a distance, the coal-like eyes looked as though they could pierce marble with their stare. Muscle rippled as he moved.

If Gwyneth's intent had been to repulse Heather away, the effect had been exactly opposite. She had never seen anything in her life so wondrously beautiful. Gryphon stood with all four of his legs squarely beneath him and faced the setting sun. He had the most noble bearing. He reared back, the same way a spirited horse would, his front legs pawing the air and his wings gently beating. Soon, he was airborne. Heather knew he was heading to the museum, hoping to find Niall nearby. Under the cloak of darkness, no one would be able to see him soaring through the skies. He looked powerful enough to cross great distances with ease and grace. She remembered he'd said he was in the country illegally. Had he been able to fly the distance of an ocean just so there would be no record of his having been in the States? Heather believed it was entirely possible, but then, she was beginning to believe anything was possible.

Of course, his parents and Shayla would need to hide what he was to protect him. In doing so, she knew he'd been lonely all his life. Her heart went out to him, the man and the beast. *He was the only one of his kind*, his mother had said. What a tragedy that such things were gone in the world, that there were still ethereal beings who couldn't spread magic and whimsy into anyone's life because they'd be hunted and harassed into extinction if humans knew of them. Heather began to uncontrollably sob. She cried for the loss of these beautiful things to mankind and for the fear in which they lived. She cried because no one would ever let her be a part of it, and she would lose Gryph forever.

If he survived the night and found the last stone, Heather knew she'd never be allowed to see him again. He'd once said that her life would get back to normal when the stones were recovered and he was able to leave. Nothing, not the smallest thing, would ever be normal for her again. How *could* it be? Her heart would fly with him when he went.

***

Gryphon flew across the city, keeping himself low to the earth, but not low enough to be detected by humans. Such was his speed that before a person could look up he would already have flown by. Still, being so near cities made him nervous. The sooner this quest could be accomplished, the better. He could see the dome of the museum in the distance. The adjoining park would be a fitting place for a battle. Earlier in the day, Gryph had scouted it and settled on a large clearing in the woods. It was far enough from human contact during the night, but close enough to the museum to lure the demon to him. He felt sure that it would respond to his wager...all three stones and the powers they held in exchange for a duel to the death.

Gryphon landed in the woods near the museum and changed back into human form. He was near the parking lot where he'd first seen Heather and the man he must now battle. Heather. Brave, beautiful and intelligent, she meant more to him than he wanted to admit. He shook his head to clear his mind for what he must do. He had no time to think of what could never be. He strode to the employee entrance where the beast had attacked him in the stairwell. He remembered, there were no cameras in that area for the security people to view him. An unlocked door gave him access. Clumsy of some security guard, especially with the criminal activity that had been taking place. Or perhaps the door and all those following were open for a reason. Climbing to the floor where the Celtic antiquities were stored, Gryphon carefully entered the hallway and made his way to the large room where McPherson's shipments had been placed. The crate with the false bottom in it was still where Heather had initially found it. Gryph knelt to see if the last stone might be there.

"YOU!"

The sound of the voice came from behind him. Gryph smiled to himself, rose, then turned around. The bait, as he defined himself, had been discovered. "Surprised to see me alive, you whoreson?" he sarcastically asked.

Niall looked at him in amazement. Sneaking into the museum earlier by distracting the guards with a false alarm, Niall had been hoping Heather would return. He hadn't planned for an appearance by a man he thought was dead. "I don't know how you survived, or who you are. But you won't live to see another day." Niall started to drop to one knee, the position from which to invoke the change.

Gryphon held up a hand. "Before you do that, you'd better listen to what I have to say. Otherwise, you'll never see the other two stones, and that's what you want, isn't it?"

"What do you know about them?" Niall muttered as he slowly straightened.

"I know what they are and what they can do. If you want them back, come take them from me."

Niall looked at Gryphon for a moment before he spoke. "If you know what they are, you wouldn't be stupid enough to bring them with you."

"Like you say, you don't know me. I may be the most foolish man you've ever met. But what you think of me isn't important. I *do* have the stones and did come to make a bargain."

Niall laughed. "What kind of bargain do you *possibly* think you can make with me? I'm a god now. I don't need to make a deal with anyone."

Gryph smiled slyly. It was as he thought. The man's self-absorbed personality had been amplified through his use of the powers. He thought of himself as invulnerable, omnipotent. "I want the powers you now possess. All I need is the last stone to enact the shape shift capabilities. You want the other two stones to keep anyone from doing so."

"So, what's your bargain, fool?" Niall sneered at the bigger man and looked him up and down in contempt.

"A fight. If you want the stones, come take them from me. Winner takes all."

Niall burst out laughing. "Do you *actually* believe you could stand against *me*?"

"I have the other two stones. I want the third badly enough to risk anything, even death. So, bastard, what's your answer?" Gryph stared at the man. His gaze never left Niall's eyes.

"How do I know you really have possession of the other two stones, that you aren't lying?" Niall leaned back against one of the crates and crossed his arms.

"You'll never know unless you agree to my bargain. Fight, or you'll never see the other two stones."

"What's to keep me from tearing your head off and taking the damned things from you right now?" Niall shook his head in amazement.

"You correctly surmised that I'm not stupid enough to actually have them on me. You'll have to follow me to get them. The question is, do *you* have the courage to bring the other stone and face me. Or can you only battle old men and women?" Gryph goaded, then slowly approached Niall until he was within a foot of him. Gryphon glared at him as his fists clenched.

"Whether you have them or not, killing you will be a pleasure. There's just one thing I'll add to the bet." Niall leaned forward, placed his hands on a box and smirked at Gryph. "Tell me where Heather is."

Gryph's blood turned to Nordic ice. Something of his feelings must have shown in his expression. Niall began to laugh.

"I see. You've had a *piece* of what she wouldn't give me." He laughed louder and put his hands on his hips. "Well, it doesn't matter. After I rip you open, I'll find that little bitch and give her something she won't ever forget." He sickeningly cupped his crotch.

Gryph hadn't wanted to come to New York to take anyone's life. Despite his anger over his own form, all creatures were sacred to him and had their purpose. But Niall Alexander had corrupted the intent of an ancient power for his own ends. Destroying him was a necessary task that had to be performed in order to save lives. And now, by threatening Heather, the man had just made Gryph's job much easier. There would never be any guilt over what had to happen.

"I'll see you to the other side of Perdition's gates before I'll let you touch her." Gryph lowered his voice, and he felt something in his chest tighten in anger and fear.

"Oh, I'll do more than touch her. I'll take her every way imaginable. Just like I did that whore in the park. Then, when I'm through, I'll eat what's left." Niall grinned and slowly licked his lips.

"Follow me, demon." Gryphon's hands continued to clench, his entire body began to ready itself for a battle. "Bring the last stone and show me whether you can fight someone who can defend himself. Or, maybe you brag so much because you're *incapable* of doing what you promise. Maybe you're as impotent as your words. Maybe Heather got in a good shot, and you're as flaccid as yesterday's cabbage. That's why you have to force yourself on women."

Niall stopped laughing and glared at Gryph. "Just tell me where and when. We'll see who's impotent and who has Heather *and* the stones by the end of the night."

"Half an hour from now, in the park where the old statues are. Be there," Gryph told him.

"I know the place. And bring the stones, Irishman. You'll save me the trouble of beating Heather into telling me where they are." Niall turned and left.

***

Half an hour passed. Gryph stood in the darkness preparing

himself for what was to come. He tried not to let his anger hinder his instincts. As the minutes passed, he began to think Niall hadn't fallen for his trap, that the man may have been more clever than expected. As he turned toward a facsimile of a large Grecian urn, Gryphon heard a sound from across the clearing. The huge, lumbering form of the demon made its way toward him. Showing no fear, he knelt down and began to change. The Niall-beast stopped, disbelieving what it saw. Gryphon's clothes ripped from his gigantic body, and he rose in the form of the *gryphon* within seconds.

Niall roared in anger and ran toward the warrior. He struck at him with his clawlike hands, not knowing his poison wouldn't work. Gryphon reared back as Niall's talons struck his left forearm. Both creatures were evenly matched in height and strength, but Gryph was fighting for more than just himself. However much they'd dispossessed him, the creatures of the Order depended upon him to win. Humankind must never know that such power existed.

The beasts fought on. Niall sunk his teeth into Gryph's shoulder. Gryphon roared in pain and retaliated by grabbing one of Niall's horns and throwing him back onto a pile of old stone. Niall stood, shook his massive head and stared at Gryph. His chest heaved with anger and exertion. Blood ran from an ugly gash on his temple. He picked up a huge chunk of granite from a nearby pile and charged.

Gryphon reared up just as the block hit him in the chest. The air was knocked from his lungs, and he stumbled backward. The beast grabbed Gryph's forelegs, and they wrestled to the ground, rolling over and over. Remnants of a retaining wall crashed as their massive bodies struck the stone from which it was made. Gryph knew if he was going to survive he had to get in the air. The gaping wound in his shoulder was not only bleeding profusely, it had cut deep into the top of one wing. Even if he could sustain flight now, Niall's strong grasp was keeping him grounded. Bleeding much more would cost him consciousness and his life. He closed his beak over one of Niall's arms and heard a resounding crunch as tissue and bone yielded. There was a satisfying taste of blood in his mouth. It dripped from his beak and down his own chest.

Niall scrambled back and screeched in agony. "SON-OF-A-BITCH...I'll have your *balls*!" He lunged, swiped at Gryphon with his one good arm and felt flesh ripping. His claws scored a long gash down Gryph's left side.

It was Gryphon's turn to cry out as the gaping wound almost eviscerated him. He limped backward, unsure now whether he would ever be able to fly again. The bottom of his other wing had almost been ripped in two. He gasped and slowly backed away. The world began to spin, and he knew but for some miracle he'd die. Niall slowly lumbered toward him, his right arm hanging by tendons.

"So...I'm not the only one who can change, eh, Irishman?" He gasped for air and kept moving toward Gryphon's retreating form. "Guess, you thought you were pretty damn smart. You feathered *freak*." He glanced at his shattered limb and growled. "You're gonna pay for this. And when I get through with you, I'll bring Heather back here and take her over and over. Right on your carcass. Nobody will hear her scream. And it'll be good...yeah, real good! I'll take her from behind and rip her open the way you've ripped *me!*

Gryphon was unable to speak in his beast form, but could understand everything Niall said. The remains of the man's blood turned bitter in his mouth. *Heather*. No matter what else happened, whether he made it out of this park alive or not, this hideous creature would never get his hands on her. The Goddess above, by wisdom or miscalculation, had given him this form for a reason. And he intended to use it. Gathering every last ounce of strength he had and ignoring the searing waves of intense pain, Gryphon moved his wings and rose upward. Niall reached for him, but was inches away from holding him down. He struggled to hold a hovering position only a few feet off the ground, but all he could think of was what would happen to an innocent and beloved woman if he didn't succeed. He lifted up further and directed his movement toward the demon in front of him. Niall swung upward with his claw hand and caught the bottom of Gryphon's leg just above the ankle. Still, his forward momentum was enough that Gryph was able to sink his talons into Niall's broad shoulder and lift.

The agony was horrible, but he neither stopped nor slowed. Higher and higher he climbed, much further than he'd ever dared to fly. The oxygen became thin. That, coupled with his loss of blood, had Gryphon sickeningly dizzy. He flew on. Niall shrieked in pain and anger.

"You can't kill me, you fool. I wasn't stupid enough to bring the other stone. It's hidden where you'll never find it." Niall coughed and spat out blood as the lack of oxygen deprived him of further speech.

The words registered somewhere in Gryphon's brain, but he kept going. The stones, his promise to the Sorceress to find them, and his promise to his parents to be careful all paled in some misty past. All he could think of was keeping Heather away from danger. *She must be safe...must protect...MUST.*

When he was as high as he could get and still breathe, Gryphon let Niall go. The man fell for what seemed like an eternity, screaming in fury all the way to the earth. His body landed on the trunk of a huge downed tree. It made a sickeningly loud thud as vertebrae broke and skin ripped. Gryph followed him down, gliding the best he could on one wing and flapping the other to slow his descent. He landed several yards away, immediately hit the ground hard and changed back into human form. Holding his shredded side, he stumbled to where Niall's broken body lay. The other man was still in his beast form. He looked up at Gryphon and tried to reach toward him.

"Who are you?" Niall rasped as blood and drool ran from his gaping mouth.

He struggled to drag in air and speak. "I'm Gryphon O'Connor, Druid Warrior of the Order of The Ancients. I tell you so you'll know who's beaten you." He paused and gasped as the dizzy feeling came over him again."By Herne's blood, you'll never touch her," he choked out.

"Go to hell," Niall spat as his eyes dimmed. He took one last, broken breath and exhaled it, long and slow.

Gryph knew he was dead. He felt no remorse. Niall would have killed him, Heather and anyone else to get what he wanted. The man had written his own fate. Leaning against a tree,

Gryphon took deep, steadying breaths and tried not to look at Niall's twisted, gory body. Suddenly, a green light began to glow from within the demon's gaping mouth. The light soon encompassed his entire body and pulsed. Gryphon backed away. Within seconds, Niall's body was gone. The power he had abused had consumed his remains. There would be no trace of the man left for anyone to find.

It took Gryph an hour to make his way back to the museum. It was a slow, tortured and staggering journey. Deprived of enough blood, his brain took him to the place where he'd met Heather. The lights of the parking lot seemed a place he should be. Someone would be there to help him. A woman with sweet, silver-blue eyes and brown hair with gold highlights. She was there. He knew it. A voice within his mind called out. Gryphon couldn't be sure if he was imagining it or not, but it summoned him to a place of healing. He laughed at the irony. It was a rasping, deathly laugh. "You can't heal a dead man," he whispered.

"*The wind will carry you,*" the voice promised. "*Rise into the wind.*"

It was the softest, sweetest sound. Like nothing he'd ever heard. "Goddess, if that's you, hear me," he prayed in agony and sunk to his knees. "Don't let me die here. Not on unholy ground in a city full of outsiders. I beg...b-beg you."

"*Rise,*" came the summons again.

Gryphon gripped the trunk of an oak tree and pulled himself into a standing position. He gazed up into its branches. "Duir," he whispered the ancient word for oak, "give me strength to leave this place. One...last...time."

He stumbled forward, went down on one knee and agonizingly made the change. Gryph staggered, turned into the wind, feebly moved his wings and began to rise. He headed toward the house where his parents waited. His flight path was very low, and he careened into the branches of trees along the way. Still, that part of him that didn't want to die where strangers would find him kept him going.

Lights of the familiar building were ahead. Gryph aimed for the ground, not able to summon enough energy to even care whether he landed safely. He was so tired. So very, very tired. One face filtered into his last conscious thought. She was so beautiful. Why couldn't he have one last lovely thing to see? Those striking eyes and sweet, generous smile. *Heather.*

Heather, still in the woods awaiting his return, gasped in horror as she saw him hit the ground hard. He changed back into human form almost instantaneously. His parents rushed forward with Shayla. James wrapped his cloak around Gryph's nude body, and they helped him inside the house. Though she couldn't see well, his poor landing was evidence of the fact that he was badly hurt. She wanted with all of her heart to go to him. But, even if she were to show up, Shayla wouldn't let her near him. Better if the Sorceress never knew she had so recently been there, but Heather desperately wanted to find out about him. He must have killed Niall, or he would never have returned. If that was true, the police would find Niall's body somewhere near the museum. Had Gryph been able to complete the job he'd been sent to do? Had he found the last rune stone?

The wind blew cold as Autumn waned. Someone was burning a wood fire nearby. Heather huddled in the darkness, hoping Gwyneth would remember she was there and come to her with news.

Hours passed, and Heather was almost beside herself with anxiety over what had happened. She stood and was about to go to the house when she heard someone approaching.

"Heather," Gwyneth, whispered, "are you still there, lass?"

"I'm here," Heather walked forward."Please, tell me what happened to Gryph. I saw how badly he was hurt. Is he going to be all right?"

Gwyneth kept her face down. She used the heavy hood of her Druid robe to conceal her expression. "I...w-wanted to let you know that you'll be safe now. Niall Alexander is dead."

"I figured that, but how is Gryph? What's happening?"

"Gryphon didn't get the other stone."

"I don't *care*. What about Gryphon? "she repeated. Something about the older woman's voice and her posture alarmed Heather. Her heart began to beat wildly, and a sense of uncontrollable fear filled her.

"Go, now, lass. Before the Sorceress discovers you're here."

"He's dead, isn't he?" Heather backed away, shaking her head.

"I wanted you to know...he had feelings for you. He's never been so close to anyone," Gwyneth whispered. "Like I told you, he was the only one of his kind. In our culture, that m-made him an outcast. Ours is an ancient culture, and we follow the old customs."

Heather's vision blurred. "Tell me, *please*."

Deliberately misinterpreting her words, Gwyneth pretended Heather wanted to know about Gryphon's lonely state among the Order, and not what had happened to him. "You worked for the museum so you should know your ancient Celtic history." She paused. "Do you know the story of Nuada of the Silver Hand?"

Shaking with grief, Heather could only nod. Nuada was dispossessed by his people when he lost his hand in battle. Only a whole man could rule and be accepted by the clans. Nuada only regained his place within their ranks as a ruler when a prosthesis was made for him. A silver hand. In the ancient, Celtic world, there were few places for a man or woman who couldn't find a tribe or clan into which they fit. Times then were horribly difficult, and a person needed to be able to count himself among the many. Not stand out. However wrong or unfair that might seem, that was the mythology of the Celts and many other cultures. Gryphon had been such an oddity that he wasn't fit to be a member of this thing called the *Order*, such an outcast that no one would get near him. That's what Gwyneth was trying to say. In his mother's mind, Gryph was finally at peace. He wouldn't be a misfit anymore.

"A man like him could never die," Heather whispered as her tears fell. "He'll be a legend forever."

Gwyneth looked at Heather strangely and approached until she was quite close. "You wanted to see him again, didn't you? Even knowing what he was, you wanted him."

Heather paused before she spoke. She knew her eyes betrayed her feelings. "He couldn't help being what he was any more than you or I can. I remember what you've told me about Shayla, but if I could have seen him once more before...just one more time."

Gwyneth looked over her shoulder, apparently to make sure she hadn't been seen leaving the house and wasn't being watched. "When I'm able, I'll try to see you again." She put her hand on Heather's arm. "Remember Heather, there couldn't have been anything between you and my son. And Shayla would have us all destroyed if she were to find out what I've told you."

"I understand, Gwyneth. I'll try to find the last stone, and I promise I won't tell anyone about any of this. People would think I'd gone insane if I did." Some part of Heather's emotions shut down. It was like she was an automaton. Repeating what she thought Gwyneth wanted to hear. Her heart was broken. Nothing she loved ever survived. Not her parents, not Ned. Not Gryphon.

"Just for the record, you'd better know that I loved your son. And there's no magic or sorcery on Earth that will ever take that love away."

"More's the pity for you both, then." Gwyneth tried to hide the sorrow in her voice for both their sakes. "Thank you, Heather. You briefly gave my son something I've never seen before. For that, I'll always be grateful."

"What did I possibly give *him*?" Heather asked, swallowing back the sickness she felt welling within her.

"Hope. For the first time in his life, I saw hope for the future in his eyes. Even if it was a slight pause in the loneliness he's known. And, though I know it was short-lived, it was more than I've ever imagined he would have."

Heather bowed her head. She was too overcome with grief to carry on much more. The whole thing had been a nightmare, ending with the loss of so much life. Such a noble life. *Gryphon's.*

She remembered that the gryphon, in mythology, was a beast born to protect and retaliate against those who transgressed. To that end, Gryphon had more than lived up to his name. "Tell those people that you go back to...that

Order...that he did his job. They should be thanking whatever Gods you pray to that he saved them. If those stones had gotten into anybody else's hands, there would be no place for your people to hide. Someone would have eventually traced them straight back to wherever you come from. The rest of the British Isles would have been dug up to find more objects like them."

"Though Gryph, his father and I spent most of our lives in Ireland, we're originally from England. We're from a forest we call the *Shire*. It's land held by the fifty-first Earl of Glen Rowan, Gryphon's father. James rules the land under the council of the Sorceress of the Ancients, as his parents did before him." There seemed no sense in withholding that information since Heather knew everything else.

Heather looked up and stared. Then, she burst into tears and turned to go. Like Nuada, Gryphon couldn't have even inherited his father's land. Not if those damned ancient legends were followed. Being the only one of his kind would keep that from ever happening.

Gwyneth stopped Heather's departure with a gentle touch to the shoulder. "Gryphon chose well. If things were different, my dear, I would very much have loved having you as a member of my family and clan. But, as it was..."

"I know. I'd never have been accepted by your Order. Just another outcast."

"Try to understand, Heather. We've much to fear. Thousands of years ago, we were almost hunted into extinction."

"'Things that go bump in the night,'" Heather sobbed and remembered she had told Gryph that she didn't believe in such things.

"Yes, I'm afraid that's what we are to you." She quickly hugged Heather then turned away. Her own voice broke, and a large lump in her throat almost stopped her. "You have to go now. I have to return to the house, or Shayla will look for me."

"Thank you, Gwyneth, for trusting me with your secrets. I won't let you down, and I'll find the last stone if I have to turn over every board and brick in the museum to do it. Gryphon's job will be finished."

"Blessed be!" Gwyneth raised her hand in a gesture of

goodbye.

"Goodbye, and...and good luck. Whatever happens, " Heather said with quiet dignity and walked away. She didn't really believe she'd ever see Gwyneth or James O'Connor again. Maybe it was better. The pain in her heart was just too great. Right now, she wanted to be dead, too, and as far away from the craziness as she could get.

TWELVE

"No, Detective. No one's seen any sign of Niall Alexander at all. Since the morning I reported him to you, he hasn't come to work. Of course, I'll call immediately if he shows up. I don't want to be anywhere near him. Yes, thank you and I'll see you soon."

Heather hung up the telephone. She knew Niall was dead, but no remains had been found. In his other form, the choices Gryph had of dealing with a body were too gruesome to contemplate. Still, Heather couldn't be repulsed by what Gryphon had done. Beasts came in all shapes and sizes. Niall Alexander had been one of the worst. Her former co-worker had made his decisions and paid for them. Gryph had done nothing more than stop the man from killing again. Heather wasn't about to tell the police anything. Not only wouldn't they believe her, but she felt justice had been served. The people Niall had killed could rest in peace. That was her wish for Gryphon.

"Heather, could I speak with you?"

She turned as Professor McPherson entered the room where some of the artifacts were being labeled. "Yes, Professor?" She turned back to the books she'd been shelving, rolled her eyes and tried to keep her temper in check. He was the last person on Earth she wanted to speak with. After she told Detective Dayton about McPherson's smuggling, and having compiled sufficient evidence to turn over to the prosecutors, the police were preparing to charge him with numerous crimes. Nothing could make up for what he'd done. Maybe it was some sense of revenge, but she wanted to be there when the man found out he was going to be arrested and the cuffs were slapped on. For several days, she'd held her tongue in his presence until the police were ready to make an arrest. They would be coming very soon, and whatever happened to McPherson was his own problem. He deserved the worst. Any trust and faith she'd placed in her mentor had been destroyed. Though she was sure he'd never intended for anyone to get hurt, people were still dead, and he'd be implicated in the murders through conspiracy.

"Some of my finds from the last trip to the British Isles are missing." McPherson took off his glasses and rubbed his eyes. "I don't seem to be able to locate them anywhere. Niall was helping me catalogue that inventory. Without him, I'm afraid I won't be able to easily locate the artifacts I want. I can't imagine what's happened to him, just disappearing like that."

Knowing Detective Dayton was on his way with a warrant, Heather lost what little control she had left. She quickly got up and closed the door to the room so that no one would hear what she had to say. "Professor, and I use the term *loosely*, most of the artifacts you're looking for have been carefully labeled, set aside where you can't get your hands on them, and will be used as evidence by the police. I've kept it as quiet as I could so you wouldn't have a chance to hide them, and to give the museum time to salvage what will be left of its reputation when all of this gets out," Heather angrily informed him.

"What? What are you talking about? What's going on?" He put his glasses back on and glared at her.

"You took most, if not all, of those artifacts without the authorization of the appropriate governmental authorities. In short, Professor, you *stole* them. I guess you thought I'd be too naive or intimidated by your position here to say anything. I've been saving everything I could find. Shipping labels, dig permits, correspondence...*everything.* And just so you know, everything I've done has been authorized by the museum Board of Directors. When the police show up this afternoon, you're going to have a lot of explaining to do," she finished.

He sighed in resignation and sat heavily on a nearby stool. "I knew I'd be caught sooner or later. It was, as they say, only a matter of time."

"Why, Professor?" Heather asked as she leaned across

the work bench toward him. "You're a renowned archeologist. Why would you risk your reputation, and the museum's, by doing such a thing. It violates everything you've ever preached to your students."

McPherson laughed. "The oldest possible reason, my dear. Money. Pure greed. You see, I've been acquiring antiquities for almost thirty-five years. I've absolutely nothing to show for it. I was scheduled to retire next April. The museum would have given me a nice plaque and little else in the way of income. When private collectors approached Niall with some very lucrative offers, he and I planned everything out. We provided false documentation about our collection data, filed the appropriate shipping information. Everything. It was almost too easy. Until a young protégée of mine started asking too many questions."

He smiled at her sadly. "I told Niall you'd catch on, that we'd never be able to get the things we stole to the collectors while you were inventorying them. Niall said we'd just pretend to have loaned the items out, or that they were in the vaults for safe keeping. We only needed the false documentation to get the objects out of their respective countries and into the States. He was going to destroy all of the paperwork, including your inventory sheets, later. You're by far the brightest of all the assistants with whom I've worked. Niall thought he could bring you around in time. He was always so confident of himself and what we were doing. I just couldn't resist so much money. It's that simple." He sighed as if a load had been removed from his conscience. "Of course, I didn't bargain on him taking off and leaving me to face the Board and criminal charges alone. I suspect that's what he's done."

"That's not all he's done. Niall is a prime suspect in the murders that have been committed. Some kind of evidence has been found that links him to the crime scenes. Nowadays, detectives can place a person in the vicinity of a crime with all kinds of forensic techniques. Some of the same procedures we use in archeology work, as it happens."

When McPherson looked up with a shocked expression and his face turned pale, Heather felt a small sense of satisfaction. Some of the same science he'd used to find artifacts and smuggle them would be used to convict him. She continued.

"That's why the police think Niall has disappeared. Several investigators believe Ned walked in on something Niall didn't want seen. So, he killed him and made it look like some wild psychopath had done it. Then, to lend further credence to the *maniac-on-the-loose* story in all the newspapers, Niall killed the prostitute in the park the same way. He just butchered them both." To her dying day, that's what Heather would let the police believe. It was near enough to the truth.

McPherson choked on whatever he would have said, and his hands began to shake. Then he broke down and wept uncontrollably. After several gasping breaths, he finally spoke. "Heather, I-I didn't know anyone would get *hurt.* It was all about the money. J-just the money. You have to *believe* me? I know it's next to nothing, but I'll tell the Board you had nothing to do with any of this. I'll take full responsibility for what I've done, and I'll cooperate."

She slowly shook her head. "Tell it to the police. I don't ever want to see you again."

As if on cue, footsteps echoed through the vast hallways leading to the room where she and McPherson had logged in so many items. She crossed her arms and glared at him in disgust. There was no pity in her, nothing left to keep the anger from pushing aside her normal sense of mercy.

"There's just one more thing, Professor."

"Yes, *anything.* I just want this to be over." He slumped dejectedly.

"Niall had a set of three rune stones stolen from Ireland. I've found where two were hidden. Do you know where the third is?"

"No, h-he was obsessed with those damned things, though. They weren't worth much as they were. Niall was at the museum using our archives to decipher them until all hours. I let him do what he wanted with them because he said deciphering their meaning would increase their sale value with the collectors." He broke into another bout of tears.

She believed him only because Niall would never have let

the Professor near enough to decipher the stones. McPherson's apparent lack of curiosity over them had probably been all that had kept him alive. But, sooner or later, no matter what ever else happened, Niall would have killed the professor, too.

Heather sighed in resignation."Well, if you can tell me where he may have had them last, I'll search that area."

"He had them in his office. That was the last place I remember seeing them."

"Open the door," an authoritative voice boomed from the hallway. "It's the police and we have a warrant,"

Heather quickly opened the door. She got her wish, watching as McPherson was handcuffed by two uniformed police officers. He turned into a sobbing mass of jell that had to be half carried away. Several other officers, including Detective Dayton, entered the room and began to carry out large boxes of Irish artifacts.

That was the part of the arrest that made her want to cry. Those antiquities might never be returned to their countries. They'd be locked away somewhere, rotting in some evidence locker, never to be seen by anthropologists. Never to peak the curiosity of school children or have their mysteries unlocked. All because a dollar sign was more important to two fools. Gryphon had been so right. If only she'd listened sooner. What if she'd taken the three stones with her the first time she'd found them? Would that have saved his life?

Heather sat down on a bench, put her face in her hands and tried to hold the tears back. Then she shook it off and began to search with new determination. No one was *ever* going to get their hands on those rune stones. Not if she could help it. Gryphon, Ned, and the unknown woman in the park weren't going to have died in vain.

***

Several hours later, Heather straightened from her stooped position and rubbed her aching back. She had systematically searched every place she could in Niall's office. The job was more difficult because she had to make it look as though she hadn't been rummaging around. She knew the police would want to go through his belongings. But there was simply no trace of the stone. Heather knew the last people who should find the stone were the police. If they did, they might want it translated, realize there were others and start asking questions. She *had* to find it.

Where would Niall have hidden an object of that kind? The last one had been in a vase from a different part of the world. Would Niall have hidden the third stone in a different section of the museum? Gryph had been right about so many things. It could take a person their lifetime searching the museum for something the size of a human palm. Glancing at her watch, Heather gasped at the time. She'd been at it for hours and was too tired to go on. She turned off the light, making sure everything was still in its place before leaving. The security guard walked her to the parking lot and left. Heather opened the door to the rental car she'd picked up after Niall had pulled the door off hers. The lie she told the insurance company about opening the car door on the street and having a passing truck pull it off had seemed to satisfy her insurance agent. *How many more lies like it will I have to tell before all this is over*?

A cold wind blew her hair across her face. She had brought up her hand to move it back when she saw the tree. In the parking lot stood a huge maple tree with a knothole a little above eye level. She remembered a part of her nightmare the last time she'd seen Gryphon and he'd held her. The tree looked *exactly* like the tree in that horrible dream. In a trance-like state, Heather felt herself walk toward it. The knothole was too high for her to reach inside and search thoroughly. A trash can sat under a lamppost a few yards away. She ran to it, pulled it to the tree and upended it. The ground was level below the branches, so it was no hardship for her to stand on the can, reach inside the knothole and pull out the stone.

She swallowed hard as her hand closed around it. How in the world the stone was in the same place as in her dream, she would never know. Perhaps it was part of the magic that had encapsulated her life since this ordeal had begun. Now, all she had to do was get the last stone to Gwyneth and James. She prayed they were still in the country and would come to her. Believing she might get them into trouble with Shayla, she dared not approach their temporary residence. Mailing the stone was out of the question. So Heather decided to keep it with her. She stuck it in her coat pocket, replaced the trash can and drove home.

***

Almost two weeks later, she still had the last Rune Stone of the Tuatha De! Danann in her pocket. Gwyneth *must* come for it sooner or later, and Heather wanted to be able to hand it to her when she did. Gryph's parents and Shayla could leave quickly and go back to the Shire, that place they called home. Then she could try to forget him. *She could try.*

Heather was walking toward her car after work when she was grabbed from behind and held by two very strong arms. A hand went to her mouth to keep her from crying out.

"Quiet, Heather. I don't want the security guard seeing me," a low, reassuring voice spoke.

When she immediately quit struggling, Gryph released her. She turned, backed away and would have fallen to the ground had he not caught her. *Alive! How could that be?* She began to tremble, her breath left her, and a mist formed over her eyes. She remembered Gwyneth had never actually said he was dead. The woman had just let her believe it was true to protect her son. That didn't matter. Nothing mattered except that he was alive.

Gryph picked her up and carried her into the nearby woods and away from the lights in the parking lot. "I'm *fine*, Heather. I'm sorry you were led to think otherwise. My mother didn't mean to hurt you. It took a while for my wounds to mend, and no one was sure I would get over them. But when she thought about how upset you'd been...well, Mother's conscience got the better of her and she helped me get back here to see you. Please don't cry so," he begged, as he stoked her hair and studied her face in the moonlight. "You'll make yourself ill."

"*Oh, God, Gryph.*" She threw her arms around his neck and hugged hard.

He winced in pain, but managed to smile. "Easy, baby. I'm still on the mend."

Heather immediately released her hold and pushed slightly

away from him. She looked up and down his tall frame, searching for the source of his discomfort. Then she half-cried, half-laughed and walked more gently into his embrace.

"There's a love. Now...don't be so upset. I'm here. It's all over," he crooned and rocked her back and forth. His heart was near bursting. *This* kind of affection and devotion was more than he'd ever hoped for. Tears filled his own eyes. He needed her so much.

It took some time for her to come to grips with his appearance. He gladly held her close while prodding her further into the nearby woods. When he was sure their voices wouldn't carry on the wind, that the security guards were gone, he slowly tilted her head back with his hands and gently kissed her. The kiss went on and on. The world could have fallen off its axis, and he wouldn't have noticed or cared. When their lips finally parted, Heather looked up at him and there was starlight reflecting in the depths of her eyes. They stared at one another until she finally spoke.

"Who was it that said, '*reports of my death have been greatly exaggerated*'?

"It was one of your own countrymen. Mark Twain."

Her eyes welled up again, and she buried her face against his shoulder.

He sighed in pure contentment. Though he knew it would be short-lived, for this moment in time, they could be happy. He held her until she backed away, ran her hands over his arms and finally took control.

"These past few weeks have been the worst of my life. Even when my parents were killed in a car accident, I could console myself with the fact that they were together. But you don't have anyone."

The statement puzzled him. How could she know about that? But Heather was still recovering from the shock of seeing him alive. She might have said anything, and it wouldn't have mattered. He was so glad to see her, hold her again before he'd have to leave. He saw her shiver when the wind blew leaves around them. She put her hands on his chest.

"You're as cold as stone, aren't you, darling?"

"Stone?" She blinked up at him, smiled brightly and reached into her jacket pocket. "That reminds me. I've been carrying this thing around for weeks now. I promised Gwyneth I'd find it."

"*Herne's antlers*, girl! You're incredible." He kissed and hugged her again as he placed the last rune stone in his shirt pocket. He paused, knowing he had to tell her. "You know I killed Niall, don't you?"

"I understand why," she said solemnly.

"Do you?" He watched her expression closely and gazed into her starlit eyes.

Heather lightly touched his cheek, wanting to be near him as much as possible. "He'd have killed others. I know he would. Nothing would have ever stopped him."

"He'll never hurt anyone again." *And never hurt you.*

She moved into his embrace and felt safe and warm there. It was as though she was meant to be in that special place. His heart beat so strongly beneath her cheek.

Gryph plunged his hand into her hair, pulled her head back and kissed her with an urgent helplessness. Knowing he couldn't have her filled him with a low, burning passion that wouldn't end. The kiss deepened, as before. Only the salty taste of Heather's tears stopped Gryphon from going further.

"Heather," he said, ending the kiss slowly, "I told you once that it was a mistake for us to get involved. There are things about me that you'd never believe or understand. I have to go, and I won't be back again. I'm sorry if I've hurt you. But, if it's any consolation, I'll never be this close to a woman again. You're all I've ever wanted. If things were different, if I wasn't..." his voice trailed away. And he was aware of the painful sound of it.

"I know," she stopped him by placing her fingers over his lips. "You're alive and that'll have to be enough."

He took a deep breath, reached inside his jacket and pulled out a leather pouch about eight inches long. "I want you to have this. It isn't much, but..." He shrugged his shoulders and handed her the bag.

Heather knew the rest. Whatever the bag contained, it was

probably all he had. And she recognized the significance of the object used by Druids to carry ceremonial items. "This is a crane bag, isn't it?"

He smiled and nodded. "I knew you'd understand. It's not much in the way of thanks, especially not after what you've been through. When you look at the contents, I hope they'll explain what I'm trying to say. I haven't words to..." He bowed his head and tried to think what his last words to her should be. "I'm doing a very poor job of this."

"Go on, Gryphon," she softly encouraged. "I'm listening."

"Whenever there's a full moon, open the crane bag and try to think of me kindly. And not as someone who's brought you pain." He placed one of her hands on his chest. "Can you do that?"

"Yeah, Gryph. Yeah, I can do that," she said softly. Then she smiled up at him and held the bag close to her heart. She was standing on her toes in order to kiss him again when a voice echoed from the woods.

"*Gryphon O'Connor.*"

"Heather, *move back*," Gryph said as he pushed her behind him.

"It's too late to protect her, or yourself. I've seen enough," Shayla said, walking out of the woods with Gryph's parents.

"Please, Shayla, it's *my* fault, not theirs. I was the one who told her. You can't punish them for something I did," Gwyneth pleaded, her eyes filled with tears.

"Mother! What *have* you done? And why are you here?" Gryph looked from his parents to where Shayla stood.

"Son...your mother...she broke the law. But I won't let *anyone* harm her," James firmly declared as he pulled his wife to him and held her close. "She only did what she thought was best for you."

Shayla stepped forward, her long silver hair billowing out behind her. As Heather watched, she felt every cell in her body freeze in fear.

Gryphon turned to face Heather. "What is it that you know?" he asked, and could hear the trepidation in his own voice.

Heather automatically backed away from him when she saw the look of intense fear and anger mixed on his face.

"*Everything*!" Shayla proclaimed. "She knows everything about the Order, about your pact to do my bidding and about your changing into the creature who protects. Your mother told her everything. And you know what the penalty must be for both your mother and the girl," Shayla proclaimed. "I will spare Gryphon only because Gwyneth admits blame."

Gryph could see pain and stoic determination were etched into the lines of the Sorceress' face. He looked away from Shayla and into Heather's eyes. Finally, his gaze fell upon his mother. He shook his head in disbelief. "You told Heather. She knows about..."

"Everything!" Shayla repeated harshly.

Gryphon faced Heather again. "Was it worth knowing, woman? Was it worth the life which will be taken from you and my mother? You once wanted to know who I was. Now see for yourself, Heather. Before you suffer judgement, see what killed Niall and made love to you." He backed away, anger mixing with his pain. He knelt.

The rippling effect began, and the clothing on his body ripped away. The shape which emerged was much larger and more intimidating up close. Gryphon rose up and roared. He waited for Heather to scream or faint with revulsion when she learned what she'd had sex with. But she stood silently and looked at him. Her lovely face mirrored something he would never have imagined. There was a kind of wonder and curiosity in her eyes. She slowly walked forward.

James shouted, "STAY BACK, GIRL! Since he was a very small child, no one has ever touched Gryph in his beast form!"

Gryph roared out a warning for her to stay away. He wasn't sure he could control his lumbering actions enough to keep from inadvertently harming her. She was doomed, anyway, but Gryphon wasn't going to be the instrument of her death. He *couldn't* hurt her. Heather tentatively put out her hand, and came closer still. Gryph began to think she had finally lost her sanity having been exposed to more than any outsider was meant to see. She was close enough to touch him, and he couldn't back away any more. His wingspan didn't allow him to venture under trees whose branches were too close to the ground. He trembled as her hand touched his feathered neck and slowly stroked down his chest.

"Amazing! You're magnificent. You're the most beautiful creature I've ever seen, Gryph. You can understand me, can't you? Oh, don't tremble. I could never hurt you or be afraid of you. After all the times you could have done something to me, I'm certain you wouldn't hurt me now." She crooned as if she were speaking to a frightened stray animal. Her hands continued to move over his shoulders and up to the base of his mighty wings. She felt him quivering.

Gryph's parents and Shayla stood by, dumbstruck. Mighty warriors had backed away in fear and awe when he'd been sent to right a wrong or settle a dispute which threatened the Order. Now, the massive gryphon stood quietly at the light touch of a willowy girl. Tears formed in his midnight-black eyes because she wasn't afraid or repelled by him. To the others, it appeared she had more courage than sense. The fact was, Heather simply couldn't fear him because she loved him and trusted him too much.

When the rippling began again, Heather backed away only because she sensed Gryph needed the space to change back into human form. When the change was over, he looked up at her from his kneeling position, and there were tears of total adoration on his face.

"You don't care *what I am.* Do you?" he choked out the words as his heart began to grow, second by second. That shattering reality broke the wall of stone around his soul, and hope began to take its place.

"No," she simply said and shrugged, "I don't."

Gryphon stood and pulled her to him so fast that there was scarcely time for her to take another breath.

James wiped tears of astonishment and sadness from his face and held his sobbing wife. "That my son has found someone who unconditionally loves him, is our dream. But the woman who has done so will soon be destroyed."

Gryphon held Heather very close and buried his face in her chest. It seemed like a long time before he finally spoke. "I won't let you hurt Heather or Mother, Shayla. I'll fight you if I have to, but that's the way of it. I love them both and can't let you pass judgement."

Heather gazed up at him. She knew every ounce of love was reflected in her face. Since she was no longer hiding anything, it would be obvious for all to see. But she didn't care.

"Don't be a fool. You can't stand against me and the forces of the Order. If you insist on fighting the law, Gryphon, the end result will be death for you and anyone who stands with you," Shayla sadly warned.

"I stand with him," James proudly declared. "My son has always done his duty to the Order, Shayla. He's never refused anything asked of him. Your part of the pact was to let him lead some kind of normal life. What life has he had that could be defined as normal?"

"Yes, what has he had except his duty to *you*?" Gwyneth asked.

"He's had the best life he could live after you meddled into things best left alone. He was born into the Order, and there he must remain or die. The choice is his."

"No. It isn't just *his* choice," Heather said, looking up at Gryphon and shaking her head. "I can't let anything happen to you or your parents because of me." She pushed away from the proud warrior holding her and walked to where Shayla stood. "If I leave right now and promise not to see Gryph or his parents ever again, will you leave them alone? Can't you make an exception just this one time?"

Shayla stared at her. "Since you'll suffer a lifetime away from the man you love, that will be punishment enough. I'll let you and the others live if you go right now, and if none of the Order finds out that I've violated the very laws I'm sworn to uphold. But I do this out of love and respect for Gryphon and because of all he's accomplished for our safety."

"Have *I* nothing to say in this matter," Gryph asked Shayla angrily. His fists were clenched at his sides. "I won't let Heather go. She's claimed me as I claim her. My parents have no say in what I do. Punish me if you will, but I'll never give Heather up or let you hurt anyone else I love."

"You've had your say, warrior. So be it." Shayla slowly and wearily raised her hands, and the wind began to blow.

"No, Shayla, NO!" Heather ran to Gryph and threw her arms about him. He held her protectively against his massive body. "Gryph, I can't let this happen. It isn't fair, I know, but I can't let Shayla do this." Heather yelled above the sound of the rising wind and backed away from him. "Have a good life, my love. *Please*, try to find some way to be happy." With that, she turned away and ran from them all.

Gryph moved to pursue her, but Shayla's power held him fast.

"Stop, Gryphon!" Shayla stepped in front of him. "The girl has done what was best for all concerned. For an outsider, she has acted quite *admirably*. If you contact her again, I'll have no choice but to send others after her who will see to her demise. You'll never know what happened to her. This way, she survives, and so do you and your parents. I will forgive the transgressions I've witnessed and your standing against me only this *one* time. And only so long as I never see or hear about that outsider again. Pray to the Goddess that she never speaks of what she knows to anyone who'll believe her or, that too, will cause her death." As soon as Shayla finished speaking the wind died down, and everything in the woods went back to normal.

Gryph gazed in the direction Heather had fled. He was vaguely aware of his father placing a cloak over his shoulders, and that James, Shayla, and Gwyneth moved away. Presumably the were giving him some time and distance to help recover from his loss. On the ground where Heather had stood, a blue silk scarf lay. It had fallen from around her neck when she ran. Gryphon knelt, saw the remains of his shirt, and found the last rune stone lying next to the scarf. He picked them both up and thought of her last words: *Have a good life. Try to find a way to be happy.*

"I'll do neither," he whispered, with only the night and the trees to hear.

THIRTEEN

Heather pushed open the door to her apartment and dropped the books she was carrying on the floor. The rain and cold outside did nothing to improve her foul mood. It was impossible to forget all that had happened. For months, every time she walked to her car after work she deliberately dawdled. There was always the hope that Gryph would be there to stop her. At night, she sometimes cried herself to sleep wondering if he was well. Though ten hour workdays and long weekends deciphering Celtic writing kept her mind busy enough, the nights were always the worst. That was when the memories intruded. Her work with the Celtic artifacts brought her the only joy in her life. It brought her closer to Gryph.

Not bothering to turn on the lights, she shook the rainwater from her coat and hung it behind the door. Half an hour later she emerged from a hot shower, wrapped in a warm robe. She walked into the small living room, lit a pink candle then brewed some herbal tea. On the coffee table lay the small leather crane bag Gryph had given her on that last night. She knelt beside the table, spread out a green, velvet cloth and carefully opened the bag as she had so many times. She lovingly placed each of Gryphon's gifts on the green cloth. There was a sprig of dried mistletoe. The most sacred of all herbs to the Druids, she knew Gryph had included it because that particular plant represented healing and overcoming difficulties. Its berries had sometimes been used in love charms. Next to this, she placed a sprig of rosemary for remembrance, a small moonstone for wishing, a citrine crystal to eliminate fear, and a perfect quartz wand for communication over distances and for balance. Then, she lovingly held the pink rose-quartz heart. A symbol of love, devotion and happiness. Last, there was a small, flat pebble with the rune symbol of an upright arrow carved into its surface. This was the rune of a warrior. For Heather, it represented Gryphon. His courage, dedication and endurance. In ancient times, Celtic warriors had painted this symbol on their shields and breastplates before going into battle. She'd seen many like it in her studies, but it had become dramatically important to her now. She placed it next to the rose quartz.

She closed her eyes and sent out a whispered prayer. "Please let him be safe. Let him be happy." The flame of the pink candle gently flickered. The little candle was her only addition to the small collection of objects. It was symbolic of love and togetherness. A representation of a hurried and dangerous relationship which had ended too soon. A relationship which had grown and intensified into something rare. In her mind, she could almost see him staring up at the moon, thinking of her. Someday, maybe the memories wouldn't hurt so much. But her world was severely deficient of legends. Heroes who did the right thing because that was all that could be done. She doubted her mind would ever be free of him, or that the pain would ever go away. Everything she touched reminded her of him. She could almost feel his gentle touch, the way he'd held her when they made love. No man had ever been so caring and demanding all at once. He'd made her want to give him her very soul. Sometimes as she slept, it was as if he was there again, moving within her, touching, caressing until she cried out for more. Then, she'd dream he was in full battle gear, charging a hill to rescue his woman from some evil force threatening to separate them forever. He'd free her from her captors and take her away to some primeval forest. There they would lay in the cool darkness and pleasure each other for hours. But the dream would finally end. Heather would awaken feeling as though she'd been cheated of something very precious. And her body would ache for his touch. In the short time they'd had, something very precious had happened. Two people didn't have that kind of connection unless some larger power had meant for it to be. But, like the Celtic gods of legend, those same powers turned cruel and laughed at their pain. There were impossible barriers placed in their paths.

That was her real excuse for working so hard. Sometimes the frustration she felt was too intense. There was no physical way to assuage it. Heather had tried everything. Work was all that was left. That was her one solace. She could be near things from his part of the world. And she was exceedingly careful that no one could ever trace any of the artifacts back to him or the Order. Heather even altered some of the paperwork before giving it to the police. Her greatest fear was that his world would be discovered. There wasn't enough tolerance in hers to accommodate such a place.

She slowly opened her eyes and listened to the thunder rumbling overhead. As soon as she was finished with the current collection of artifacts, she had decided to turn in her resignation and move on. Maybe to California or someplace bright and hot. A place where there could be a new life. Nothing about New York appealed to her anymore. Everything of real importance was gone. She blew out the candle and stood up. Flashes of lightning lit the darkened room.

Something instinctively warned her she wasn't alone. The hair on the back of her neck stood up, and her mouth went dry. Heather carefully turned to face the door. A slender female figure stood there, watching her. The woman was robed in white.

"You studied Druid traditions well, though you've forgotten to acknowledge the elemental spirits and close the ceremony properly. You should be more careful about that. Goddess knows what you'll invite into this room." She waved a hand, and the candle flickered back to life.

"*Shayla*," Heather gasped. Her heart pounded out a heavy rhythm, and a horrible dread filled her. "Gryphon. Is he all right?"

"Why are you so concerned?"

"Just *tell* me," she demanded.

"When I left him, he was in tolerable condition. Though I believe he misses you as much as you seem to miss him."

Heather stared at the older woman, trying to gauge whether there was a hint of a lie or subterfuge in her words. Every instinct she had told her Gryphon needed her as much as she needed him.

"If you're not here to tell me something's wrong, why have you broken into my apartment?"

"I might have approached you somewhere else, but you're always at work or here. So, I decided to speak with you where we can be alone." She paused and walked toward Heather. "And, like all outsiders, you haven't been paying much attention to your surroundings, or you'd have noticed you've been followed."

Heather swallowed hard. "Why? By whom?"

"Some of my people have been keeping an eye on you. I told you what would happen if you ever went to anyone about us."

"I *haven't...*"

Shayla held up a hand to silence her. "I know. You'd already be dead if you had."

"Then why are you here?"

"Sit down. I have a proposition to put to you."

Heather sat on the sofa while Shayla regally positioned herself in the opposite chair. The older woman untied a white bag from around her waist and carefully placed the contents on the table next to Heather's stones and herbs.

Heather groaned and shook her head when she saw what lay there. "Why did you bring those damned things back here? Gryph almost died getting them to you."

Shayla carefully arranged the rune stones of the Tuatha De! Danann so the symbols faced Heather. "I take it you have a passing familiarity with these?" Her voice dripped with sarcasm.

"Yeah. I know 'em," Heather snapped back and moved farther away from the stones.

"I intend to put them where no one can ever find them again," Shayla informed her.

"They're not staying in my apartment. And I've got a real good suggestion for just where you can put them," Heather sniped.

"You're rude, girl."

"Well, you've broken into my apartment, which is something

I really hate about you people, and you've brought those . . those pieces of crap back into my life." She nodded toward the stones. "I never wanted to see those damned things again. Why don't you throw them into the deepest part of the ocean before someone else gets killed?"

"I intend to use them one more time. At least, I intend to *watch* them being used."

Heather stared at Shayla for a long moment. "Are you out of your friggin' mind?"

"I'm going to excuse your rudeness once more. But only once."

Heather got up, marched to the door and opened it. "Get out. And take those God-awful things with you."

"*Sit down* before I lose my patience, and you lose the one chance you have of being with Gryphon." Shayla quickly stood up.

Heather jumped as the woman raised one hand and the door slammed shut behind her. "You *can't* be serious," she choked out the words as she walked back toward the Sorceress.

"*Think* girl. The Order isn't ready to accept outsiders, though we'll someday *have* to. For now, using these stones may be the only way that an outsider can safely enter our world. To convince those of my kind that some of *your* kind can be trusted."

"What do you mean?" Heather shook her head in confusion.

"It's a simple matter of a closed society with limited genetic resources. Once there were hundreds of thousands of us. That's no longer the case. Over the centuries, our numbers have decreased as the land needed to sustain us diminished. We currently have physicians all over Europe who've secretly reported back to us on their findings. No one knows these men and women are part of the Order, and we've taken great pains to keep it that way. But their research undeniably concludes that our numbers are too few to sustain a healthy gene pool. Unless, of course, we start taking in new blood from time to time." Shayla looked pointedly at her.

What she was saying suddenly hit home. Heather would have collapsed to the floor if the sofa hadn't been behind her.

"And...and you want...you want *me...* "

"Yes. I want you to use the stones as Niall Alexander did. Hopefully, the outcome will be somewhat more acceptable. If everything turns out well, it may no longer be necessary to resort to such magic. Selected outsiders might be brought in without..."

"Without endangering their lives," Heather interrupted.

Shayla nodded. "Yes. The stones could turn you into something evil that I'd end up having destroyed, or you could die while using them. Those are two possibilities."

"I am *not* your guinea pig."

"Do you want to be with Gryphon, or not? The choice is yours. And, if you'll recall, a *third* possibility does exist." She walked to where Heather was sitting and looked down at her. "If your heart is good, you'll end up as a creature reflecting the true nature of your soul. Since you're the only person who can judge whether you're worthy or not, I leave the choice to you. But we must eventually have new blood in the Order. Whether it's you or someone else makes no difference to me. It would simply be easier on *all* concerned if we took advantage of this opportunity. *You* already know about us and have accepted one of our members. We might have to search a very long time to find another outsider trustworthy enough to approach."

Heather looked up into Shayla's face and shook her head. "You are one cold-blooded..."

"*Don't.* Don't you even *think* of saying it." Shayla picked up the rune stones, safely returned them to her bag and walked toward the door. "Consider the possibilities, Heather. You could be with Gryphon, or continue on as you have been. I have an entire population to save. Now make your choice. I'll be in the museum park tomorrow at midnight. If you aren't there, I'll assume you want nothing more to do with any of us."

Heather watched the woman walk out the door. It opened and closed without the Sorceress having touched the knob. Her brain went numb, and it was hours before she moved. Dawn had come before she finally stood up and tried to gather her wits. First, she paced. Then she put on some jogging clothes and ran until she couldn't take another stride. It made no sense trying to eat or rest. How could a person remotely consider such mundane tasks when faced with a chance of gaining everything or dying?

It finally came down to a series of questions, the main one being did she love Gryphon enough? Heather closed her eyes, and she could see his handsome face. He'd smiled so seldom. There was a sadness about the man that made her want to hold him close, though he'd hate such contact if it only came out of pity. He was too proud for that. He'd love the same way he did everything else, with determination, nobility and passion. That's the man she'd come to know, the one she had come to love.

Heather sat in front of her apartment building and watched people walk up and down the street. Some were parents with small children. Some were couples holding hands and others talked on portable phones, making deals and carrying on businesses. An infinite number of cab drivers, pedestrians and couriers dodged each other in a continual melee. All were totally oblivious to the magic that existed on Earth. How sad it was. They were all so consumed with their own problems and fears that life was passing some of them by. She could see it in the harsh expressions on some of their faces. Could she rise above her own fears and give up the reality she knew for the chance of a lifetime? And what would await her in that other world if she did?

The questions came, but they always circled back to one conclusion. It was the hardest decision she'd ever made in her life. Having made it, Heather went back into her apartment and for the last time closed out the world she knew.

***

Shayla waited in the cold darkness. Her white robes had been exchanged for brown to better conceal her presence in the dark. Over them she wore a hooded cape to break the biting wind. She pushed back the hood when a slender figure wearing blue jeans and a leather jacket approached.

"I was wondering if you had the courage."

"So was I. But I thought about it all night and all day. I guess I love him too much." Heather stood up straight, fought back the fear and held out her hands for the stones. "I assume you've had these translated so that I won't have to?"

The Sorceress nodded. Seeing an outsider showing such bravery was beyond her experience. She pulled the stones from her bag, handed them to Heather and backed away. "Last chance, girl."

Heather shook her head. "I'm doing this."

"Very well, then. Repeat after me, *exactly*." She paused only a moment, making sure Heather was ready. When she nodded, Shayla began. "Goddess Dana, give me the power of your race. Ceridwen, give me knowledge. Cernunnos, empower me with the spirit of your chosen beast. Test my soul for your purpose. Find it worthy."

Heather repeated the translation. For a second, nothing happened. Then her surroundings began to blur. She felt her body heat, go numb, and heard her clothing tear. Somehow she found herself on the ground and could see the Sorceress backing away. There wasn't any pain. But there was a strange sense of displacement accompanied by dizziness. Bright light permeated the darkness, and she could see the older woman's face. Shayla's expression of horror terrified her. Would Gryphon want her if she was a monster? Would *he* be the one sent to destroy her? That was her last conscious thought before sinking into oblivion.

Shayla stood in the darkness and trembled. The last of the light died away as the beast sank to the ground. The creature Heather had become lay still, its gargantuan head twisted to one side, the body splayed at an odd angle. The rune stones lay where Heather had dropped them.

Shayla picked them up and turned her face toward the night sky. "By the Goddess above, I swear I'll never let these be used by another soul." Her gaze fell back to the beast before her. "I'm sorry, girl. So very sorry. You made your decision. Now it's done. So mote it be." Shayla took off her hooded cloak and carefully placed it over the creature.

FOURTEEN

Gryphon downed the last of the bottle in one smooth swallow. He passed a hand over his unshaven face and staggered toward an open window. The cool night air did nothing to alleviate the effects of the whiskey. Small fires dotted the forest landscape as the Samhain moonlight beamed down upon hundreds of revelers. It was the most sacred time of the year for all members of the Order. He could hear the sounds of merriment from the tall parapet of the ancient castle. This was the place his father and mother called home. To the outside world, it was just another of a thousand old European castles inhabited by a secluded member of an outmoded upper class. To him, it was a residence he could never own. One more thing that left him bitter. Without a mate, the rest of the Order would never let him be the next Earl. For generations, one of his father's bloodline had inherited the land and had taken care of its forests under the Sorceress' council. Without an heir, there would be no one to inherit. He was good enough for the Nymphs to play with, but not to find a mate, handfast and have a child. What woman would want to take the chance of producing a small replica of a half bird/half lion or take the risk that the child he fathered would be stillborn? No. He would see that even the promiscuous Nymphs who occasionally happened his way never got pregnant. It was far better to never, under any circumstances, take that chance. The sacred herbs Druids knew about, and that he gathered every month and ate, assured that none of his seed would ever prove fertile. And Nymphs knew how to take care of things like that. Because they had sex with virtually anyone, they had ways of their own to counter pregnancies, as did all of the inhabitants of the Shire. Children should be wanted and have parents who loved them. Not accidents whose coming was feared or resented.

Whether it was because he was drunk or because he was tired of hiding away like a frightened fawn, Gryph knew he'd finally had enough. He threw the whiskey bottle across the room and watched it shatter against the stone wall. Then, he stumbled toward the door and the stairway beyond.

"I should have as much right as anyone," he muttered. Wasn't he a member of the damned Order, too? Why should he hide during the most sacred time of the year? Even his parents were out there among their friends. They'd invited him but, as always, he'd stayed behind. That was before the alcohol dimmed his sense. He wasn't staying cloistered anymore.

Being so inebriated, getting outside was an ordeal. Several times he fell. Once he struck his head against the marble railing and had to stop and steady himself, almost falling down four more flights. In an effort to rid itself of the copious amounts of whiskey he'd consumed, his body broke into a hard sweat. Gryph stopped to pull his shirt off and threw it to the floor below. Like a fine blue wraith, Heather's silk scarf floated to the floor with it. He hurried down as fast as he could, sat on the bottom step where it had landed and held it tenderly in both hands. It was the one thing he always carried.

"What would you think of me now, my girl? Would you look at me with those beautiful eyes and still give a damn?" he spoke to himself. "I'm a disgusting, pathetic mess, and don't seem to care."

"*Gryphon*! You look like something a cat should bury." The voice echoed off the cold stone walls and through the foyer.

He looked up, but his vision doubled, and all he could see were several tall figures weaving before him. "That you, Da? Who's with you?"

James shook his head and knelt in front of his son. "It's just me. You've drunk so much you can't even see straight." He paused. "How, by Herne, did you cut your head open like that?" He started to look at the wound only to have Gryph push his hands away.

"It doesn't matter. Help me outside, Da."

"Not like this, Son. Let's get that head looked after and clean you up."

Again Gryph pushed his helping hands away. "*No*. I want to go outside. That's where the party is, isn't it."

"Don't do this, lad," his father pleaded in a soft voice.

"Do *what*? Didn't you want me with you and Mother tonight? It's been a long time, hasn't it?"

"Gryph..."

"Let's see...how old was I when we last went to the Samhain celebration together? Eight? Was I eight years old?" He wrapped Heather's scarf around the palm of one hand. "No, it was more like I was ten. That's right, I remember. Ten."

James sighed. "Let's go upstairs, Gryphon. That was a long time ago, and you were too young to understand."

"Understand *what*, Father? That a bunch of intolerant bullies ganged up on me, and I had to *change* to kick some of their butts all the way back to Scotland? Or wherever they came from."

"Can't you *ever* let anything go? It's useless talking to you in this irrational state."

"Yes, I remember quite well, now. I was all of *ten* when five *grown men* decided to have a little fun with the *freak*."

"No one will ever do anything like that again, Gryphon. That's over, in the past. Let it go."

"I almost killed one of them before the Sorceress stopped the fight." He stopped and looked up at his father. "I wonder what ever happened to that jackass?" His question was a ploy. He knew very well what had happened. His father just wouldn't admit it.

James remained silent and watched his son carefully touch the blue silk scarf in his hand. The man he was referring to had died. This was the first time since that incident Gryphon had ever spoken of it. The entire scenario was always hanging over them every year at this time. But no one ever said anything to bring it up again. Neither Gwyneth nor he had ever told Gryph what had happened to the man. Likely as not, the Sorceress would have had the men involved in the incident put to death for attacking a child. Since the one had died at Gryph's hands, however, it was decided to let the lesson be a hard one for all concerned. The others who had attacked Gryph quickly left for other sacred areas and hadn't returned to the Shire. They had probably been as drunk as Gryphon was now and had let their intolerance go too far. In the future, his son could very well become what those men had feared. A monster. And James agonized over it. He watched as Gryph studied the scarf with a soft expression on his face.

"Is this about Samhain, or is it really about something else?" James asked. "You're missing that girl, aren't you?" He paused. "Son, I know this past year hasn't been easy for you. I wish there was something I could do to take the pain away."

Gryph smiled bitterly. "What pain, Father?"

"You're not going to sit there and tell me you're not in love with her?"

"That was a dream, Da. It would never have worked. Even if, by some miracle, Shayla *had* allowed us to be together," he paused, "could you imagine Heather going outside to celebrate Samhain with me? The Order would never accept her. She'd be in constant danger from their machinations and spells. No. It was only a dream. I know my place within the Order, and the woman would never have fit in. She is an *outsider*. She belongs in her world. I in mine."

"And that?" James pointed to the scarf Gryph held tightly in his right hand.

"It's just a reminder of a mistake I almost made. I keep it as a sort of souvenir, no more," Gryph lied. He used the railing to pull himself up, then stumbled toward the massive oak doors that guarded the foyer.

James quickly followed. "Where are you going?"

"Outside to put an end to this one way or another. And don't worry. I won't kill anyone *this* time."

James gasped and stopped walking.

Hearing his father's response, Gryphon slowly turned to face him. "You didn't know I *knew*, did you, Da? It's just another game we play. Pretending everything's all right." Gryph stopped talking as his vision cleared slightly, and he saw his father's stricken expression.

"Your mother and I thought you were too young to feel responsible for such a thing. It wasn't your fault." James bowed his head.

Gryphon walked over to him and put his arms around the older man. "Don't you know there are no secrets in the Shire? Some of the other children taunted me about being a murderer a long time ago. It's one of the reasons they weren't allowed to be around me. Parents didn't know what would spark my change."

"I just never...we never asked how you felt about it," James mumbled.

"Of course not. You didn't want to know, and I didn't want to tell you. That's the way it is." He rubbed the back of his neck with one hand, shoved the scarf into his pants pocket with the other and turned toward the doors again. "Come with me, Da. I want an end to this."

James nodded. "Perhaps you're right. I should have been more aggressive about standing by you. Let's find your mother first."

"Fine. But I do my own talking. My own way. Understood?" Gryph said as he staggered outside.

***

Shayla stood by the central fire and threw in the herbs which blessed the celebration of the end of one year and the beginning of the next. Fairies, Sprites and Pixies played music while Druids, Elves, Gnomes, and others danced and indulged themselves. Large quantities of food and wine had been prepared. The celebration would go on for days, and everyone was expected to enjoy themselves to the fullest.

The music suddenly stopped, and she turned toward the darkness. Others did so as well. Gryphon, flanked by his parents, stepped from the surrounding forest, and it was apparent the man had been drinking heavily. He stopped in the light of the fire, staggered, and slowly looked around.

"So, you've finally decided to join us, have you?" Shayla loudly announced.

Gryphon strode purposefully forward, glaring at the Sorceress. He made his way to a rough-hewn table, sat and propped his booted feet upon its surface. Then he stared back at the faces of those nearby and smirked. *They look as though the Banshee just arrived.* "Bring me wine," he loudly commanded.

A young girl carrying a tray of blue crockery mugs came forward and quickly set the wine before Gryphon and his parents. He guzzled the potent red-berry wine then ordered her to pour him another.

"This is a celebration, isn't it?" the Sorceress' voiced boomed out when everyone maintained their silence. "Musicians, play."

As she commanded, the music began again, and the crowds slowly gained their previous momentum. Some still stared at Gryphon, but most went about their business. Shayla made her way to the O'Connors' table and took a seat opposite Gryphon. "Well, that was quite an entrance." She paused, waiting for him to make a comment. He simply looked in another direction and continued to imbibe more alcohol.

"Gryph, haven't you had enough?" Gwyneth placed her hand on his arm in an attempt to keep him from swilling down yet another mug. "You've been drinking too much lately."

"I agree," James remarked. "I don't like seeing what you're doing to yourself."

Gryphon carelessly shrugged. "Then don't watch. There are other places to sit."

Gwyneth gasped at the rude remark, stood up and marched away.

James stood and tossed his mug aside in anger."Say what you want to *me*, but if you continue hurting your mother like this, then it might be better if you headed back to Ireland. I don't know what's gotten into you these past months, but I'm sick and tired of it." He stopped when it became apparent Gryphon was staring off into the distance, too drunk to focus. James turned to Shayla. "Excuse me, Sorceress. I leave my sot of a son to you. I'm through trying to talk sense into him." James marched off, following Gwyneth.

Gryph's conscience hit an all-time low. But making his parents angry with him would help them get through the future. The confrontation he'd spent his whole life avoiding was at hand.

For a few moments, Shayla said nothing. She watched Gryphon's gaze move to a group of laughing Fairies and their mates. One tall man picked up a girl and swung her around as she screamed in delight. They began to dance and sing while others clapped in amusement. Something in Gryphon's eyes went cold. Then he picked up an entire jug of wine and began to drink from it.

"It's *she* isn't it?"

Gryphon wiped his mouth with the back of one hand. "Who, Sorceress?"

"That woman in New York. You've still got your mind on her."

"Been looking into your magic mirrors again, Shayla?" Gryphon grinned sarcastically and waved his hands in the air in a cryptic gesture.

Her eyes narrowed. "You're a good man. Too good to let you ruin your life like this."

He laughed. "Yes, and *popular*, too." He glanced around at the nearby tables that had emptied. Their occupants having left shortly after his arrival.

"You *could* be if you weren't so self-absorbed, insisting on living like a hermit and making a fearsome image of yourself."

Gryphon placed his palms on the table and leaned toward her. "You see that man over there*?"* He nodded toward a Druid glaring at him across the clearing. "I'm not clairvoyant about some things like you. But I'll bet money he's thinking he'd like to pound my head in for chasing him down last summer. Never mind that he wouldn't work, left his mate and children to run off with an Italian Fairy, got *her* with child then refused to admit it. *You* sent me after him. Remember, Sorceress? *You* had the Whip Master give him ten lashes, but he blames *me*."

"I remember," she said in a bored tone.

"There are two Brownies whose families were feuding over land in Scotland. You sent me to settle that, and it ended in my having to beat one of their sons half to death when he came at me with a knife."

She sighed. "Your *point*?"

He stood up, grabbed the end of the table and violently pushed it aside. Crockery, food and utensils went flying. "My *point*, you old hag, is that I'm sick of your orders. Sick of policing people Clan Leaders should deal with, and I'm damned well through with you! I don't care if you take back whatever spell you have on me, and I change back and forth every two minutes. It can't be worse than being completely ostracized by the entire Order. I'll take responsibility for the way I behave, for living like a hermit, as you put it. But if you can't get your *children* to play nicely with each other," he nodded toward the large gathering of revelers, "it's not going to be my problem any more." He stalked angrily into the nearby woods.

The entire assembly had heard every word.

Shayla watched the others as a poignant hush continued. Such a disrespectful outburst shouldn't be ignored, but she hoped someone...*anyone*...would step forward in his defense. That he'd openly defied her wasn't a surprise. The man had been aching for a fight ever since New York and had found the perfect opportunity to pick one. Having made his feelings so public, he knew she'd be forced to judge him. Gryph's parents were presumably back at the castle by now. They shouldn't be the ones to constantly come to his aid. The confrontation from a hurt, albeit drunk and angry man, should have elicited some response. But no one came forward except the Fairy Leader, Lore. She held up her hand to stop him when he would have spoken up for Gryphon and waited. There seemed to be no one else. It was disheartening to think feelings among the Order could be so callous. So, now it was time to hear *their* side.

"Is there nothing to be said?" she loudly asked. The long silence continued, and she grew angry. "There are those of you he's helped." She scanned the crowd. "Torbin, when your granddaughter ran away from home, it was Gryphon who brought her back before she could end up in London in Goddess knows what kind of trouble. And you, Marceau. When the rain almost ruined your crops last year, Gryphon flew to a quarry and brought back stones for a retaining wall. It saved your harvest. He did this without being asked. Did you thank him? Did you offer him a meal or ask him to stay for the night as you would have done anyone else?"

The man bowed his head. "He's not like the rest of us, Sorceress. He's...*different.*"

"Look around us, you fool. Who among us *isn't*? The way you're all responding to his difference is exactly how the outside world would respond to us if we were ever found out. We either stand united or we'll cease to exist. There aren't enough of us to fight off the advancement of a world which presses in on us every year. It's our differences that make us strong, and all you can do is wallow in intolerance the same way as the outsiders. Thousands of them die every year because their skin is differently colored or their eyes aren't the same. Are we no better than they? Have we learned nothing?" She paused. "Some or our traditions should be questioned. Especially anything that keeps us separate from one another."

"How do you mean, Sorceress?" a woman curiously asked and moved forward. Others moved with her.

"I'm saying that our magical powers are growing weaker every year. By the end of this century, there won't be enough new blood to promote genetically healthy offspring. I intended to make the announcement later, but now is appropriate. We should rid ourselves of the idea that we can only mate with our own kind."

The crowd gasped and immediately began to converse with one another.

"The Sorceress is right," came a voice from the forest. Lore, the Fairy Leader, approached Shayla and stood beside her. "The law says that we should mate with our own kind. But that rule could be interpreted as mating with *anyone* who's a member of the Order. Not just Fairy with Fairy or Druid with Druid."

"He makes a point," said a Satyr. "There are only a few of us left. Not enough to breed with after the next ten years."

"But won't that diminish our powers?" asked a man in the crowd.

"It might *increase* them," said Lore. "Either way, we have no choice. All our numbers are dwindling."

Shayla let the discussions continue. After a time, she raised her hands until there was silence. "So let it be. Anyone wishing to handfast and mate with anyone outside their own race or Clan has full blessing. And some of you should find O'Connor and speak with him. What he's done in the past was at my command. From this moment on, Clan Leaders will be responsible for their own people." Many in the crowd smiled in agreement while others discussed the possibilities of the Sorceress' edict.

"What of Gryphon? Will you punish him for his disrespect to you?" the Fairy Leader asked in a low tone.

Shayla smiled and shrugged. "All he really did was toss a table aside. There are those present who've already done that while celebrating a bit too much."

Lore laughed. "True. But, he *did* call you an old hag in front of everyone."

She frowned and placed her hands on her hips. "Yes, and that *will* have to be addressed. First, find him and make sure he's all right. The man had more liquor in him than a Dublin pub."

"As you command," Lore bowed slightly, grinned, then raced off to find Gryphon.

***

Gryphon fixed his blurred gaze on the moon. "Are you thinking of me?" he whispered to the night sky, hoping his question might reach the right person. Then he pushed his hair off his face with both hands and held his aching head. If only he could get her out of his mind. All he had to do was see some large stone with Celtic pictographs on it, and he'd start thinking how Heather would love to explore the Shire and all the ruins. There were crystal caves below the forest, where semiprecious stones glittered. The castle housed a huge collection of medieval tapestries and scrolls. She could spend a lifetime exploring his world and never see it all. How would she react upon meeting a Leprechaun? He smiled as he pictured the scene.

But she didn't belong in this world any more than he could belong in hers. Despite his disfavor with the Order, this was the only place he could live. Or *exist.* That was all he was really doing. Marking time until life was over. He sighed and resigned himself to leaving for Ireland as soon as he had slept off the booze. After what he'd done tonight, the Sorceress would call him back for some kind of punishment, and it would be severe. Gryphon couldn't bring himself to care.

There was a rustle in the bushes near him. He growled and slowly slid down the trunk of an oak, hoping its healing powers could alleviate some of the ill effects of his drinking.

"What do you want?" he spoke to the figure in the undergrowth.

"It's just me, Ursula," the Nymph responded as she moved forward and sat next to him. She pushed her silver hair off her shoulders.

"I told your sisters to leave me alone. Now, I'll tell you the same..."

"Please," she interrupted, "don't send me away. I didn't come to annoy you."

The expression on her beautiful face was uncustomarily serious for a Nymph. Her green eyes glittered in the moonlight. "What, then?"

"I wanted to apologize for the way they've acted."

"Who?"

"My sisters. They've been making some crude comments."

There were very few times in his life anyone had ever apologized to him for anything. It puzzled him into silence.

"They'll apologize to you themselves when I can find the little vixens," she promised.

Gryph swallowed hard and waved a hand in dismissal. "I-it's all right. Guess they only thought of it as a joke."

"Betting on the size of someone's um...well, it isn't funny."

"Wasn't to me. But it's over."

She was silent for a few minutes and watched him stare up at the full moon. "Who is she?"

Startled by the perceptive question, Gryph turned his complete attention to Ursula. "Who's who?"

"The woman. When a man sits alone in the forest staring up at the moonlight, there almost *has* to be a woman involved."

"If *I* had a woman problem, you'd most definitely have heard about it." There was no lack of gossip in the Shire. The *gryphon* having a female would have been the focal point for months.

"Then, it's a *lack* of a woman, isn't it?"

Gryphon sighed. "Look, I'd really rather be alone. I appreciate your trying to be friendly. That happens seldom enough. But this isn't something I want to discuss."

"We don't have to talk." She sidled closer and put her hand on his forearm, then slowly moved it up his arm and pushed his hair back over his shoulder.

In his inebriated, pitiful state, Gryphon was only thinking of one woman. And only she would ever do. "You should go."

"You're lonely."

"I'm drunk."

"I know. It doesn't matter. It doesn't even matter if you're thinking of someone else." She placed her hand on his cheek, turned his face toward her and leaned into him. She started to kiss him.

He leaned away and stared at her."This isn't right, Ursula. You shouldn't be with a man whose attention isn't on you one-hundred percent. I *am* thinking of someone else."

"I don't care," she repeated. "If you can't be with her for some reason, maybe she'd understand."

That was the trouble. Heather *would*. She'd want him to be happy, but rolling in the moss with a Nymph wouldn't replace the emptiness he felt. And a woman should have more self-respect than to want to lie with a man just to satisfy her lust.

"Do you want this woman to be happy?"

He closed his eyes. "Yes."

"Then, you'd want her to find someone, wouldn't you?"

The thought of it filled him with jealousy. Especially when he knew no one cold ever love her the way he could. She'd someday lie with some man who'd open her creamy, soft thighs and pleasure her all night. Would she be thinking of *him*?

"Gryphon, we aren't handfasting. We'd just be giving each other a fantasy for the night. No strings attached. You could even pretend I'm this other woman," Ursula suggested.

He turned his head away. "I could never do that. There'll never be anyone for me but her," he solemnly announced.

"If that's the way it is, then I'll go, warrior."

"You should find someone who's sober. Someone who'll care for you, Nymph. There's nothing worse than being with someone just to ease an ache or to tamp down the fires of lust. Without love, there's nothing. Nothing but emptiness. I know. I'll always know."

She gently touched his hand. "I'll ask the Goddess for a favor on your behalf."

"Ask, beg, plead. Won't do any good. Not on my behalf. She doesn't listen. So, save your prayers for yourself." To his ears it sounded pathetic but true. There were no other words to describe the situation. Without Heather, he'd spend the rest of his existence in a kind of living hell. He'd want her, but could never even touch her face again or see her smile. Perhaps she was even getting on with her life as he sat around in a drunken stupor. But he just couldn't think of going on. And he could never take one woman when another held his heart in her hands.

"I'll go now, Gryphon."

"It's best you do. And please ask your sisters to never make a joke out of me again. It's painful, and I have my limits."

Ursula nodded, backed away, and left him to his pain.

After the Nymph left, he undressed and sprawled beneath the moonlight. At least he could try to dream of her. No one could take away dreams. And maybe, some time in the future, his life could end while visiting his dream world. And he could be in a place where outsiders and those of the Order could live as one. A dream of forever.

FIFTEEN

"I'm sorry, Sorceress. This is how I found him." Lore shrugged.

"Get him up and dressed," she angrily ordered. "I've had enough of this."

Lore shook his head as Shayla strode away. "You're in for it now, old sod." He bent down and roughly shook Gryphon awake. "Come on, man. Wake up. The Sorceress wants you, and I mean *now*."

Gryphon slowly pushed himself to a sitting position as Lore threw his clothing at him. "Tell her to go bugger off!"

Lore leaned back and howled with laughter. "Not in *this* lifetime, old friend. I like my balls right where they are, thanks."

Every nerve in Gryph's body screamed in pain. His head felt like a blacksmith's anvil, and his movements were slow and clumsy. All he wanted to do was go back to sleep until the booze wore off. But Lore didn't look as though he was going anywhere without dragging *him* along, too. He glanced at the tall man, pushed his hair off his face and used a tree to help himself stand.

"Did she send you to babysit?"he grumbled.

"You can say that. Now, hurry up," Lore urged.

Despite his friend's insistence, Gryph took his time dressing. Then he walked to a small brook to throw water on his face. The reflection in the water didn't remotely resemble the man he used to be. The one he knew *she* cared for. He shook his head in self-disgust then stood up. Lore, standing some yards away, beckoned him to follow. Gryphon almost turned and walked the other way out of sheer contrariness. But it was quite possible the Sorceress would punish Lore for not bringing him back, just to make a point. In the past, the woman had had men beaten for less.

He couldn't quite remember everything he'd told the Sorceress last night, but he *did* recall saying he wasn't doing her bidding any longer. No matter. He was tired. Tired of being someone's bloodhound and sick of having no more relationship other than that which could be gleaned from a tawdry night on the forest floor. All that was finished.

"Come on, Lore. Let's get this over with." He strode ahead of the Fairy Leader, determined to get it through the Sorceress' head that she didn't control him.

They found her in the middle of the great clearing, watching some of the men practicing with medieval weapons. For thousands of years, such practices had been taking place. Though the weaponry and the use of it was ancient, there was still no better way to silently defend the Shire and its inhabitants. Unlike a gun, a sword made no noise, and was lethal to any outsider who wouldn't leave when told to do so.

Shayla turned to face them when she sensed their approach. Lore bowed and, with an almost imperceptible nod from her, the Fairy Leader left. She glared at Gryphon and walked toward the woods, confident as ever that he'd follow.

Gryph watched Lore leave and wondered why a man with such pride would humble himself before a woman as cold as winter ice. He stood his ground and waited for her to realize he wasn't going to follow. Not now or ever again. He watched the furious expression on her face grow as she had to retrace her steps and walk back to where he stood.

"I'll have you beaten to within an inch of your life for being so insolent," she growled.

Realizing she was speaking about more than just his refusal to follow her like a puppy, Gryphon carelessly shrugged. "I don't give a flaming rat's ass."

Truly shocked by his lack of respect, she moved to within a foot of him and stared up into his unshaven face. "You really don't care *what* I do to you."

"If the most you can do is have me killed, there are worse things." A calm came over him. At that instant, he knew he really *didn't* care.

"And what about your parents, Gryphon? Don't you care that they'll suffer if I punish you?"

"They have each other." He sighed. "They'll get over it."

Shayla walked around him in a slow, methodical circle. He ignored her movements and stared straight ahead, a dead look in his eyes. She wasn't sure she'd ever seen a man look so unconcerned about himself. When she faced him again, she gazed into his dark eyes for some time before speaking.

"It occurs to me that a man without a reason to live is a dangerous thing." She paused before continuing. "I'll give you something to worry about."

Gryphon took a slow, deep breath, refused to rise to the bait and kept staring into the distance. She couldn't argue with someone who simply wouldn't let himself be manipulated any more.

"In two weeks, at the end of the Samhain celebration, I want you before the bonfire. You'll stand before the Order and accept my judgement. Will you show up on your own and accept it like a man, or will I have to have you dragged there in chains?"

Gryphon sharply turned his head toward her and glared. "I'll be there, Sorceress. Don't send anyone for me unless you want them dead." He quickly turned and stomped into the woods.

She watched him go, sadly shook her head and murmured to herself. "You're making things so much more difficult than they ever needed to be, my lad. And you're going to feel quite foolish before it's all through." With that thought still on her mind, she smiled and walked back toward the castle.

***

Gryphon took one last long look in the mirror. Only out of pride and respect for his parents had he showered, shaved and put on his best black leather. He'd painted his face with the blue woad marks of his Celtic forebears, braided his hair as a warrior and belted on his broadsword. Though he had no intention of using his weapon, he was still a Druid warrior, member of a noble lineage and would take his place for judgement looking the part. Whatever happened, he was determined his mother and father wouldn't have any reason to feel any more shame on his behalf. He looked out the castle window, grabbed his black cape and turned toward the door.

Upon hearing he was to be judged, his parents had pled with him for days to apologize to the Sorceress for his behavior. James had railed on about the need for conformity and how the safety of the Order as a whole depended upon obedience to her will. Gryph had heard it all before. Obedience had never gained him a thing except contempt from the very people he'd tried, albeit grudgingly, to serve. And he couldn't conform when there were no standards for being a *gryphon.*

The worst of it was watching his mother sit and silently cry. To her he had apologized. It almost broke his heart, what was left of it, to hear her beg his forgiveness for meddling with his future. He shook the thoughts away and kept walking.

Judgements usually meant beatings or worse. As he approached the bonfire, he couldn't see any sign of Legion, the Whip Master. That meant he was due for the *worst.* It just didn't matter any more. He stood at the fringe of the crowd, pulled Heather's blue scarf from his leather jerkin and tied it around his left bicep. As members of the Order saw him and word quickly spread that he'd appeared for judgement, the crowd silenced and parted. He heard murmured whispers about the scarf, and it gave Gryphon one last moment of perverse pleasure. Tied as it was, the scarf represented the medieval favor of a woman and would cause gossip and confusion as to who its owner might be.

Before them all, the Sorceress stood on a large stone platform. Flames from the fire reached far overhead and provided an eery background for her. The wind blew her long silver hair and white robe as she raised her hand and beckoned him forward.

His parents stood to the Sorceress' left, several other hooded figures to her right. Gryphon moved forward, climbed the steps and faced her with his head held high. He could hear his mother crying and was sorry for her sake. He was vaguely aware of his father pulling her close. There had been no other way things could end. He simply didn't belong.

Using her powers over the wind, the Sorceress amplified her voice so that everyone could hear. "Face the crowd, Gryphon O'Connor."

He turned and looked into the faces of those nearest him. Lore looked back and slowly shook his head. There was true regret in the Fairy's eyes. As others moved a little closer to the platform, Gryphon imagined he could see that some of them wore the same expression. Perhaps that was just his subconscious trying to make it easier. His brain's way of making final preparation.

The Sorceress' powers were awesome. She could destroy him with a wave of her hand. He took a deep breath, looked straight ahead and cleared his mind. No matter what anyone thought of him now, he was a warrior, and frost would form at the hottest regions on Earth before he'd show fear. His ancestors had fought alongside King Arthur. Gryphon was determined that his last actions wouldn't shame that history or himself.

Shayla stepped forward and stood beside him. "Have you anything to say, O'Connor?"

He stared straight ahead, kept his mouth shut and let the crowds think what they would. His last thoughts were his own, and they were thousands of miles away with a woman he loved and wouldn't ever see again.

"What I do now is for your own good and that of the Order." She stopped, lifted her eyebrows in an imperial fashion and caught the blue scarf as it fluttered in the Autumn breeze. Then she turned and addressed one of the hooded figures across the platform. "Does this belong to you?"

The figure came forward, walked in front of Gryphon and turned to face him. "Yes, it's mine."

As if it were happening in a dream, Gryphon slowly lowered his gaze from the horizon and stared into her face. *"Heather,"* he mouthed. His voice had deserted him.

James and Gwyneth rushed forward.

"You brought her here to watch our son's judgement? An *outsider*?" James angrily whispered.

"You'll get her killed," Gwyneth gasped in a low voice.

"Hush, both of you, and step back. This is among Gryphon,

this woman and me. And a judgement doesn't necessarily mean punishment."

James reluctantly pulled Gwyneth back.

Heather and Gryphon hadn't heard the exchange. They stared, fixated, at one another.

The crowd began to mill about, and a murmur of voices rose over the confusion on the platform. Shayla turned to them, raised her hands and loudly announced, "This woman claims the right to handfast with The O'Connor." She quickly walked toward Heather, pulled her away from Gryphon and pushed back the hood of her green cape. In the blaze of the fire, everyone could see her face.

"She's *lovely*," someone said. "Who is she, does anyone know?"

A general commotion began among the Order. Shayla waited and watched.

Still too stunned to react, Gryphon stood and tried to focus. *What in the name of Herne is Shayla doing*? Some instinctive part of him screamed out that he should get to Heather. Protect her. Another part of his brain was telling him that judgement had been passed, he was in the next life and she was there with him. It made no sense. For the first time in his life, his mind and body just wouldn't connect. It was all like some alternate reality.

"Since O'Connor doesn't seem to have anything to say, I'll challenge him for the girl," a loud voice rang out. A tall man in a black, hooded cape stepped from the back of the crowd. Everyone gasped and backed away.

"Valerian," Shayla acknowledged, "come forward."

He sauntered toward the platform, mounted the steps and bowed before the Sorceress. His gaze drifted toward Heather, moved up and down her slender form appreciatively, then back to Shayla. "I want her."

Heather began to shake. The man was dangerously handsome, but his green eyes held no warmth at all.

"You don't even know her, man. Why do you challenge?" Shayla asked.

His eyes met Heather's. "She's just too damned beautiful to let the *gryphon* have her."

The sound of a sword being drawn caused the crowd to gasp. The blade of it came within inches of Valerian's chest.

"Back away from her, or you die," Gryphon snarled. He'd finally been propelled forward by the overwhelming need to protect what he saw as *his*.

Valerian threw back his cape and quickly drew his own sword.

"Not on the platform," Shayla warned, then turned to the crowd. "Clear an area."

The Order moved back.

Gryphon backed the man down the steps of the platform by holding his sword to his chest. The instant Valerian's boots hit the ground, Gryphon was on him with a ferocity he'd never before felt. He swung his blade in a high arc toward the other man's skull.

Valerian raised his to block, then swung low toward Gryphon's chest. The tip of his sword caught Gryph breast high and slashed a long mark through the leather of his jerkin. Steel cut into his flesh.

The wound was minor, but the feel of his own blood being drawn energized Gryphon, and he swung his blade even harder. In accordance with ancient law, it was forbidden for any member of the Order to shape shift when a challenge such as this was made. Gryphon wouldn't have changed whether that rule existed or not. He wanted blood drawn with his own *human* hands. Years of frustration and anger poured out of him. Over and over he pummeled the man with blows and barely gave him a chance to do anything but block. He was fighting for everything he ever wanted, and *no one* would stop him.

Heather watched in horror. One of them would die while fighting over her. She would have moved into the fray, but James quickly pulled her back and pushed her into Gwyneth's embrace. The older woman held on to her. Though Heather tried to break away, Gwyn was stronger, and James came to his mate's aid. They wouldn't let her free. Wouldn't let her get to Gryph.

Fighting for his life, Valerian thrust his broadsword toward Gryphon's abdomen. Gryph jumped back, and the other man charged. Valerian hit him in the face with his elbow, and Gryphon fell backwards and to his knees.

Valerian saw it as a way to finish Gryphon off, moved to his rear and swung down toward the kneeling man's head. Gryph blocked the blow by bringing his sword up and parallel to the ground. In a split second, he was on his feet, swung around and sliced his attacker's thigh open.

Valerian dropped his weapon and hit the ground. Panting, Gryphon moved over him and placed the blade of his sword to the man's chest. The beaten man raised his hand.

"I yield, O'Connor." He sucked in air as his open wound continued to bleed. "You must want her very badly."

For a moment, Gryphon wasn't sure he'd let it end. That *anyone* would challenge him for Heather angered him beyond control. He moved the blade across the man's chest and over his heart.

"Stop it, Son. He's yielded." James came quickly down the platform and grasped his son's sword arm. When it appeared the *yield* would be ignored, James placed his hand on Gryphon's shoulder and attempted to pull him away. "Stop, *now*."

Gryphon turned to the crowd. "Anyone else?" he shouted.

Those nearest to him quickly moved away. Gryph glared at them in contempt and slowly backed away from Valerian. He watched as if in a daze while his father ordered others to take the injured challenger to the castle and have his wound tended. When the elder O'Connor turned to face him, Gryphon stared into his father's face.

"I don't know what in bloody blazes is going on either, Son," James answered Gryphon's silent, expressive plea for an explanation. "Come on."

They mounted the steps to the platform, and Heather rushed forward and threw her arms about him. He dropped his sword to the stone beneath his feet and held her. She tilted her head back and gazed up at him, and he was lost.

"Handfast them quickly before someone *else* challenges," James pleaded.

"After what your son just did, I don't see that happening." Shayla smirked. "Still, that's what she's here for. Best to get on with it."

She pushed the couple apart, clasped their hands together and held them with one of hers. From her pouch, she drew a long silver ribbon and wrapped it around their joined hands. "Before the Goddess and all creatures, I bind you in one heart, mind, body and soul. Blessed be."

When Gryphon stood, trance-like, and stared at Heather, Shayla impatiently pushed them both toward the steps. "*Goblins teeth,* man!" Shayla groused. "You've got her. You're handfasted. Now, take her away someplace so the rest of us can get on with the Samhain celebration."

Without even glancing at Shayla or his parents, Gryphon took Heather's hand, strode down the steps and into the woods.

SIXTEEN

He walked until they were some distance from the clearing then dropped her hand and stopped. He didn't want to face her. Gryphon was afraid she wouldn't be there, that she was some illusion and this was another of the Sorceress' ways to punish him. And, if she wasn't real, this particular retribution was worse than killing him outright. Shayla had been right when she'd said, '*I'll give you something to worry about.*' If he turned and Heather was gone, he'd go mad.

Heather placed her hand on his back. "Gryph?" she whispered.

He swallowed hard and slowly turned toward the sound of her voice. Moonlight poured over the tiny glen where they stood. She pushed the hood of her robe back, and something deep inside him broke loose. Gryph roughly pulled her into his embrace and held her as tightly as he could. She responded by wrapping her arms around his neck and nuzzling his cheek with her own. The warmth of her soft flesh told him she was real, and he held on for a very long time. His mind wasn't able to grasp the *whys* of the situation. She was *real*, and that was all that mattered.

Finally, Heather pushed herself away far enough to gaze up into his face. "Guess you're wondering what a girl like me is doing in a place like this?"

He began to breathe hard. For the first time in his life, Gryphon actually believed he was going to have what people referred to as an anxiety attack. Words left him as he stupidly tried to get his brain and his vocal chords to connect. His experiences had never left him ready for such a situation.

Heather put her hands on either side of his face and smiled. "I missed you so much. I couldn't wait to see you again."

Gryphon pulled her head against his shoulder, held her again and groped for words. "I don't...why...how..."

She smiled. "That's about as *inarticulate* as I've ever heard you." She pushed away and disconnected from the embrace. Gryph was really having a hard time with seeing her in the Shire, and her heart went out to him. Here was a man used to having some control of the situation, and Shayla had pulled a rug right out from under him and the rest of the Order. Later, they'd laugh about this. Right now, it wasn't funny. Not for him. She could only guess at what was going through his mind. Since for the moment he couldn't seem to pull himself together, she'd have to do the talking.

"Shayla brought me here to be with you."

He put a shaking hand to his head and tried to speak again. "You can't...you can't be here. It isn't safe."

"It is now." She nodded in the direction from which they'd come. "Shayla is back there explaining a few things to the rest of the Order. About the rune stones and what happened in New York."

He grabbed her by the shoulders as his panic finally found a voice. "You aren't one of us, Heather. You *can't* be here."

"Maybe you'd better sit down," she spoke calmly and pushed him backward. His knees buckled as he came up against the downed trunk of a tree. He sat and looked at her. The dazed expression wasn't like him and she started to worry a little. Now, it was her turn to help *him* through a crazy situation.

"After you left New York, the Sorceress came to see me and she gave me a choice. I could stay there or come here." She paused, took his hands and slowly continued. "She wants to bring outsiders into the Order. I'm the first, Gryph."

"Why?" He shook his head when the question came out a little too harsh. "I...I mean...why is she doing such a thing, and why *now*?"

"Simple matter of numbers. In a hundred years, the Order won't be here if you don't bring in some new people. You can't inbreed, and that's what it'll come down to. As to why she's doing this now, I think she finally found someone she could trust to bring in and a way to do it."

"She's using you to see if her crazy plans will work?" His gaze moved around the clearing, and he stood and started to pace. "They'll never accept you. If they won't regard *me* as one of their own, what in the name of Herne does she think they'll do to you?"

She shrugged. "Nothing."

He abruptly turned. "You're not in New York anymore, or haven't you noticed? Just because Shayla, Sorceress of the Ancients, wants something doesn't mean everyone will abide by her decisions. That's exactly why I've had to go after some of our own people on occasion. What in the name of Danu does she think she's doing? No Sorceress has *ever* done anything like this." He raised his hands in exasperation and continued to stalk around the glen. "No Sorceress in our history has ever..."

"Gryph?"she tried to interrupt his ranting.

"I've got to get you out of here."

She pulled her arm free when he tried to lead her away. "I was going to save this until later, but I don't think you're going to listen to me until you know everything."

She quickly backed away and pulled off her robe. "I was going to break this to you differently, a little more tactfully. But I just don't see any other way. Shayla's right. You've sometimes got a head like a brick."

The shocked expression he wore prompted her to act fast. Heather knelt on one knee and willed the *change*. It was much easier now that she had hours of practice behind her. The first time had been hell. It had taken her body a while to get used to the transformation. Now it came as easily as breathing.

Gryphon backed away as he saw the beginnings of the transformation. "NO! Goddess, Heather, what have you done?"

The answer came to him almost immediately. She'd used the damned rune stones, and Shayla had allowed it. He continued to watch as a bright white light haloed Heather's slender form. From within, a shape formed, grew and emerged. He fell to his knees in absolute wonder. She changed into the most enchantingly beautiful thing he'd ever seen. And the stones had, true to legend, transformed her into a creature which reflected the true nature of her soul.

A graceful white gryphon, sizes smaller than his own alter ego, stood proudly before him. In his other form, he could easily spread one of his own wings and shelter her beneath it. Without pausing, he walked forward and placed his hands upon either side of her noble head. For a long time they stood there. Tears formed in his eyes, and it took a while before he could speak without sobbing uncontrollably. He leaned into her neck, and she brought up one silver claw and gently wrapped it around his shoulder. A hug.

That did it. He plunged his face into the sparkling, opalescent feathers at her neck and openly wept. A small chortling noise issued from her throat, and he stroked one perfectly white leonine shoulder. Her wings glistened like diamonds in the moonlight. Something on the feathers had a sparkling quality. Like Fairy dust. He'd seen his own reflection in mountain lakes and pools. Compared to her, he was like a dark shadow. But *she* was exquisite. An absolute wonder. No one in the Order would ever look upon her as a monster. But he sensed a great, noble strength. It would have taken those attributes in her character to make her so light and ethereal. She was a complete match to his masculine, dark side. A great calm came over him, and love swept away his doubts.

She gently nudged him back with her silver beak. As soon as he was far enough away, she changed back and slowly looked up from her kneeling position. Heather chewed at her lower lip, waiting for what he'd say or do.

Seeing her worried expression, Gryph's heart went out to her. She wanted acceptance the same way he had. He'd give her more than that. So much more. Swallowing back the remainder of his tears, he held up his head and grabbed her green robe from the ground. He knelt down beside her and wrapped it carefully around her body. "You're shivering," he whispered and pulled her close. "I'll have to make you a larger crane bag so you can carry clothing and..."

"Oh, Gryph," she cried out and threw herself into his embrace.

"Easy now, little one. It's all right," he comforted her and closed his arms around her form. "You didn't know how I'd respond, did you? How could I do *anything* but love you," he told her as she tearfully snuggled into his chest.

"You're not angry with me for using the stones and changing?"

Heather needed his reassurance what was done could not be undone. "I could never be angry with you for any reason, love. I just don't want you to ever have any regrets."

She shook her head in denial. "I wanted to be with you. And...and I *like* what I've become, Gryphon. The first time I flew, it was as if I could reach out and touch the stars. It was wonderful. I'm part of a world I've only dreamed about."

"And the Sorceress intends on letting others use the stones to come here?"

"No." She shook her head and gazed up into his dark eyes. "Unless your heart is right and you're absolutely sure about what you're doing, the stones can kill you. Or turn you into something horrible. She means for me to change people's minds about the outside world, so we'll be accepted without the use of magic. We're not all so frightening, you know."

He rubbed his nose against hers. "Not so frightening at all," he agreed.

"You know, the Sorceress thought I was dead the first time I changed."

"You were hurt?" He plunged his hands into her hair, and his gaze swept over her face and body.

"Only unconscious for a while." She mischievously grinned. "Shayla almost had an aneurysm when I woke up. I scared her half to death."

He laughed and hugged her harder. "Good for you." Maybe Shayla needed a little frightening. She'd meddled in others' lives far too much. But, if she hadn't, he wouldn't have Heather with him now. He wondered if that was what the Sorceress had wanted all along, and if he owed her an apology. Part of his heart softened toward the older woman.

"She told me she's going to put the rune stones where no one will ever find them," Heather explained. "And there are other objects that need to be retrieved. Some as powerful, some not. But they still don't need to be out in the world."

"Let me take a guess." He smiled and rocked her back and forth. "She wants us to find them and bring them back."

"I'm handfasted to a very smart man," she teased and held on to him tighter.

"Not smart enough, apparently. You're freezing." He chaffed her hands and rearranged the robe around her body. "We can talk about all this later. Right now, we need to get you warm. You aren't used to being outside in the night air."

She snuggled even closer as he picked her up and carried her farther into the woods. He finally stopped under a tremendous oak and lowered her next to it. "Stay here. I'll gather some wood."

Heather watched as he gathered small dead branches from the forest floor and quickly circled the pile of branches with stones.

He closed his eyes. "Duir, I thank you for the use of your branches. Peace be with you and on all nature." He opened his eyes, glanced at Heather and saw her smile brightly. There were many aspects about life in the Order which she'd have to learn. It helped that she had an extensive background in ancient Celtic ways.

"What are you thinking?" she asked.

"How wonderful it's going to be. Teaching you everything about the Order. Watching you learn and just...just *being* with you." He passed a hand over the dried wood, and a warm flame reached for the sky.

"I don't think you can teach me *that*," she grinned as his hand rose to strengthen the fire.

He moved toward her, pulled her back into his arms and softly murmured, "I can teach you how a man of the Order receives his new mate. I was so shocked at seeing you that I'm afraid you weren't properly welcomed. Forgive me?"

Before she could respond, his mouth closed over hers, and his hands pushed the robe away. Gryphon took one of her hands and gently placed it over that part of his body which was rapidly hardening. "Help me with my clothes," he breathed. "If I don't take you soon, I'm afraid I'll wake up and all this will have just been some wonderful dream."

Heather quickly undressed him as his hands caressed her body. He placed his own cloak beneath her to make a soft bed, then covered her body with his. She stroked the muscles of his bare chest with the tips of her fingers and placed a tiny kiss over his heart. Gryph moaned when her lips teased at his nipple and hardened it. He drew in a swift breath at the touch and felt even more blood rush into his groin. He grasped her shoulders and held her to him, letting her touch and taste where she would. The feelings were so sensuously erotic that the world around him began to dim and waver. Long, graceful fingers enticed his manhood, and every cell in is body *ached* for her.

Heather wanted to touch every part of him and to have him touch her. Every muscle in his body gleamed in the moonlight. He was as hard as iron and as ready for her as she was for him. A bronzed Celtic god for the taking.

He softly stroked between her thighs and saw her chest rise and fall as her breathing became heavier. He intended to love her until sanity left them both. Gryphon pushed her breasts together and circled each nipple with his hot tongue.

"I'm going to take you now," he huskily breathed. "Nothing and no one on Earth is ever going to come between us again. I *swear* it."

She opened her thighs for him and he quickly stroked forward. Heather cried out and clung to him, tangling her hands in his long, thick hair. Their moans of delight were the only sounds besides the small chirping of night insects. Gryphon felt her tighten convulsively around him.

"Not, yet, girl." He withdrew slightly wanting to make sure the moment was right for both of them.

"Yes, Gryphon. It's been too long. *Please,*" she begged.

He smiled down at her, then moved slowly forward again. "All right, love. Here I am." And he knew he was ready. The look in her silver-blue gaze captured him.

She gripped his hips and began to moan with each stroke. This was what he'd been waiting for all his life. A woman with fire enough to love him no matter what. Gryphon plunged into her, and she cried out as her body and his fit together perfectly. He released, and his cry of complete ecstasy joined hers. He thrust all the way through his intense climax, and she held him until his senses returned.

She lay trembling in his embrace, and he cuddled her close. He'd never felt more wonderful and he wanted to know she felt it, too. "I love you, girl. Don't ever, ever doubt it."

"I love you, too, and missed you so much." She kissed his temple as he snuggled his head into her shoulder.

"We're together now. That's all that matters," he breathed. "And you're *mine*."

He covered her body with his to keep her warm, then pulled her robe over the lower half of them. It was the most perfect bed he'd ever enjoyed. "I had a fantasy about making love to you in the woods. In a soft bed with the stars out."

She looked up at him, and they softly kissed. "Love me again."

He chuckled softly. "My *pleasure*. Anything you want."

He took her more slowly, savoring every inch of her form, kissing her slim thighs, running his hands down the soft length of her and feeling her stroke the muscles of his back. When her fingers skimmed over the scars formed when he fought Niall Alexander, she frowned. But he quickly kissed the frown away.

"It's nothing," he told her. "There isn't any kind of wound that hurts like those inflicted on a heart."

Tears pooled in her eyes for him. "My poor darling."

"No, my love. Don't cry for me. You're very quickly mending every wound I've ever had."

She pulled him to her, and they made love until dawn.

***

Shayla and Gwyneth silently crept through the woods so the sleeping lovers wouldn't awaken. Gryphon's senses would alert him to danger, but as neither of the women posed such a threat, he slept on. Unconsciously, he pulled Heather more protectively into his embrace and placed a gentle kiss against her hair. Gwyneth watched with loving indulgence as her son held the sleeping woman in his arms. Her family had just increased by one.

"We'll leave the food here," Shayla pointed to a low, flat

stone which could serve as a table. "I'll restart the fire for them."

Gwyneth nodded while carefully rearranging Heather's robe over them. She placed Gryphon's sword against a nearby stone, knowing that it was part of the ancient ritual that he emerge from the forest with it strapped to his side. As a finishing touch, she place a bottle of wine on the makeshift stone table. Shayla placed changes of clothing nearby so that Gryphon and Heather could take their time coming back to the castle.

"There now," Shayla whispered, "this is as cozy a spot as I've ever seen for a handfasting to be consummated."

Gwyneth agreed, looking around the small clearing at their handiwork. "Yes, they could easily stay until tomorrow night if they wanted. Everything they could need is here."

"Come, Gwyn. I know you're anxious to get back to James, and these two should be left to um, *sort things out*, so to speak."

Gwyn took one more look at her son and new daughter. Pride in them both filled her heart. "I was shocked to learn she'd given up so much to be with Gryphon. I mean...risking her life using those stones. She must really love him. Do you think he knows what she's done?"

"I'm sure she's told him. But I'll never let those cursed stones be used again. She could have been changed into something...well, there's no use going into it. Everything has turned out far better than I expected. The woman learns fast. My people in the States tell me she's nothing short of brilliant. They've been teaching her for weeks before she arrived here. And, depending upon how she behaves in front of the Order, it'll make things much easier for the rest of the outsiders who'll follow. Every other problem of a personal nature must be worked out between the two of them. Now, come along," Shayla advised. "Let's let them be."

Some time after the women left, Gryphon woke to a warm, brightly burning campfire. He smiled, knowing his mother had been present. Only Gwyneth would have thought to bring his sword. He glanced down, Heather snuggled closer to him to absorb some of his warmth. Resting on one elbow, Gryph began to trace a lazy finger down one of her smooth white shoulders.

That was when he noticed for the first time the Celtic marks on her arms. They exactly matched his except for being much smaller in size and more feminine. He touched them gently.

"Love," he whispered in awe, "that you would go through the pain it took to make these..."

"Mmmmm , it wasn't that painful. Besides, I like them," she murmured sleepily. "Keep me warm, Gryph." Heather smiled as she moved even closer into his chest.

He immediately pulled her beneath him and rested his weight on his arms. "I have a way to keep you flaming," he grinned mischievously.

Heather opened her eyes, smiled and brought her arms up to encircle his neck. "Then quit talking and let's see a little action."

Gryph pushed her heavy, silken hair back from her face and kissed her slowly. Heather responded by rotating her hips against his sensitive erection.

"Woman, you awaken beautifully." He felt he could drown in the cool depths of her silver gaze.

She pushed him until their positions reversed. *She* was now on top and wanted to watch him as she slid onto his erection. "*Ahhhh Heather*, you're more lovely than a spring day on the moors," he gasped, closing his eyes and letting her soft sheath surround him.

Her hands touched, caressed, and massaged his body, lingering on the Celtic designs on his arms and moving down to those on his inner thighs. He held her firmly on him by placing his hands around her waist and her back. She rocked back and forth, slowly bringing him close to release. Gryphon suddenly sat up and moved with her. Their gazes locked, and Heather felt a wonderful pressure begin deep within her womb. The feeling was so incredibly satisfying that she feared the intensity. Gryph's breathing deepened and matched hers.

"Gryph...I can't...it's...ooooooh," Heather cried out.

"Don't stop, love. Don't..." Gryph never finished as he lost himself within her. Heather fell against his shoulder, crying out when her own climax began and went on long enough to render her completely sated.

They clung to each other as their breathing began to slow and their pulses calmed. Gryphon lay back down into the soft leather cloak beneath them and pulled her robe back over them both. "It will always be this way between us, love. Hot and intense. I love you, Heather. With all my heart and soul."

Heather raised her head to look into eyes as dark as the night. "Gryphon, my sweet, sweet warrior. I can't believe all of this is real, that you're here with me and we're finally together. I've wanted you so badly. Some nights the hurt wouldn't stop. I love you so much."

"Ah, little one, there'll be no more hurting," Gryphon promised and pulled her back into his embrace, gently rocking her. "We've both done our share of that."

She let him hold her and watched the fire burn. The silence they shared was so peaceful, and Heather never wanted it to end. Her body tensed as she heard bushes rustle several yards away.

Gryphon reached for his sword, then stopped. What he sensed was small and defenseless. No threat at all. "Who's there?"

"Just me," a small voice answered.

Heather grabbed her robe and quickly made sure she and Gryphon were modestly covered. A small girl, probably about three years of age, walked out of the bushes. She had soft golden curls trailing down her back, and her dress was a shift made from some gauzy green fabric. It sparkled in the light. Heather smiled at the little figure. She was absolutely darling.

"I was just hunting berries," she explained.

"You're Lily, aren't you?" Gryphon smiled at her.

"Uh-huh. And you're the *gryphon*." Lily pointed at Heather. "Everyone says she's an outsider. Is that so?"

"She came from outside, but she's one of us now," Gryphon said.

"She's pretty."

"Yes. Yes, she is." He turned to look proudly at his new mate. "Her name is Heather, and she and I were handfasted last night."

There was a gentleness in his eyes that made Heather's

heart fall into her stomach. He wasn't angry or upset with the child's interruption. Just patiently explaining. The girl had obviously used the berry hunting excuse to see the outsider. For the first time, she realized how closed off these people had been. Lily had probably never been allowed out of the Shire.

"Can I watch you fly sometimes?"

Gryphon chuckled. Lily had bounced to a completely different subject. "Of course you can. Heather is a gryphon, too. And she's much more beautiful than I. You could watch us *both*."

Lily smiled and nodded. "Goody! I get to be the first to see you both fly. I'm gonna' tell Merrybelle. She said you'd say no."

The little girl ran off to find whoever Merrybelle was, and Gryphon smiled at her tiny, retreating figure. Heather watched him closely.

When he turned back, it was to see Heather's face with a particularly intense expression, and he immediately knew what she was thinking. His heart began to sink. So much happiness had been offered. So many things had happened in the last day. Now, the final challenge to their relationship would come, and he wasn't sure the newly formed, sweet alliance could withstand her questions. He turned away.

"You like children," she simply stated.

"Yes," he sighed. "But they're usually afraid to be near me."

"Lily wasn't."

"Her curiosity about you overcame that."

"Gryphon?" She placed a hand on his shoulder.

"Don't, Heather. Please don't ask."

"You don't want to have children of your own?"

He swiftly turned back. "Of *course* I do. But I don't want a child born like me. Not if it will have to go through...never mind."

"Gryphon, I want you to listen to me." She took a deep breath and continued. "In the future, there are going to be a lot of children born here who might or might *not* have the powers their parents have. They may even look different. But something tells me their parents won't care once they're holding them in their arms. It's going to happen. The Order will be extinct unless it does. What if we have children and they *are* gryphons? Or what if they don't have any powers at all? Would you love them any less?"

"I'd love my children no matter what," he replied with intensity. "And no one would ever hurt them. Never."

She sighed. "Then what's your problem with having them some day? Everyone *else's* will be different, too. And, even in the outside world, there aren't any guarantees about how a baby will be born, what it will look like, or whether it's healthy. The best people can do is hope and pray. The Order doesn't have a monopoly on fears about their kids and what will happen to them, you know. But life goes on, and things usually work out pretty well."

He gazed into her eyes for a long moment. Something inside him finally tore away and flew free. The last of his fears. She'd broken down the final barrier, and the love he felt couldn't be more pure or strong.

"You're right," he whispered as a dozen scenarios came to mind. Sons and daughters to watch grow, and an Order full of children who tolerated each others' differences. Plans of a future he'd never thought possible flooded his brain and he smiled again. "And you'd love our children, too." It was a statement rather than a question. She'd make a wonderful mother.

"Yes, I'd love them. Just the way I love you. And, trust me on this, there's no limit to it, Gryphon. No limit and no strings attached."

In the deepest part of him, he knew she was speaking the absolute truth. Why would she have risked her life to be with him otherwise? He touched her cheek with his fingertips and softly kissed her. "I'm the luckiest man on Earth."

She moved into his embrace and held on tight. "*I'm* the lucky one. Now, hold me. Never let me go."

"Not even after a million lifetimes have passed, Heather. I'll never, *ever* let you go."

***

"Forgive me for disturbing your work, Sorceress." The young girl curtsied as she entered the castle room where Shayla was preparing for her full moon prophecy.

Shayla looked up from the scrying bowl she had been preparing. "What is it, Lyla?"

"*The O'Connor* is here to see you. He says it won't wait."

"Very well." Shayla waved a hand. "Show him in." She watched the girl walk into the hallway and heard her speak quietly to someone there.

Gryphon walked into the room and knelt before Shayla. Two of the most perfect weeks a man could ever imagine had just passed. But there were things that needed to be said, and his heart and conscience demanded that he leave Heather long enough to confront the Sorceress with his feelings.

"I expected you'd still be in the abbey with Heather. I hear things are going better than hoped," Shayla said as she looked down at the large man's bowed head. When he looked up into her eyes, she saw the face of a man whose life had been transformed. The worry, anger and defiance had left his dark gaze. In place of those emotions Shayla detected contrition, and there was a sense of deep, abiding peace. She smiled at him, motioned for him to stand and was rewarded with a winning grin.

"I'm sorry I haven't come sooner, Sorceress. My only excuse is that Heather and I have been...well, we've been quite busy."

"Whatever the reason for your visit, you've always been welcome here. And people have been saying good things about her presence in the Shire. The outside world isn't nearly so frightening to many now that she's been introduced."

His guilt increased that much more. "She loves it here."

"Of course she does. This is where her heart lives."

Gryphon knew she was speaking of *him* as much as anything else. He nodded and prepared himself to bare his soul. It was the only way to ease his mind, and Heather had been in full agreement with his confronting the Sorceress with his declarations. They'd spoken of it at length. So much had happened that he felt he had to make amends for his behavior.

The callous man he'd been no longer existed.

"I take it this isn't a social call?" she asked.

He shook his head. "You know it isn't. I've come to beg your forgiveness for my behavior. I've been a pain in the ass since this whole thing began."

"Oh, you were that and then some, young man." She smiled to take the condemning sting from the words. "I take it being in love has somewhat mellowed your attitude?"

Gryphon smiled and nodded in agreement. "You've still had every reason to punish me. Instead, you've made my dreams come true. I can't think why the Whip Master hasn't paid me a visit. I deserve anything you can think up in the way of punishment."

"I don't want you beaten, Gryphon. What I've always wanted, and still need, are your loyalty and obedience. Those aren't qualities I could instill in you at the end of a whip. With people whose heads aren't quite so hard, that particular punishment might have worked. But not on you."

He sighed. "You and Heather are in total agreement over my stubborn nature. I wish I could say it was the Irish influence. Truth is, I was wallowing so much in self-pity that reason, logic and awareness of what I was doing to myself and everyone around me was unimportant. But you have my loyalty and my obedience from this moment on. I'll never question your motives or actions again. And there are others to whom I owe apologies. Beginning with my parents." He raised his hands, palms up, in a supplicating gesture. "There are no words to...no way I can articulate my shame. It'll take me the rest of my life to make up for my actions. You were right about my distancing myself from everyone. I let a few bad instances in my life negatively influence my behavior and my judgement."

"You weren't entirely to blame. It was wrong of me to ask so much of one man. And wrong of the Order to treat you so harshly. Being different from everyone else on Earth *should* have made us that much more tolerant of one another." She sliced her hand through the air in a gesture of denial. "That has to stop. If we're to survive, we must unify. Ignore everything but our common goal to perpetuate a way of life as old as time, and all the magic that goes with it."

"I'll do everything I can to help. All you need do is ask. And Heather has promised to do whatever she can."

Shayla saw before her one of the most penitent and ingenuous hearts she'd ever known. Here was the man he was *truly* meant to be. A warrior with a peaceful heart. She'd heard the rumors that Gryphon had been in the Shire talking with others and gaining acceptance. If bringing in one understanding, gifted outsider could accomplish so much, there was great hope for the future.

"It's amazing what love can do, isn't it?"

"Not to me," he said. "Nothing seems impossible any more. Every day is...I can't tell you how much..." His voice became so thick with emotion it was difficult to continue.

She took one of his hands in hers. "It's all right, Gryphon. I understand. And your apologies are accepted. Now, go back to your mate with my blessings. I'll talk with both of you soon."

Gryphon swallowed hard. "Thank you, Sorceress. You're the wisest of all who've preceded you. You have my eternal gratitude and my *love.*" He kissed her hand, smiled and walked quietly out of the room.

Shayla sniffed back tears and walked to a window. She saw him exit the castle's front entrance and embrace a lithe figure which ran to him in the darkness. Such happiness was the stuff of dreams. But there were others waiting for *their* dreams to come true.

***

Shayla gazed into the black scrying bowl. Great changes were coming. One of the events she saw made her smile broadly. A tiny white gryphon peeked from around her mother's front claw leg. The larger white gryphon nudged it forward, but it shyly stepped back beneath her again. Other children of the Order beckoned for it to come and play. Gryphon, in his Druid form, strode from the woods. Seeing his mate standing in the Goblin Meadow, he opened his arms wide in welcome. The baby gryphon quickly changed into a sweet little girl with blue eyes and long brown hair. She happily ran into her father's embrace, and he lifted her high into the air before gently lowering her to the ground. Their laughter rang out, the joy on his face would have melted the coldest heart. Heather joined him as she wrapped a soft, blue robe about herself. Gryphon pulled her close and kissed her, slow and long. Then, they walked away and laughed merrily as they tried to get the squirming child dressed. Soon, the little girl joined the other children. Gryphon and Heather sat at the edge of the meadow and watched. Other parents arrived, and it seemed the entire meadow was filled with laughter and song. Twilight came and the summer breeze invited Pixies to make their rounds gathering flower nectar.

The scene faded. But it left the Sorceress with a wonderful feeling of contentment. "That's as it *should* be," Shayla smiled and murmured to herself. "Now, on to the others. First, there's that matter in New England to take care of. I can't imagine the man doesn't even know he's a member of the Order." She made a *tisking* sound, emptied the water from the scrying bowl and straightened her white robe. Then, the Sorceress of the Ancients royally flounced out of the room, making plans as she did so. She needed to call her advisors together. It seemed that a Sorceress' work was never done. There was so much to do, so little time in which to do it.

ABOUT THE AUTHOR

After having worked as a Police Officer for eleven years, and on the back of an ambulance as a Crew Chief and crew member for about eight years, I got pretty used to things that go 'bump in the night'. Sometimes . . . I was what went 'bump in the night'!

I love paranormal, futuristic, fantasy, time travel, shape shifter, anything out of the ordinary romances. Having read romance since the age of about thirteen, I've seen every conceivable story. But all the romances with the supernatural elements or those involving Celt or ethereal magic are still what's best for me.

I'm currently the senior woman on the U.S. Kung Fu Team and exhibited in China, at the request of the Chinese Government, in November 2000. I hold an International Martial Arts Competition title from 1997, and was awarded the Medal of Putien and the Statue of Tao from the deceased Grand Master of Nan Shaolin Kung Fu in China, Grand Master Chee Kim Thong. (So, I like the kicky, throw-you-down down stuff!)

I live in Alabama with my exceedingly patient husband and seven children in the form of three large dogs and four cats. I love to garden, have an extensive daylily collection and a bird making a nest right outside my writing room window! Autumn is favorite season of the year.